ORIGINS
BOOK 2

DISCLAIMER

This is a work of fiction. Names, characters, businesses, places, events and incidents are either the products of the author's imagination or used in a fictitious manner. Any resemblance to actual persons, living or dead, or actual events is purely coincidental.

All rights reserved:

No part of this book may be reproduced or transmitted in any form or by any means, electronic or mechanical, including photocopying, recording, or by any information storage and retrieval system, without prior permission in writing from the author.

Translation:

Don't steal the stories I worked so hard on, and occasionally cried over. Don't get upset at the absolutely made-up story lines: this is a romance, so of course it isn't realistic, duh! Don't be petty and hate on it because it isn't your kink. We've all got different tastes and there's no shame in that.

Warning: Author is dyslexic as hell.

The editing and beta reading team: Martha Collins and Lauren Meghoo

Profession Editing: Chrisandra's Correction

Check out my website for links to free books, social media, and updates on the lates news:
www.RK-Munin.com

CONTENT WARNING

-Rain and her siblings lost their parents before the story begins. --There's nothing on page but they do talk about them and experience sadness at the loss.
-One of Rain's siblings experienced child abuse, nothing on page.
-Two of the siblings verbally fight—a lot! They're involved in one physical altercation.
-There is violence and fighting on page that results in death.
-Two characters are drugged and kidnapped.
-There are graphic scenes of consensual sex.

CHAPTER 1

Rain

Perching on a support strut on the top of her crawler gave Rain the best view of everyone filing off the small passenger section of the long-haul ship. Her position was a little precarious, but nothing she hadn't done before. Standing like this allowed her to see everything without being forced to drive the crawler closer to the port.

Omanal's only port was small, with a single building that doubled as a place to store equipment and living quarters for the small staff that ran the place. Due to the complete lack of anything else that could be classified as a city, this one was simply called Omanal Proper, and the port was Omanal Port. As the passengers filed off, the more important cargo was being unloaded from the belly of the ship: crates of proto-plants, bags of bog binding agents, and other items necessary to farm on Omanal.

Beyond the ship, the port authorities held off the Gorlag Gang. The port was the last place where they couldn't get access, and it was only because the employees who ran the place were better armed than the gang. But they were the only ones. Everyone else on Omanal had to figure out how to coexist with the growing Gorlag Gang problem.

Putting the planet's troubles aside, she focused on the people shuffling out of the passenger compartment at the very top of the ship. As she expected, there weren't many.

Omanal wasn't a place you traveled to for fun. There were no centers of learning, large bustling cities, or gorgeous geological views. There was nothing here but bogs and farms.

A loud squawk made her blink in surprise. Dorincs, the tall, feathered species that made up most of the inhabitants of Omanal, weren't prone to making their loud, warning call unless feeling very threatened.

As she watched, a Dorinc rushed out of the ship's hatch in a flurry of feathers and practically galloped down the ramp, the sound of his four feet pounding loud enough to hear even at this distance. He was casting anxious looks over his shoulder the entire time and almost ran into a group of Dorincs ahead of him.

"What's got his neck-feathers all ruffled?" she murmured to herself. When she shifted her gaze back to the open hatch, she saw what caused the Dorinc so much alarm. A species even more massive than a Dorinc emerged to make his way down the ramp with a calm, metered stride.

This had to be the reason she was here.

According to the transmission she'd received only yesterday, his name was Hesarium, a Talin who'd responded to her job posting. His brief message had included an arrival time. She'd half expected no one to show up, but here he was, looking large and threatening.

He was already capable of doing most of the job she'd posted: look dangerous enough to keep the Gorlag Gang from bothering them too much. The second part of the job was to refrain from hurting any of the humans on her little farming settlement. As she took in his intimidating appearance, Rain worried she was a fool. Anyone willing to take a job like this for food and a bed was probably the same type that would hurt and steal from them.

She'd probably added to her community's problems instead of solving them.

Torn between climbing off the strut to pilot the crawler home before he saw her and going down to greet him, Rain remained in place and stared at the large male. Dear god, he was impressive!

He stood a little taller than the Dorincs, putting him somewhere around eight feet. Unlike the winding cloth Dorincs wrapped around their bodies in complicated patterns, or the hardy pants, shirt, and boots she had on, this male wore only pants made of some kind of gleaming black fabric. This gave her a good view of his broad chest and muscled arms. He had several packs slung over his shoulder, and although they looked heavy, he carried them with ease.

Everything about him screamed strength and confidence, including the way he ignored the chittering Dorincs at the bottom of the ramp all glaring at him. Around his waist was a thick, dull gray belt with a pouch hanging off one hip. Then he shifted one of the bags and she could see an expensive Identification Cube hanging from the belt at the other hip.

The sight of that Identification Cube made her pause. The tech was new, hard to get, and pricy. Why would someone with enough wealth to own an Ident accept a non-paying job offer on a backward agricultural planet?

Hesarium hadn't provided much information about himself in the short missive he'd sent accepting her job. Only a low-res capture of his face, species, place of origin, and list of skills. The skills he claimed to possess were impressive. Expertise on many different weapons and even passable knowledge of battleship systems. That spoke to a high level of training and probably positions of command in a military.

Omanal didn't have a Unibase for people to access data, and sending information requests to the nearest station with a Unibase was prohibitively expensive. This kept her from researching him as an individual or his species as a whole. All she'd found out from asking around was that the Talin Empire was in the process of expanding into nearby areas. They'd recently won a war against the Orlok, another species she'd never heard of. One Dorinc had claimed they had rigid social protocols and not adhering to them could get a person killed.

The last one would've been helpful if the Dorinc telling her had any information on what Talin social protocols were! Things like that could vary greatly even within the same species. She could deliver a serious insult simply by looking him in the eye or avoiding eye contact. She let out a long breath, trying to relax her shoulders. The key was going to be flexibility and asking questions.

Unless questions weren't allowed among his species.

A slight headache was developing behind her right eye as she watched him slow then stop behind a line of Dorincs. He was the last to disembark, so he was stuck waiting for each Dorinc to complete the ceremonial movements they performed every time they returned from a trip. To her surprise, he didn't act impatient at being slowed down or tell them to move.

The Dorinc who'd squawked had pushed past everyone, done a very short form of the ceremonial movements, and run flat out for home. The rest of the Dorincs kept wary eyes on him but didn't speak to or look directly at him.

Ignoring the chirping Dorincs, Hesarium surveyed the port until his gaze landed on her. Still standing on the strut meant she was easy to spot, and she wasn't surprised when his found her. She expected him to keep looking around, but the moment he saw her, his focus was absolute. He didn't seem to notice anything else as they stared at each other.

Rain's breath caught in her throat. She suddenly felt like prey.

What was wrong with her? The urge to jump down off the strut and run was strong. He wasn't even doing anything threatening, only looking at her, but to her refined instincts for survival, Hesarium screamed menace.

That was a good thing, wasn't it? If she was this intimidated by his gaze alone, then there would be no need for actual battle to take place in defense of their farms. The Gorlag Gang might decide he wasn't worth testing and simply leave them alone.

Yeah, and Sunny might learn to use the kitchen-prepper and Rain would never need to make another reconstitutor tray ever again.

Thinking of Sunny's perpetual allergy against indoor chores brought a smile to Rain's face and helped her pull in a deep breath. She wasn't the only one who needed this Talin. Everyone's future rested on Hesarium. This was going to be fine.

She could hear Cherish's perpetually angry voice in her head, "Unless, of course, he turns out to be a murderer looking for his next victims."

Great, now she was having thoughts as grim as her thirteen-year-old sibling. Pushing all thoughts of murder and mayhem out of her head, she focused on climbing off the strut and onto the seat below.

It was time to be a polite host and go meet Hesarium. She couldn't drive the crawler onto the port, but it was only a short walk to the edge of the area where the ship was located. From there she'd be able to get his attention and wave him over if he hadn't already realized she was the human who'd posted the job.

Trying to put her apprehension aside, she made her way to the back of the crawler and down the short ladder. She was on the second to last rung when strong hands grabbed her around the waist. Startled, she kicked back with her legs and tightened her grip with her hands.

"Be at ease, human. I've got you," a deep voice assured her as the hands holding her tightened and continued to pull her away from the ladder. Either she let go or hurt herself by continuing to cling the metal rungs.

Releasing her grip, she expected to be dropped unceremoniously to the ground. Humans were some of the smallest and weakest species in the universe and most didn't realize how delicate they were in comparison. This wouldn't be the first time someone had tried to "help" and ended up hurting her by accident.

"Don't drop me," she belatedly announced seconds after letting go.

"Never," the deep voice assured her, accompanied by a sound that made Rain think of purring. The world tilted and whirled. Then she was being cradled against a broad chest and looking up into Hesarium's fierce face. "See? You're perfectly safe."

For a split second she thought he might be angry, but she quickly realized that his species didn't have mobility in their faces. Dorincs didn't have facial expressions either. They displayed emotions though moving their feathers, especially the ones on their head and neck. She would need to learn how these Talins showed what they were feeling or risk being constantly worried Hesarium was upset, especially with the hint of sharp teeth she could see when he talked.

Then she saw his eyes. They were a red so deep it tricked the eye into thinking the color was purple. Tyrian purple. The color of the wealthy and affluent. When compared to the lavender-gray coloring of the keratin plating on his skin, his eyes appeared even more otherworldly. It was as if he was staring directly into her soul.

She was intrigued, and not a single one of the emotions flowing through her was fear.

The silence must have lasted too long for Hesarium. "Are you broken, human? Can you not speak?" The purring sound stopped, replaced by something that sounded a lot like a hatch whooshing open and shut repeatedly.

"Oh, uh, right. Yeah, I can speak," Rain answered, shaking herself out of all the fanciful thoughts about Hesarium's eyes. What was she, sixteen again? This guy was here to do a job, not act as the star in her personal fantasies. "I'm Rain, the one who posted the job. You can set me down."

"Why were you on the ladder?" he asked, ignoring her suggestion to set her back on her feet. "I saw that you observed me from your high perch. Why would you risk a fall by descending?"

"I was trying to be polite," she answered, feeling suddenly amused by his questions. Unlike humans, most species didn't show friendliness by displaying teeth, so Rain made sure not to smile. "I was going to walk to the edge of the port and wave. And I thought you might like some help loading your packs into the crawler."

"You thought I'd need assistance?" he asked, and the whooshing noise abruptly ended. For a brief moment, it sounded like there was a swarm of angry wasps coming at her. Then an uncomfortable silence.

She'd bet her last stash of sweets that the last sound was one of annoyance. Less than five minutes in, and she'd already upset him.

"Humans help each other," she explained, working on damage control. "It's considered rude not to offer assistance."

The purring started up again. "I see. Among my people, it's considered rude to let a hu—one of a smaller stature to labor when someone larger and stronger is at hand."

Before she could ask him about his slip, the sound of poorly tuned sonic engines hit her ears. Looking over Hesarium's shoulder, Rain saw several Rasts come to a screeching halt at the entrance to the port and jerkily lower to the ground with loud thumps. The Dorincs riding the old and poorly maintained Rasts were wearing sickly greenish-yellow winding cloth, as if running around on the inefficient and impractical Rasts weren't indicators enough that they were part of the Gorlag Gang.

Even being against Hesarium's chest she couldn't what was going, but she didn't need to. They were probably about to confront the port authorities again, and that never ended peacefully.

"We need to go," she declared. There wasn't much in the way of weaponry on Omanal, but the Gorlags had gotten good at creating improvised weapons.

Hesarium turned slightly to see what she was staring at. "They look disorganized and aggressive."

"And you'd be right on both counts," she said, wiggling in his hold. "But if we can get into the bog before they notice, we'll be safe."

"We're going to be traversing a bog," he commented, his arms tightening around her slightly, "on foot?"

She snorted. "Of course not, in the crawler. If you put me down, I can climb up first and you can hand me your gear."

"No."

No? Just *no?* How did he think they were going to get into the crawler if he didn't set her down?

Without another word, he rearranged his grip on her. Instead of cradling her with both arms, she was now being held like a toddler with her legs on either side of his waist and her butt resting on his arm. Unsure of this new position, she wrapped her arms around his neck to steady herself.

She might have been worried about being dropped, but he wasn't. He had no problem bending at the knees to pick up the bags he'd dropped, holding both handles in one hand. With ease she envied, he lobbed them up into the crawler without much apparent effort, never once jostling her. Then he grabbed hold of the ladder and climbed up with her still held tightly against him.

It was during the climb that she noticed the quills on his forearm. They were long and looked deadly sharp, but right now they were all folded flush with his arm. Between the hard plates covering his body, sharp teeth, and now thick, wicked-looking quills, it seemed this male was designed to fight!

Unsure what to do and worried about distracting him, Rain remained quiet and clung to him until they were on the flat top of the crawler. Even after he'd finished his ascent he didn't set her down. Ignoring his bags, he traversed the long vehicle and sat in one of the only two seats.

He didn't set her down on the other seat but kept holding her as he lowered himself down. After he was seated, he arranged her in his lap so she was sitting sideways and even kept his arm around her to keep her in place. Rain tried to ignore how good the Talin's muscled bulk felt around her, and she absolutely resisted the impulse to start running her hands all over his body.

What was going on? Did he think she was a child? It was a common mistake many species made when first meeting humans.

"I'm a fully grown human adult," she told him as he swung the seat around to face the control panel.

"I know," he answered and started making that purring sound again. Now that she was so close, she could feel the vibration of the purring where her shoulder was pressed against his chest.

"I could sit in the other seat so you can have this one to yourself," she offered.

"You could," he agreed but made no move to shift her off his lap as he peered at the crawler's control panel.

For simple traveling, a person only needed to use the handheld controller to pilot the crawler. Hesarium obviously didn't know that because he stared with intensity down at the complex control panel that took up space in front of both seats, but he didn't touch anything.

He must have realized he wouldn't be able to pilot the vehicle. Without any comment, he arranged her in his lap so she was facing forward. He wrapped both arms around her waist like a living seatbelt and kept purring.

"You may take control of the crawler," he announced, as if doing her a big favor.

"Gee, thanks," she muttered, reaching into the breast pocket of her jacket for the small hand controller. He followed her movements with his eyes as she retrieved the controller then initiated a simple pre-programmed command. The crawler jolted to life and started the slow turn. The bog wasn't far away, so once they were turned around, the crawler took off at top speed to the safety of the brackish water. Not that top speed was all that fast, but it was better than trying to walk in the deep and dangerous bog.

As they moved, Hesarium took in the area around them. She couldn't be sure, but thought he might be keeping watch for trouble. It gave her hope he'd actually be able to help them.

When the crawler hit the bog and the wheels sank almost all the way down, Rain relaxed on Hesarium's lap. The Rasts couldn't navigate even on the edges of the bogs, making the dark, smelly, briny water dotted by small clusters of trees the only truly safe place on Omanal. For a short while, the gang owned an expensive hover-runner. That vehicle was capable of going anywhere, including the bog. To everyone's relief, they'd crashed it within a few days of owning it. No one had been surprised. The gang destroyed everything they touched sooner or later.

Now that they were safe and had an hour of travel time ahead of them, it seemed like a good time to get to know Hesarium.

Of all the things she could ask him about his culture, history, or skills, she commented on the first thing that popped into her head.

"Why do I smell sugar cookies?"

CHAPTER 2

Hesarium

Hesarium wasn't prepared for that question. He froze, trying to decide what to tell her.

Her bright, brown eyes were focused on him, brows wrinkled in confusion. A few tight coils of dark, honey-colored hair stuck out from under the hat protecting her from the cold. Between the hat and the bulky clothing she was wearing, he couldn't tell much about her except she was small, like all the humans he'd met so far. And she looked far healthier than the mining crew he and his squad had stumbled upon half a solar ago. Unlike those miners, her cheeks were round from having access to plenty of nutritious food.

It appeared that this group of humans had access to enough food, which was one positive thing at least. The skin of her face and hands were a dark brown tone without any obvious signs of sores or discoloration. Another sign of overall good health, but he'd feel better once she could be looked over by a healer.

"Um, Hesarium? You okay?" she asked, reminding him that she'd noticed and asked about his scent. "Have I confused you? Was the INT unable to translate something?"

Hesarium worked on keeping up his soothing rumble even though Rain's question made him want to rattle with excitement. First he needed to make sure it was him she was smelling. Then he needed to know if she considered *sugar cookies* a good or bad smell.

"Not confused at all." He pointed to the side of his face where his scent glands were located. "Is the scent more powerful here?"

He leaned over so Rain could put her nose to the spot. Even the brief touch of her soft skin brushing against his made his scent gland ache. He pulled away before bonding oil could start seeping from the glands.

"Wow, you smell exactly like sugar cookies!" she exclaimed. Her voice sounded excited, but she wasn't smiling. Just like Ari and the miners, she must have taught herself not to show teeth while interacting with non-humans.

"Do you dislike sugar cookies?" he asked, struggling with the strange human *shuug* sound in the first word. The INT in his head couldn't find an acceptable translation for the human word, so he had no choice but to speak human as best he could.

If he hadn't been watching so carefully, he might not have caught how Rain's mouth twitched, as if she wanted to display her teeth in a smile. It was an excellent sign that she was already regarding him favorably.

"I love sugar cookies," she answered. "They were one of my favorites back when we could still get the ingredients."

Her words made his comforting rumble grow so intense it almost dipped into a sexual rhythm. She liked the smell of his bonding oil! Between her accepting his embrace and her favorable response to his bonding scent, he was sure this human would come to love him.

If he was careful, he could have a human of his own! Now he understood how Bazium had bonded with Ari so quickly. When you held the right human in your arms, you simply knew.

"I can see about getting the ingredients so you can make the sugar cookies again," he offered.

He watched her cover her mouth with her hand, hiding her teeth. "The way you say sugar is cute."

"Were you going to bare your teeth at me?" he inquired so he could explain that it was okay to smile around him.

Instead of admitting to the smile, Rain slapped both hands over her mouth. Her eyes went wide as she spoke through her fingers. "No! If you saw my teeth, it was only because I was talking. I'd never show a threat display to you."

Realizing he'd caused her distress, he focused on making his rumble louder so she could feel the vibrations as well as hear them. Ari and the other humans often said the sound and sensation of Talins' comforting rumbles were soothing.

"Be at ease, Rain. I know humans show teeth for many reasons and none of them are threat displays. If you feel the need to, uh, present your teeth, I won't take it as a challenge or an act of aggression."

Her eyes stayed comically wide as her hands dropped to her lap. "You know what a smile is? Wait, you've met other humans?" she gasped.

Had he given too much away already? His entire reason for being here was to talk these humans into joining the ones he and his squad had already relocated to Talarian, the Talin homeplanet. The very clever human, Ari, had warned him repeatedly that he needed to gain the humans' trust before he started telling them about relocating. She'd explained that talking about humans being pets too soon would cause the humans to reject his offer outright and maybe even demand he leave.

"I've spent time with a group of human miners," he explained, settling on half-truths. "Your species have expressive faces and I'm familiar with some of their meanings."

A broad, uninhibited smile split Rain's face. "That's a bit of a surprise. It's not like there are a lot of humans out there. I'm glad the universe sent you to us."

"I'm also thankful for the Ancestors' guidance," Hesarium agreed. "I'm looking forward to meeting the other humans in your settlement. How many are there?"

"There are thirty-two of us," she answered promptly. "A few years ago, our number was double that, but uh, things happened."

They'd lost half their number in only a few years? Poor humans!

"Tell me about the rest of your herd," he urged.

"We call ourselves a community, not a herd," she answered with a chuckle. "And they're curious to meet you too. You'll be staying at my family's domicile, so you'll meet Sunny, Wind, Cherish, Royal, and Auntie today."

A horrible thought occurred to him: what if one of those names was her mate? "Are these humans all related to you?"

"Yes, they're all my siblings," Rain answered. "Well, except for Georgia who is my father's younger sister. That's why we call her Auntie."

Relief and sadness filled him. Rain didn't live with a mate but had obviously lost her parents if they weren't being named as members of the household. "How should I greet them? By name or do they have titles?"

"No titles around here," she answered while frowning at the crawler's control panel. She kept talking as she fiddled with some settings. "I won't have time to take you around to meet everyone today, but tomorrow I can make introductions and show you the extent of our farms."

The comment about the farms brought Hesarium back to the reason he'd found these humans to begin with. "Tell me about why you need protection. The job posting I saw was rather vague."

Rain let out a long, heartfelt sigh while still staring at the control panel. "The short answer is the Gorlag Gang."

"Gorlag Gang? I believe I'll need further explanation," Hesarium pushed.

Looking up from the panel, she met his eyes. "It started a few years ago after the bog expanded and took a lot of farmland with it. The wealthy farmers left the planet, but those who couldn't afford to, stayed. There isn't much in the way of work around here unless you're a farmer or own a business. Jorc, one of the Dorincs that lost their farm, started the Gorlag Gang. Now they basically run everything except the port."

Hesarium was outraged. "Are there no centralized authorities to deal with this issue?"

Rain shook her head. "This is a throwaway colony. The Massoc who own it want maximum profit for minimum investment. That's why the bog keeps expanding. The terraforming was done fast and poorly; it was only stable for the first hundred years and now it's starting to change rapidly."

"Does the Gorlag Gang steal from you and the other humans?"

"Yes, they demand we pay them a percentage of what we make," she explained. "We were able to pay last year, but only barely. The crop yield is looking worse this year. If we have to keep paying them, we won't have enough to survive on, and there's no place for us to go. It's a bad situation all around."

I have a place for all of you, he thought, but kept it to himself. Patience and timing would be key to this mission.

"If we could, we'd leave, but we'd end up as slave labor somewhere," Rain continued. "Even before the bog expansion and the rise of the Gorlag Gang, it would've been hard to find a place that would let a bunch of humans live there. With how little wealth we have, it's impossible now."

Before he could ask more questions, the crawler jerked violently and came to a grinding halt. Hesarium tightened his hold on Rain to keep her from flying off his lap. He couldn't bear thinking of the damage she would've sustained if he hadn't been there. Nothing on the crawler was padded and there were sharp edges and hard planking everywhere.

"Rot!" Rain exclaimed and jabbed a finger at the control panel diagnostic chart. "We're in a tweshi trap. She must have built it while I was waiting for you at the port because it wasn't here earlier."

He didn't like the sound of that. "Tweshi trap?"

"Tweshi are native predators to this planet; big, scaly girls that live in the bogs," Rain said.

"Girls?" Hesarium questioned.

Rain held her hands apart, indicating something roughly the size of her shoulders. "The boys are too tiny to worry about. The females build traps by digging up an area and letting it fill with water to create a hidden low spot. An animal foraging in the bog will fall in and splash around."

Hesarium tensed and glanced over at his duffle, now resting against a far corner of the crawler. "How dangerous are these female tweshi?"

Rain didn't look concerned. "They rarely attack something as big as a crawler. I'm going to need to climb over the side to pour some pink around the trapped tread."

Had his INT mistranslated her words? "You're going to pour pink into the bog water?"

She finally looked up to meet his gaze, huffing soft breaths out of her mouth that condensed white in the cold air around them. He froze, letting the sound sink into him.

Laughter. She was expressing human laughter. He'd heard it with Ari and her humans, but Rain's was different. The sound of her laugh struck a chord in him that caused happiness to flutter through his chest. He wanted to hear it more. He wanted to feel her chest expand against his as she breathed out her sounds of happiness. It was a desire so strong, he had to fight the urge to grip her even more tightly against his chest.

If he thought his scent glands were aching before, he'd been wrong. They were so full of bonding oil they were throbbing with the need to expel it all over Rain.

"I guess that must sound weird to someone who doesn't live here," she said, completely unaware of the profound effect her laughter had on him. "We have a powder called pionious loose-earth solution that we can pour into the bog to solidify it for a short time. It allows us to walk on it or unstick equipment."

"And you call this powder pink?" he questioned as she wiggled around on his lap. At first he thought she was turning to face him, as Ari would do when sitting on Bazium's lap. When Ari did it, she often wrapped her arms around Bazium's neck, or snuggled her face against his chest. It was something Hesarium longed to experience but none of the humans in the mining group had been interested in touching him.

To his disappointment, Rain only looked up into his face, and she didn't try to clutch her arms around his neck as she'd done when he carried her. "You'll see why we call it pink in a minute, but first you need to let go."

With great reluctance, he dropped his arms, allowing Rain to slide off his lap.

"Thanks for keeping me from taking a tumble," she commented as she opened up one of the floorboards and pulled out a clear package the size of her head. There was a white powdery substance inside. "Let me climb down and dump this out. It works fast so we'll be ready to move soon."

Standing up, Hesarium plucked the bag from her hand. "Let you climb down into the bog? Absolutely not."

She looked up at him with confusion. "Do you want to stay stuck?"

When she reached for the bag, he held it up out of her reach. "I'll pour the contents where they need to go."

Giving up on getting the bag, she stepped back and crossed her arms over her chest. "This would go a lot faster if you let me do it."

"No." His single word response made the corner of her lips stretch to the side. It almost looked like the beginning of a smile, except it was paired with a furrowed brow. "Are you happy with me?"

"Annoyed," she answered, then pointed to her face. "You guys don't do facial expressions, right?"

He made a rattle of agreement, then remembered she wouldn't know what it meant. "That sound indicates I concur with your statement."

"Huh, it sounds like water dripping on metal," she commented, then circled her face with a single finger. "I'd describe this expression as a grimace."

"Your displeasure doesn't change my intent," he informed her, striding to the lower corner of the crawler. "I'm still assigning myself this task. Now please explain to me how to accomplish my goal."

"You talk really fancy for someone willing to work for room and board," she said, moving to stand next to him. He wasn't sure if that was an insult or a compliment. She pointed down at the submerged tread. "You'll need to climb down and sprinkle it on the ground. Whatever you do, don't get it on the wheel or anywhere on the crawler really."

Hesarium eyed the powder. "What happens if I get it on the crawler?"

"Once it's on, you can't get it off, and it eats holes clear through within a few days. It won't do anything to you or your clothes, unless your stuff is infused with non-binding, polarized metals."

His armor, safely tucked away in the duffle, would've been in danger, but nothing he was currently wearing could be affected. It was also helpful to know that even if he accidently got the powder where it shouldn't be, it would take rotations before any problems would develop. He could deal with crawler issues later, without having to worry about some bog beast trying to eat either of them.

"I'll be careful," he promised and tucked the bag in his belt. "Anything else I should know?" Rain bit her lip, a clear sign of anxiety in a human. He wanted to draw her into his arms again and sound a soothing rumble.

"Only about a million things," she grumbled. "But here are the two most important: don't fall into the bog, and if the bog starts to bubble, climb up fast."

"I'm strong and swift," he promised her. "This simple task isn't beyond my skill set."

Rain moved her shoulders up and down in a small motion a single time and mumbled something about pride and falls. Ignoring her, Hesarium swung his leg over the short railing and found a foothold. Soon, he was climbing down the corner of the crawler, a task made easy by all the small indentations on the outside surface of the vehicle specifically designed for the activity.

Once he was close enough to the bottom, he maneuvered until he felt secure enough to let go with one hand and pull the bag free from his belt. The rotting smell of the bog was bad enough while sitting on top of the crawler, but down here, the stench was nearly overwhelming. He kept a strong hold on the crawler; falling into the disgusting muddy water wasn't an option.

Using his teeth to tug off the release seam, he opened the bag's funnel and started sprinkling the powder onto the ground. The reaction began immediately, and he understood why they referred to the substance as pink. A bright version of the color marked the ground, glowing briefly as it dispersed.

It took him longer to finish than he expected, and his body was protesting being forced to hang at such an awkward angle for an extended period. Tucking the empty bag back in his belt, he reached for a hand hold when bubbles started breaking the surface of the bog not far from where he'd distributed the pink.

Cursing under his breath, he pushed his body to move faster. Long, yellow limbs covered in short, fat spikes emerged from the bog, reaching for him. The tweshi was far bigger than he expected. Judging by the length of its limbs alone, it probably measured twice his size or greater. He wasn't going to get away from it in time, so defense was the only option.

Lengthening his claws, he embedded one hand into the side of the crawler and reached for his military knife. His hand met nothing. It wasn't there. He'd taken it off and stowed it in his duffle to appear less threatening when first meeting the humans.

Cursing himself for not retrieving it before climbing over the side of the crawler, he focused on his natural weapons. Bristling the long quills on his forearms, he pulled back his teeth and sounded a war rattle with his back plates.

The thing that surfaced was mostly tentacles, all connected to the body like the spokes of a wheel. The center mass was cylinder shaped with a large gaping hole at one end ringed with small waving tentacles. Each tentacle had a hook on the end to help drag prey into its large mouth.

Two of the legs found him and started tugging on his foot. Slashing down, he left a deep gouge in one leg but didn't manage to do any damage to the other. As he battled the first set, two more reached up and clamped down on his thigh. It hurt, but he ignored the pain and prepared to slash again. If he couldn't get the legs off him, he'd be forced to drop down on the beast and kill it directly instead of trying to escape.

"Hes, hold on!" Rain screamed from above. He looked up to find Rain leaning far over the edge of the crawler.

For the first time, fear spiked through him. If she fell, the creature might hurt her before he could do anything. He opened his mouth to yell at her to stay back. He didn't even get a sound out. She pulled back her arm and threw something. Her aim was perfect, and it landed directly in the tweshi's gaping mouth.

The creature let go of him to claw at its mouth. Flashes of bright pink told Hesarium what Rain had tossed. The beast disappeared back into the earth, leaving a faint coloring of pink on the surface of the watery bog.

"Are you hurt? I told you to watch out for bubbles!" Rain yelled down at him. She already had one leg over the side of the crawler and looked ready to climb down to help him.

"Stay there," he barked. "Don't distract me by climbing down." Despite the pain in his leg, he hurried to finish the climb up before Rain decided to disobey him.

Dealing with the humans at the Orlok mining compound had taught him and his fellow squad members that humans were far too ready to put themselves in danger. Humans were often a foolishly brave species. The problem was, there was an inverse relationship between their courage and ability to withstand damage.

Rain grabbed him the moment he was within reach. Her small hand did little to haul him the last bit of distance into the crawler, but he didn't try to pull free. Once he was standing there, she let go of his arm and started running her hands all over his body, looking for damage. She spoke the entire time, her words rapid and high pitched from worry.

"That was a big one. I haven't seen one that size in years! But of course it's just my luck that we fall into her trap. I can't believe how strong you are. She had you with four legs. Four! And you were still able to hold onto the crawler; that's amazing. The cuts look bad though." She was on her knees in front of him, examining his thigh. "There's some bleeding. She got past your natural plating. I don't have much here but we can go—"

"I'm not badly injured. I can wait until we reach your home to assess and treat the damage," he interrupted her, touched by her concern. "You called me Hes."

She looked up at him, her expression confused. "What?" Then her confusion cleared. "Oh, yeah, I did. I was rushed and you've got a long name."

"Shortening my name is a nickname, correct? It's a sign of comradery and affection. We are friends now." After all the time it had taken to earn the humans' trust at the Orlok mine, Hesarium was delighted to gain Rain's acceptance so quickly. Of course, they weren't dealing with the same language barrier because Rain obviously had an INT, but this was still amazing progress.

One side of her mouth slanted up. "Sure, Hes. We're best buddies."

Her words made it easy to ignore his discomfort. He reached down to help her to her feet and his leg nearly collapsed. Numbness was starting to spread at an alarming rate.

"Let me help," Rain insisted, as she scrambled to her feet and draped his arm around her shoulder. "Don't worry about the dead feeling in your leg. I've got some tweshi antivenom in the box under the control panel. We get bit by the males occasionally, because they'll come out of the bog to hunt little game in our fields."

Gritting his teeth, he staggered to the front chairs and focused on not putting weight on her small frame. She kept up a monologue about how fast he was while fighting the bog beast as she collected the antivenom and a temporary dressing for his leg.

He was disappointed when she didn't voluntarily climb back onto his lap even after she'd applied a temporary skinpatch bandage. Even after he'd assured her that he wasn't in any pain, she absolutely refused. He reminded himself they'd already made great strides because she'd remained in his lap before his tangle with the tweshi.

Rain would soon want to be his human. He was sure of it.

CHAPTER 3

Rain

Rain internally winced as she led Hes into their domicile. A burned smell hung in the air, telling her Sunny had used the temperamental kitchen-prepper. Rain couldn't be angry. Sunny was a growing girl and was hungry all the time these days.

Rain wished the slightly unpleasant smell was the worst of it.

The main floor had an open plan which gave Hes an excellent view of the mess the moment he followed her inside. Every surface had items piled high. There was a line of parts in need of repair or replacement along the far wall. Twenty boxes of next year's proto-plants were stacked high in one corner. The floor was dirty from children and teenagers forgetting to take off their muddy boots. At least half the illumination panels in the ceiling were dim from old age, so the mess wasn't showcased in perfect bright light. Unfortunately the poor lighting made everything appear even more dingy and older than it was.

The food area was the worst. The counters and table were covered in empty rehydration packets, dirty reconstitutor trays, and bits of dropped food. The kitchen-prepper's door was wide open and the blackened remains of something were still inside. The reconstitutor's door was also open, giving them a clear view of the big splotches of food covering the interior walls. Someone had used the wrong setting and a meal exploded inside.

With a sigh, Rain turned to face Hes. "If you want to run away screaming, I totally understand."

Hes was silent for a moment before speaking. "I sense no danger and you aren't acting with fear. Were your words meant to be humorous?"

Rain barked out a sharp laugh. That was the first time she'd laughed in a year. "Let me try again. Your room is upstairs, clean and ready for you to occupy."

"Am I displacing anyone from their room?" he asked, surprising her.

"It was my room but don't worry about it. There was a spare bed in Auntie's room, and I'm used to sharing space," she assured him, then remembered the guy was injured. She swept everything off a nearby chair then pointed. "Here, sit down. I'll get the med kit."

He made a sound reminiscent of glass marbles clinking around in a bag as he dropped the bags he'd refused to let her carry. He sat gingerly on the chair, as if worried it might break under his weight. It creaked but held.

Straightening his wounded leg out, he looked up at her. "If you have even a basic kit, I can care for myself."

"It's upstairs. I'll be right back," she said, heading for the ladder a few paces down the wall from the front door. All the two-story domiciles had ladders instead of stairs. Many species, including the Dorincs, could easily jump from one story to another—the ladder was something the humans had to add. It was just another example of how out of place humans were compared to most sapient species in the universe.

Guilt ate at her as she rushed back down with the med kit. Setting it on the floor next to Hes, she pulled up a stepstool and sat down. "I hope these aren't your only pair of pants. None of us are great at mending clothes, and the nearest shop with professional tailoring machines is the Hub. That's a long trip for a pair of pants."

He didn't react to her attempt at a joke. "What about clothing stores? You can't possibly produce everything you need."

"There used to be a few stores, but the Gorlag Gang kept harassing them, so they packed up and left. Now we have to order everything from the Hub, but that's only in range once every year," she explained. He watched her closely as she pulled the ragged edges of his pants apart and assessed the wound.

"It isn't a bad injury," he said, leaning over to peer at the wound. "With my superior Talin physique, my body will rapidly heal as long as the wound is treated properly."

"Then I guess I better do a good job," she said with a smile and sprayed her hands and then the wound with disinfectant foam. Hes didn't react even though she knew from experience the foam stung.

"So you're forced to purchase everything all at once?" he asked. "What if the Hub doesn't have it in stock?"

She dug around the kit, looking for a binding agent. "The Hub always has everything in stock. The problem is the figure-eight orbit the Hub is on. If they aren't in the section near us, they charge extra to send anything over to us."

Hes made a sound that reminded Rain of a hatch whooshing open and closed. His next words told her that sound was one of concern. "So if you require something immediately and the Hub isn't close, what do you do?"

Rain shrugged. "We go without."

"Even food and medicine?" Hes pushed.

"We try to use our medical supplies carefully, but we never have to worry about food. Eighty percent of what we grow is a cash crop. The remaining twenty percent is enough to provide for the community."

"Smart," he commented as she worked to clean up the edges of the wounds.

She wrinkled her brow as she examined the hard keratin plating around the wound. "Do the loose or broken sections need to be removed?"

"Yes," he answered, pointing to a jagged bit of keratin. "Any plating like this needs to be excised to allow the skin underneath to heal cleanly."

She nodded and went to work. Although she tried to be careful, the muscles of Hes's leg quivered slightly when she pulled off the last plate in a line of damaged ones.

"I'm sorry I don't have any numbing agents left," she apologized. "We used up the last of them when Gris tried to repair one of the machines while it was still running and got his hand caught."

Hes made the worried sound again and touched her shoulder, drawing her gaze up and stilling her movement. "Is Gris still alive? Does he need immediate medical attention?"

"Gris is fine. It happened a while ago and he's all healed up now," Rain assured him.

Hes removed his hand from her shoulder and placed it on the side of the chair. "Tell me if anyone else becomes grievously injured. I can help."

That was unlikely unless he had a portable medical suite in his duffle, not that she'd ever say that out loud to Hes.

"I wouldn't worry. We're a hardy group," Rain assured him as she went back to work on his leg. Guilt made her offer up one of their scarce resources. "I've got some jomjil juice. It's not a strong analgesic, but it's good for taking the edge off the pain."

Hes made another sound before going back to the purring. "No need."

Rain paused and looked up. "Do the sounds you make mean anything?"

"Yes, they can express emotion or intent."

Hoping to distract him from the pain, she pushed for more information. "What does the sound you're making right now signify?"

"It's a rumble of comfort," he answered, tapping a finger over his chest. "Rumbles come from our chestbox." He made the *tink, tink, tink* sound of water dripping on metal. "Rattles come from our backplates."

Finished cleaning the wound, Rain spread binder gel on the edges of the cuts then held them together until the gel sealed. She still needed to cover the entire thing in a clear coat of overskin, but first she wanted to appease her curiosity. Standing up, she circled the chair. The back of the chair only covered Hes's lower back, giving her a full view of the rest.

As she watched, the plates all moved in a wave motion starting just below his neck and moving down past where the chair obscured her view. The movement created a soft wind chime sound. Then they moved in a different pattern, creating a hatch-whooshing-open sound.

"That's amazing," she murmured. Fascinated, she put her finger on one of the plates that hadn't moved on his neck. "These ones don't make sound?"

"The ones at the back of our neck can't move independently," he explained, dipping his head forward and separating the plates. "That's as far apart as they go."

She ran her fingers down one of the smooth plates, then slipped her fingers between them to touch the skin underneath. Hes's skin was unbelievably soft, and she found herself stroking her fingertips back and forth.

The smell of sugar cookies filled her nose, stronger than before. The scent was comforting and familiar but also made her want to touch Hes more. That was weird; she'd never had a smell affect her like this.

His purring changed to a lower pitch with a longer note. "What's this rumble mean?"

Hes didn't answer right away. She thought he might be struggling to describe what it meant. After all, some things were hard to translate from one culture to another. While waiting, she was content to pet the small bit of Hes's skin she could feel and breathe in his sugar-cookie scent.

"Rrrrraaaaain! I'm starving!" Sunny wailed as the front door slid open and the sixteen-year-old stomped the mud off her boots before coming inside. She froze at the sight of Hes's large figure, her eyes going comically wide and one foot up in the air.

"Damn, you're big and spikey!" she whooped. "Those podheads aren't going to be messing with us anymore!"

Wind, Cherish, and Royal were stuck behind her, unable to come inside because she was blocking the doorway.

"You're not the only one who's hungry!" Cherish complained loudly and shoved her sister hard in the back. "If anyone's a podhead, it's you! Now move!"

Sunny's excited expression turned to anger in an instant and she swung around, hands balled into fists. "You're the podhead, podhead!"

Most times, Sunny and Cherish's fights were nothing more than short, heated exchanges, but occasionally they grew to a battle of epic proportions. This sounded like one of those times, pushing Rain to stop them before they really got started.

"Shut it, guys!" she called out. "We've got company, and this is how you act?"

Both girls turned to face Rain, mouths shut and expressions mutinous. Before they could turn their anger on her, she started issuing orders. "Cherish, I need you to start dinner. Sunny, you're on clean-up duty and toss whatever is still sitting in the kitchen-prepper into the bog."

"If we're lucky, it'll kill a tweshi," Wind murmured as he tried to slip past his angry siblings only to get blocked when Cherish put her hands on her hips, elbows sticking out.

"That's not fair," Cherish started to say, then went still and stared at Hes. She'd finally noticed the giant male sitting dead center of their domicile. "What are you?"

"Cherish! That's rude!" Rain admonished as Cherish finally let Wind nudge her aside and Sunny moved all the way inside.

The siblings stayed tightly grouped together as they met the newest member of the household. "Everyone, this is Hes. He's the Talin who accepted the job I posted. Hes, this is Sunshine, but we all call her Sunny. Next to her are the twins, Wind and Cherish. The little guy partially hidden behind Sunny is Royal. Say hi, everyone."

Sunny and Wind both greeted Hes at full volume. Cherish glared without saying a word, and Royal ducked behind Sunny and hid while whispering a barely audible greeting.

Rain sighed. Cherish's anger was usually quick to burn out. She would warm up to Hes within a few days. But little Royal would probably take a lot longer. He had some trust issues Rain couldn't fault him for.

"The only person you haven't met is Auntie," Rain said. As if waiting for the perfect moment to appear, Auntie was the next one through the door. There was a new stain running the length of her old coat, her hat was missing, and her face was haloed by a tangle of tightly curled black hair.

"You must be Hesarium," Auntie boomed out in her cheerful, enthusiastic way. Auntie rarely met people she didn't like and never passed up a chance for a friendly conversation. She'd even managed to de-escalate a situation in town involving members of the gang at the general store before it closed. She'd simply kept asking genuinely interested questions about the men until they were all friends, and everyone left the store without anyone getting hurt or things being stolen.

The scariest part was that Auntie hadn't even realized what was going on.

With her signature eagerness, Auntie strode up to Hes with her hand out. She'd been taught as a child to clasp right hands when meeting someone new and never broke out of the habit. Unsure how Hes would interpret her move, Rain was quick to put herself between Auntie and Hes.

"Not human," Rain hissed.

"Oh, well, yes," Auntie stammered, dropping her hand down. She looked up as Rain heard the faint rustle of clothing. A glance over her shoulder showed Hes was standing up, staring at Auntie.

"Were you going to hit me?" he inquired, sounding calm and curious.

"No!" Auntie shouted the denial. "I was going to shake your hand, in uh, a traditional human-greeting type of way."

He held out his left hand. "That is acceptable."

Curious to see what would happen, Rain stepped aside. Trying hard to grin without showing teeth, Auntie slipped her left hand into Hes's and moved their joined limbs up and down rapidly as she spoke.

"Welcome to our home," Auntie trilled. "Are you hungry? What types of food do you like to eat? We don't have much variety, but I'm very good at cooking in volume. It's a good thing too, because you're a large one. I make the best—"

Hes watched her intently as she spoke, but as the monologue kept going, he glanced at Rain. It was clear he was looking for help and it was adorable.

"Speaking of food," Rain interrupted Auntie. "Shouldn't you get started on dinner?"

"Yeah! Food!" Sunny cheered. "I'm sure I'll die if I don't eat soon."

"We can only hope," Cherish mumbled. Thankfully, Sunny ignored her. Rain didn't bother admonishing Cherish. The teenager was angry at the universe and nothing they did seemed to change her attitude. They could only hope this was a phase and Cherish didn't stay irritable and peevish for the rest of her life.

Auntie let go of Hes's hand in mid-motion and clasped her hands to her chest, letting out a dramatic gasp as she swung around to face Sunny and the other kids. "We can't have you dying! If you're gone, who'll fill the house with such a lovely perfume? What do we call this one, Distracted Sunny?"

"Hey, it's not my fault!" Sunny declared. "I swear the kitchen-prepper is out to get me."

"That's what you said about the reconstitutor," Wind pointed out, hiding a grin behind his hand.

"I'm sure it's a conspiracy of food machines," Auntie commiserated, draping an arm over the teenager's shoulders to lead the younger woman to the messy kitchen area. "Let's go. You can clean while I fix food."

Sunny let out an exaggerated moan as they walked away.

To Rain's absolute shock, when she turned to face Hes, Royal was standing in front of the massive Talin. She'd been distracted by Sunny and Auntie's exchange, so she hadn't noticed him move.

Royal was staring up, clutching his multi-tech tool to his chest. His little five-year-old face was set in determined lines, and although his voice shook when he talked, he didn't stutter.

"Hello, Hes. I'm Royal. We can be friends. But if you hurt my family, I'll hurt you."

She heard audible gasps from Cherish and Wind, which matched the astonishment she was feeling. Where had the shy, fearful Royal gotten the courage to confront the large and imposing Talin?

Hes started purring again and sank to his knees. Even then, he was much taller than the child, so he sat back on his heels to put them on the same level. With the wound on his leg, that couldn't be comfortable, but he hadn't hesitated or made any sounds of pain.

"Your words mark you as a male of worth," Hes intoned. "It's an honor to meet you, Royal. I swear to you, I'll protect you and your family for as long as life remains in my body."

Then Hes made a fist and struck his chest hard enough to make a loud sound of impact. Royal jerked at the noise but didn't move away. Lowering the multi-tech tool, Royal held it in one hand and put his fist against his chest with a soft thump.

Rain felt tears burn her eyes. She was doing a great job of not letting them flow down her face until Royal held out his tool. "Here, you can use this if you need it."

With great reverence, Hes accepted the tool he probably didn't even know how to use. He pretended to examine it with a critical eye. "Thank you, Royal. This is a fine item. I've never seen one as nice." He held it back out to the little boy. "Would you show me how to best use it tomorrow?"

Royal snatched the multi-tech back and tucked it against this chest with a sigh of relief. "Okay." It looked like he used up all his bravery because, after that, Royal scampered away and up the ladder.

"We'll check on him," Wind said as he and Cherish hurried after Royal. Cherish grunted and nodded at Hes as she passed. It was the sullen teenager's version of a stamp of approval.

Now Rain was the only one standing next to him. She noticed his wound was seeping a little blood, telling her she'd missed a spot with the binding agent.

"Sit," she ordered. "Let me finish with your leg."

He obediently sat. Before she knelt next to his leg, she leaned in close and put her mouth near his earhole.

"Thank you, Hes. The way you treated Royal means a lot to us," she murmured. The smell of sugar cookies filled her nose, and she had to fight the urge to rub her face against him. Hes's purring grew louder, and the need to touch him was almost overwhelming. It took a lot more willpower than she expected to pull away and focus on his leg.

Feeling a little shaky, she concentrated on applying the gel and then applying the overskin. At best, she'd hoped someone intimidating would show up that wouldn't hurt the family. What she got was a guy who was protective of her, fearless, and kind to a fearful little boy with a multi-tech.

Her heart was in danger of getting seriously attached.

CHAPTER
4

Hesarium

Hesarium sagged against the crawler and took a moment to gauge how much more of the vertical fields he had left to do. How could there still be half to be done? They'd been working for six marks. Shouldn't they be finished by now?

"Hes?" Rain called down from the top of the crawler. "You need a break?"

He didn't want to say yes. Rain was sweating and had taken off her heavy outer coat but didn't appear tired in the least. If he agreed to stop for a rest, he'd be admitting he couldn't keep up with her, a small delicate human.

Still, he was having problems catching his breath. The last time Hesarium had worked this hard for an extended period of time was during general training in the Talin Empire's military. Each night he'd collapsed on his bunk, laying there, listening to the labored breathing and groans of the other trainees. At the time, he'd thought nothing else could be as physically straining. He'd been wrong. Being a farmer was far harder than he'd ever thought possible. Even with the mechanization the humans had, the process was still labor intensive.

Not that he considered quitting. He'd excelled in military training, he'd excel here.

His leg made everything more difficult. The binding gel held the wound closed, but it still hurt every time he moved. He'd been forced to keep weight off that leg, but now his good leg throbbed from the added strain.

Ancestors, he wanted to rest, but pride kept him on his feet. He was a Talin warrior. A member of an elite squad. There was no—

"Here, drink this."

He blinked his eyes open to find Rain standing in front of him. He didn't remember closing his eyes or hearing her climb down. He'd been too busy standing there feeling sorry for himself to be situationally aware. It was inexcusable. He needed to do better.

Seeing her sweat-dampened hair and the soaked top of her shirt didn't help his sense of guilt. She was working as hard as he, and yet she didn't appear tired, only slightly winded.

"Hes?" She jiggled the canister. "Come on, buddy. You should drink. Then I'm taking you back home for a break."

Pride had him straightening up, but his wounded leg made him stumble a step. He was forced to grab onto the crawler to stay upright.

"Woah!" Rain exclaimed, dropping the canister to grab his arm with both her hands. "Let's sit down. It's been a long morning, and we deserve a break."

The only reason he sank to the ground was because Rain went first. If she needed to sit, then he'd join her. Once they were both seated, she picked up the fallen canister and handed it to him. "Drink up."

Hesarium accepted the container and drank deeply. The tea inside was cool and the subtle flavor was refreshing. Unlike Rain, who wore layers of clothing to deal with the cool temperatures of the planet, he hadn't been bothered. The work had heated him up enough to force him to open his backplates in order to regulate his body temperature. Even now, as he sat with the chilly breeze washing over him, he didn't lower his backplates.

"We got a lot done," she commented.

He grunted and took one last swallow before trying to hand the drink back to her. "Do you normally do this alone?"

"Denise, Jenni, and Tam usually help me with this field, but they're dealing with greenhouse three," she explained.

He pictured the four uniform buildings he saw grouped together when Rain had taken him on a walk around the property that morning. He'd met most of the humans and noticed everything they had, from the hand tools to the buildings, looked old and worn, including the greenhouses. It was no surprise they were having issues.

"What's wrong with it?" he asked. Between the drink and the breeze, he was starting to cool off. After so many years spent in the perfectly controlled atmosphere of ships and stations, he'd forgotten what it was like to feel like this. The humans must be uncomfortable all the time considering the narrow range of temperatures they could handle.

Rain let out a deep sigh, signifying she was more tired than she appeared. "A swarm of mun bugs got into the building. Before we caught them, they destroyed the automated systems and all the crops. We're scrambling to keep them contained while we exterminate them so they don't get into the other greenhouses. Losing one greenhouse is fine, we always produce extra. But losing the other two would be really rough."

He could see that small losses created large consequences here.

"What happens if you lose all the greenhouses?" he asked.

"Our diet gets a lot more restrictive until we can get them up and running again. They're part of the twenty percent of the food we produce for ourselves," she explained. "It's unlikely though. We had trouble with them before and Jenni is really good at dealing with them. I'm sure she won't leave a single one of those little bastards alive."

Rain might be smiling, but it didn't reach her eyes. Despite her confident words, his little human was concerned.

He'd never dealt with bugs or greenhouses, but he felt obligated to offer his assistance. "Should I be helping them?"

"No way, I need you here," Rain said, looking off toward the unfinished section of the field. "We'll do the rest of the vertical beds tomorrow morning."

"I'm fine to continue harvesting today," he argued, a determined rattle coming from his back plates.

Rain shook her head. "We need to process what we've got before we gather any more. Auntie should be making the midday meal by now. I'm sure the kids are already heading in from the border field to eat. We can join them, then after the meal, we can process what's in the crawler while the kids have their lessons."

"Lessons?" He inquired.

"Carter and Nova have an old teaching-station at their domicile." She pointed in a direction and Hesarium assumed it was where they lived. "There are about ten kids who take turns using it during the day. Wind, Cherish, Sunny, and Royal have their turn in the afternoon."

"Yours and your sibling's names are inconsistent with the other humans I've met," Hesarium commented. "Rain, Wind, Cherish, Sunshine, and Royal aren't typical human names, are they? Is that common with the other humans here?"

To his surprise, Rain's expression turned sad. "Mom named us after what she considered the most important things to farming. Rain, Wind, Sunshine, and Cherish, because you have to cherish the land or nothing can grow."

"Where does Royal's name fit in?" Hesarium pushed.

Rain's expression tightened, her melancholy morphing into something more like anger. "Mom didn't name him, Debra did. She moved in with us a few years after Mom died. Dad didn't love her, but I think he was lonely, and a year later, she gave birth. Because he was her son and not a stepchild, he was better than the rest of us and she wanted everyone to know it, so she named him Royal." Her mood suddenly lightened. "Joke's on her though. Despite her best efforts, Royal is the sweetest kid you'll ever meet."

"He is a kindhearted child," Hesarium agreed. "And now I understand why he doesn't look like the rest of you."

"Yeah, Royal has his mother's lighter skin tone and straight hair." Rain gave him a smile that didn't reach her eyes. "But enough about all that. The important thing is we're all doing our best and getting along—mostly."

Hesarium couldn't mistake her words for anything but an attempt to end this line of questioning. There was a painful story here, and he had to trust she'd tell him more when she was ready.

"It's good to know the young humans are receiving an education," he commented, hoping to steer the conversation back to a more neutral topic. That morning, he'd been deeply dismayed to find out that all four of them were heading out to check one of the fields. He'd hated seeing the young humans all gathered on top of a crawler with Sunny piloting them away. He'd refrained from saying anything but only barely.

None of them should be working but most especially not the young ones.

"Sunny loves her time on the teaching-station, but Wind, Cherish, and Royal are a lot less interested," Rain volunteered as she patted her head to check that her mane was still in place. Unlike yesterday when she kept the tight curls under a hat, today it was tied up in two fluffy groupings on either side of her head.

That morning, he'd watched with fascination as Auntie and Rain had helped style all the siblings' manes while they ate breakfast. After they were done with the kids, the two women took turns eating while the other put their mane into a similar style. Although the texture of their manes were different from the humans he'd met before, he was sure he could learn to properly care for them. He looked forward to the day he could help the humans maintain their manes, especially his beautiful Rain.

The sound of young voices shouting and laughing in the distance made Rain perk up. Getting to her feet, she held out her hands to him. "Sounds like the kids are almost back to the domicile. It must be later than I thought. We need to get going or they'll eat everything before we get there!"

Ignoring her offer of help, Hesarium heaved himself to his feet and laboriously climbed up into the crawler. Stifling a groan, he laid down on a bed of harvested seedpods while Rain piloted the crawler back to join everyone for the midday meal.

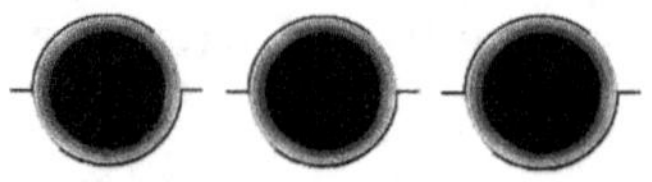

Rain

Rain didn't like how Hes was shuffling when he walked. He was in pain and refusing to admit it or take it easy. The rest of today wouldn't be a problem. The sorting job could be done seated. The question was, how was she going to keep him from working tomorrow?

"Hes, you should eat more!" Auntie said as she pushed the large platter of food sitting in the center of them further toward him. "Don't worry, there's always plenty to eat. The only thing we don't run out of is food. You're not depriving anyone if you take your fill."

"My species usually only eats once a day," he explained, looking down at the communal platter.

"But you didn't eat much at breakfast," Auntie argued. "When do you normally eat your meal? Morning? Evening?"

"It depends on our duties. What meal is the most important for you? The humans I knew believed the evening meal was the one everyone should attend."

That comment caused a flood of questions about the humans he knew. All the kids and Auntie spoke on top of each other, not giving Hes a chance to answer.

"Enough!" Rain barked out. "One question each and then no more questions."

"You mean no more questions today," Sunny countered. "Can we all ask one question tomorrow?"

Rain smiled. "Sure, but Hes doesn't have to answer anything he's not comfortable with. If you ask and he doesn't want to talk, then you don't get to ask another question. Got it?"

"Sure," Sunny agreed then focused on Hes who'd remained silent for the exchange. "Where did you meet humans?"

Hes hesitated before answering. "They were working at an Orlok mining colony."

Everyone waited in silence for him to elaborate, but he didn't add more details. Turned out, Hes wasn't a chatty guy.

Auntie jumped in next to ask her question. "How many humans were there?"

"Seventy-six."

Rain felt a little excitement and blurted out a question of her own. "Do they need more help? We might not be miners, but we can learn, and I'm sure almost all the thirty-two people here would be willing to move."

"They no longer work the mine," he told them, his tone as gentle as his rumbling purr. "The mine is now owned and run by Talins."

Wind frowned. "The Talins kicked them out?"

Hes's rumble went silent as he rattled out a negative sound. "We didn't make them leave. We relocated them."

It was Auntie who pressed for more details. "To where?"

Again, his answer was much too brief. "Most went to Talarian."

"Whatever you do, don't give us too many details," Auntie grumbled under her breath. Rain couldn't blame her. When she'd instituted the one question limit, she hadn't expected Hes to be so taciturn. If she didn't know better, she'd think he was trying to hide something.

Cherish and Royal were the only ones with questions left. Sitting back, Cherish crossed her arms over her chest with a challenging expression on her face.

"You probably could've gotten a good paying job in a lot of places. Why did you come here to work for nothing but a place to sleep and food you don't eat?"

Although it wasn't what Rain expected from Cherish, it was still a good question. Rain shouldn't be surprised. Cherish was one for insightfulness. All Rain could think was that she'd been too scared to ask Hes the same question.

They all stared at Hes as he regarded Cherish. Then he shifted his gaze over to Rain, staring intently into her eyes. She couldn't look away, and a strange excitement flared through her body.

"I was seeking my purpose," he answered, slapping down his back plates once in a decisive sound. "Money is not a purpose."

Why did those words tug at something deep inside of her? And why couldn't she look away? Before she could figure out what was going on with her, Royal spoke up.

"Hes?" Royal called out from his safe perch on Auntie's lap. "I have a question for you."

Hes rumbled out a purr as he looked at the youngest of them. "Yes, little Royal?"

"Can I sit in your lap?" Royal's question made everyone chuckle, even Cherish's sneer turned to a smile for a brief moment.

Hes opened his arms up in invitation. "The answer to that will always be yes."

Auntie lifted Royal off her lap and passed him over to Hes. The little boy snuggled down, telling Hes all about his multi-tech and how it was the best tool anyone could ever have. Purring the entire time, Hes listened intently while also urging Royal to eat between sentences.

What was that she heard? Yup, that was the sound of her ovaries exploding!

CHAPTER 5

Rain

    Rain couldn't sleep. Staring up at the stained ceiling of her bedroom, she debated getting up and making herself a warm drink or continuing to lay there with anxiety curdling her stomach and poisoning her thoughts.

    Stupid brain, she thought, throwing off the covers. She sat up and tugged the edges of her bonnet down her forehead a little. She had to feel around with her feet for a bit, but she managed to find her house shoes. With the heaters set to the lowest setting during the night, the air was chilly. She didn't want to risk waking up Auntie by turning on a light, so she wrapped a blanket around her shoulders and shuffled out of the room.

    It was almost perfectly dark upstairs, but she didn't bother turning on a light even after the bedroom door quietly slid shut. After so many years, she knew every inch of this domicile. A misstep was unlikely.

    With the blanket half falling off, she climbed down the ladder and made her way to the kitchen area. Once there, she activated a single light, blinking at the sudden brightness filling her vision.

    As usual, Auntie had left the kitchen immaculate. Rain smiled at the sight and loved Auntie a little more. The woman was an absolute blessing. There weren't many people who would agree to live with a bunch of orphaned kids, but Auntie hadn't hesitated. When the Jonas family took Royal away, Auntie fought alongside Rain to get him back.

It still brought tears to Rain's eyes when she thought about how Royal had been treated for the six months he'd lived with those horrible people. When their abusive treatment came to light, they'd run away. In a stroke of justice, they'd been murdered by the Gorlag Gang while trying to flee the planet.

Good riddance to those three horrible humans.

That was a little under two years ago, and Royal still had nightmares about his time with them. Guilt weighted heavily on Rain. She should've fought the community harder to get him back. She should have broken into the Jonas's house and stolen him.

"You can't change the past so focus on the future," she muttered to herself as she gathered the items to make what the kids called her can't-sleep drink. It was warmed pod-milk mixed with a little seedpod flour. Once it was thickened, she'd add in a hit of Zuri's moonshine. Some of the elders claimed it was similar to warmed Earth milk with a bit of whiskey added in.

It didn't take long to prepare the drink. The first sip slid down her throat, leaving a trail of comforting warmth. Turning off the single light, she shuffled over to a low, overstuffed chair. It was an ancient piece of furniture and perfectly worn to suck people in and refuse to let them out. Settling down, she arranged the blanket around her and took another sip. If she fell asleep in the large, comfy chair only to have someone wake her up in the morning, it wouldn't be the first time.

She was halfway done with her drink and making mental lists in her head when a sound at the front door made her tense up. It was almost pitch black in the room, and she debated about getting up and rushing to turn on the lights. If it was a male tweshi on the trail of prey, then the lights would scare it off. It was rare for even a male to travel this far from the bog, but it happened enough that everyone was careful walking outside at night.

Before she could decide on a course of action, the distinct sound of the door lock disengaging hit her ears. Whatever was out there had hands and the intelligence to open a door. That whittled her choices down to human or Dorinc.

Going still with fear, her heart pounding in her ears, Rain listened to the door softly swish open. A member of their community would be calling out by now or stomping their feet and wrestling to get their boots off. All she could hear was barely perceptible footfalls. That was the sound of someone sneaking around.

It had to be one of the gang members here to hurt them!

Fear had her scrambling out of the chair, causing her to spill the last of her drink down her front. Her legs got tangled in the blanket and she fell hard on the floor. Something rushed to her. Flipping over on her back, she looked up at the shadow looming over her, a scream bubbling up in her throat. A familiar purr filled her ears at the same time as the smell of sugar cookies hit her nose, stifling her scream.

She'd been wrong; there was a third option! How had she forgotten about the addition to her household?

"Hes?" she whispered, relief making her slump down on the floor. "What are you doing outside at this time of night?"

"My kind require only a few marks of sleep. I decided to make good use of my time while I waited for everyone to wake up for the day. I was out assessing the landscape at night. Did you hurt yourself?"

She couldn't make out any of his features as he knelt down next to her. "I'm fine," she assured him, sitting up. "You scared me, is all."

Hes pushed his arms under her body and lifted her easily to his chest. "I'm sorry, Rain. That was never my intention. If I'd known anyone was awake, I would've called out."

"My fault too," she said and pulled in a deep breath through her nose as Hes's warmth surrounded her.

She should've insisted he set her on her feet or back on the chair, but it felt good to be cradled in his arms. She hadn't been ready to be a parent, sibling, head of the household, and a community leader all at once after her father died. The last few years had been exhausting, and snuggling up to Hes seemed like an innocent break from her worries.

It didn't hurt that he smelled so damn good!

"Are you sure you're uninjured?" he asked, sitting down in the same chair she'd fallen out of. While it had been big enough for her to curl up sideways, Hes barely fit. It forced her to stay nestled against his chest as he settled her weight on his lap.

"Only my pride," she answered with a half laugh. "It's embarrassing, but when I heard the door open, I froze. I should've been going for a weapon or at least getting up to turn on the lights a lot sooner."

"Remaining still to assess a situation is often both viable and wise," Hes told her. His warmth and purring were doing what the drink hadn't, lulling her into a relaxed state of mind. "Tell me why you're down here when everyone else is sleeping?"

"We need equipment," she said after a brief internal debate. "Several of the vertical planters need to be replaced and one of the crawlers is barely usable. Two of the houses need new energy plants and our grow-starters all need to be replaced. It's all falling apart, and no matter how much I work the numbers, I can't get us everything we need and pay the Gorlag Gang."

After a few minutes of silence, Hes asked a question. "What about leaving this planet? You could all start somewhere new."

Rain let her head drop to Hes's shoulder. "That's harder for us than most. Humans are a species with no homeworld. That means we don't have a viable government. No one to hold other species accountable if they mistreat us. There were over a hundred humans at the Hunak station. Last time we heard from them, there were only five. There might be none now."

"Are they leaving the station?" Hes asked.

"No, they're dying," Rain bluntly corrected him. "The station assigned the most dangerous jobs to the humans and barely paid them enough to survive on. After they realized how bad it was, they wanted to come here."

"Why aren't they here?"

"Money," Rain answered. "They couldn't save enough to leave the station. My guess is they've all died out by now and that's why we haven't gotten a message from them in over a year. When you don't hear from a group of humans for a while, it's always bad news."

Hes placed one big hand on her back and gently stroked up and down her spine. For such a big individual, he was surprisingly gentle.

"What if there was a place you could go where you wouldn't have to labor?" he asked.

A harsh bark of laughter came out of Rain. "What you're describing doesn't exist."

"I know a place," he insisted. "The humans there don't work. Everything they need is provided to them."

She frowned. "Sex work is still labor."

Hes hissed out a breath, his body going tense, and his hand pulled away from her back. "No one is forced to have sex either."

Rain had too much experience with the cold reality of the universe to take his claim at face value. "Are you trying to tell me there's some kind of paradise where humans can live without having to contribute? I find that hard to believe."

His body relaxed slightly, and his hand went back to petting her. "They contribute."

Now she knew he was making it all up. "How can they contribute if they aren't working?"

"It's hard to explain, but you must believe me," he answered.

"Sure." And just like that, she brushed off the whole thing.

This had to be a cultural misunderstanding. The same thing had happened to her during a meeting many years ago. She'd been young and learning how to negotiate and put together contracts with her father. That was back when buyers would still visit the planet. There was enough being produced to create competition, and the buyers who showed up in person to negotiate always got the best price.

A Marshet buyer had offered Rain a job at the end of the negotiations. Thinking it was a mark of her improved skillset, she proudly told her father she was going to accept the job and send money home.

It'd been a harsh blow to find out the *job* was one of wife. Among the Marshet, everything was a job. When they reproduced, their offspring had the job of *children*. A short conversation with her father asking the right questions revealed that the Marshet wanted her as a fifth wife for his second husband.

That day she learned two things. The first was that Marshet marriages were complicated. The second and more important was that she needed to be cognizant of even the slightest cultural differences in other species or risk major misunderstandings.

"Someday I'll be able to prove it to you," Hes murmured, taking her silence for continued disbelief.

"Maybe," she responded stiffly. She really didn't like this topic and was relieved when Hes moved on to a different line of questions.

"The maps you have for this area indicate there's only one viable road, is that correct?" he asked.

"Yes, that's right," she answered. "When the bog expanded the second time, it took out the two other roads. If you've got a tall crawler, you can make it through, but the Gorlags don't use crawlers, only those Rasts."

"While I was out, uh, walking around, I found Rast displacement tracks. They'd been created within the last few days. From what I could see, the vehicle sat in one spot for some time. It was at the high section of the road, just as the fields start."

Rain didn't like the sound of that. "Do you think they were watching us?"

Hes didn't hesitate to give her the bad news. "Yes. I also found evidence of older spots were Rasts have been parked in the area before. Do you know why they'd be observing you like that?"

With a sigh, Rain sat up so she could look him in the eyes. The dark made it difficult, but they were close enough for her to make out the shape of his face. "They're waiting for us to finish the harvest. They want to make sure they get what they demand."

"You're referring to a percentage of the crop?" Hes asked.

Rain rubbed her forehead, feeling the onset of a tension headache. "They probably won't want a bunch of processed seedpods. They're watching so they know how much we've produced. That tells them how much money they can demand from us. I thought it was bad when all we had to deal with was weather, tweshi, and bad batches of proto-plants. But now I realize that was all easy compared to the present."

"I'm here to help." Hes's arms went around her, drawing her back against his chest. "I'll do my best to keep the community safe."

Rain wasn't surprised when a single tear managed to slip out of her eye. "It's not supposed to be like this! I know life isn't fair, but does it have to keep getting worse? This is bullshit."

"I'm unsure what an herbivore's excrement has to do with the inherent difficulty of your situation."

"It's an Earth saying," she explained with a chuckle. "We humans are fond of using animal excrement as descriptions. Horseshit denotes a lie. Dogshit means it's not worth anything or badly made. Batshit is used to describe someone who's crazy. Oh, and a person who's acting like a coward is chickenshit."

"Does this mean bullshit is used when dealing with difficult or impossible situations?" Hes asked. She could hear the humor in his voice.

"Bullshit is the most versatile of the shits," she answered, barely keeping from laughing at the absurd conversation. "In this context, it means the whole system is rotten."

"I believe your description is accurate," Hes responded, as he interrupted his purring to sound the clinking-glass-marbles rumble of amusement. When he spoke again, his tone was soft but serious. "Leaving this place seems to be your best option."

"I know, but like I said, there's no place to go and very little money to get there," Rain reminded him, gloom settling over her again. Her head was resting on his shoulder, close to the base of his neck. She could see a slip of exposed skin, not covered by the hard keratin plating. Giving in to impulse, she put her nose and mouth against that skin.

She sighed out a breath at how soft it was. Hes tensed and his purring stopped. Worried she'd caused him discomfort, she went to move away, but his hand came up and cradled the back of her head, keeping her there with gentle pressure.

"It felt good," he whispered. "Please don't move."

If anyone understood the importance of the little comforts in life, it was a farmer. Nuzzling that spot of skin, she kissed it. The smell of sugar cookies became even stronger, and Hes started purring again.

No, not exactly a purr—a rumble. It was slower and throbbed more than his purr. This was the first time she was hearing it, so she should probably ask what it signified, but a wave of fatigue washed over her.

She felt warm and safe nestled in Hes's arms. His smell, rumbles, and embrace were all doing what the warm pod drink was supposed to. Sleep, more peaceful than she'd experienced in years, overtook her, and she slid into unconsciousness. The Talin's rumbling and sweet, sugar-cookie smell followed her into her dreams.

CHAPTER 6

Rain

Waking up to the smell of sugar cookies was much better than burned reconstitutor packs. Rain breathed deep and smiled before she even opened her eyes. Then she tried to stretch but found she was trapped.

Blinking at the bright daylight flooding the room from the automated transparency panels, Rain realized she was on the main floor in the same position she'd curled up in last night. Moving her head back, she looked up to find Hes with his eyes closed and his head held straight and level, despite his apparent sleeping status.

"Hes?" she whispered in case he was prone to startling awake. She didn't want to get launched, but she couldn't get herself untangled from the blankets and off his lap until he moved his arms.

Watching a Talin wake up was fascinating. First his eyes popped open, and then he focused on the room in front of him. He went from fully asleep to awake in a second. There was no bleary-eyed blinking or confusion. Next, he dropped his head forward and she heard his neck plates slapping down. That's how he must have kept his head still while asleep. Then he moved his head and assessed his surroundings before looking down at her.

As his gaze settled on her, the sound of a distant bass drum rumbled out of him. "Are you in distress?"

Why was that the first thing he asked her? She never looked her best first thing in the morning, but no one had ever accused her of looking ill!

"I'm tangled," she answered with a half-smile at his concern. "It's morning and I should get up so I can dress and start the day."

He lowered his gaze to take in the blankets and his arms wrapped around her, but he didn't move. "It's early. Can we not remain like this for a while longer?"

Had he gotten as much comfort from their cuddles as she did? It hadn't occurred to her until this moment that this Talin might be in need of the same warmth and emotional support as a human. If he'd been on his own for a long time, he could have been starved of touch.

Memories of him with Royal in his lap, listening intently as the little boy listed all the things the multi-tech could measure, floated across her mind. At the time, she thought he might be doing it simply to get along with everyone, but now she thought he might miss his family. He had to be far away from home, and it was a harsh, cold universe out there. Warmth, affection, and kindness could be hard to come by.

The more she thought about it, the more she decided they had a lot to offer this wandering warrior.

"You're safe here," she murmured.

"You couldn't hurt me," he scoffed. She didn't take offense at his tone. At the moment, he reminded her a little of Cherish. The teenager used her attitude to hide her vulnerabilities just as Hes was trying to hide weaknesses behind physical strength.

"We're a safe group to love because we'll always love you back," she whispered, pulling a hand free from the blankets to cup his cheek. She felt something warm and viscus on her palm but ignored it. The scent of sugar cookies permeated the air, and Hes started purring. "We might not always get along, but this family is fiercely loyal and unrepentantly affectionate. If you stay with us, you'll be folded right in. That's both a promise and warning, Hes."

"What if I don't know how to do this?" he asked, his voice barely above a whisper.

Her heart broke for the big male. What had his childhood and life been like to create someone who didn't understand love?

She drew his face closer to hers. "We'll teach you," she murmured, then brushed her lips against his. "Here's your first lesson: that was a kiss. We only kiss on the lips with someone we're romantically or sexually interested in."

"Does that mean you want me in that way?" Hes asked, his purr changing pitch and tone. It was deeper and slower now, like the thrumming of a massive, distant engine that shook the very ground.

"I do," she answered. "In some ways, I'm lonely too. We could comfort each other."

"Think I want to do more than comfort you," Hes responded.

Something trickled down her palm and onto her wrist. She pulled her hand away from his face to find an oil-like substance on her skin. Curious, she looked to his face to see the same substance beading on the skin of both cheeks. The sugar-cookie smell was so strong she'd swear there was a fresh plate of them right under her nose.

"It's bonding oil," he explained, watching her closely as he talked. "We Talins have scent glands in our cheeks. They produce an oil with a unique smell, and we spread that scent on our partner so they smell like us."

His voice never changed as he spoke, but Rain heard the subtext to his words. His explanation was a request for permission and a plea for acceptance. Without hesitation, she rubbed the bonding oil from her hand onto her neck and shoulder. Hes pulled a sharp breath, and his arms came around her back.

"I need—I want—" he stuttered.

"Show me what you need," she urged.

She was expecting a kiss or something like that. She was surprised when he ignored her lips and pulled her body tight to his, leaning down to rub his cheeks into her hair. At some point during their night of cuddling in the chair, her bonnet had ended up on the floor, giving him access to all her hair. She could feel the warm oil saturating it, all the way down to her scalp.

All the members of her family and many of the community used oils to soften and protect their hair and skin. As circumstances had grown worse, access to those oils had slowed. Last year it had stopped all together, as wealth and trade diminished. The combination of the sugar-cookie smell and the sensation of luxurious oil being worked through her hair all the way to her scalp made Rain's body start to heat.

It didn't take long for the rumbling and his touch to cause her body to tense up with neediness. She wanted to strip down, lay back, and let Hes rub his oil all over her body. She wanted his hands touching her everywhere, and she wanted to feel his body press against hers.

All these sensations and impulses were a first for her!

She'd had exactly two relationships in the past, one with a woman and then one with a man. They were both lackluster and brief. After they parted ways, each person went on to marry others and start families of their own. She'd never been jealous of either of them, but she wished she understood why everyone else was so excited about sex. Those two lovers felt like trying on coats that didn't fit. At the time, she thought maybe she was simply asexual. Now she knew better.

It turns out she wasn't asexual, she was Hes-sexual!

Moving a little, she tilted her head to give him access to the back where he hadn't touched yet. She moaned a little as he rubbed his face against her skin. Conflict rose up in her, she wanted him to touch her in other places, but she also didn't want him to stop what he was doing.

Hes pulled in a deep breath, as if smelling the subtle change in her scent when his bonding oil soaked into her skin. It was hard to describe, but the closest she could think of was that she smelled like frosted sugar cookies now.

"You like this?" he asked, his mouth at the nape of her neck.

His warm breath ghosting through her damp curls and across her saturated scalp made her shiver. "Yes. So much."

"Can I do the same thing to the rest of your body?"

She didn't even hesitate. "I might need to kill you in your sleep if you don't!"

The marbles-clinking rumble of amusement briefly interrupted his sexy, thrumming rumble. He pushed the edges of the blanket out of the way and tugged at the hem of the overlarge shirt she wore as pajamas.

Living in a crowded house meant Rain wasn't normally self-conscious, but with Hes's eyes roaming her body, she had to fight the urge to cover her chest with her arms.

"You're beautiful," he breathed, making her insecurity vanish. Supporting her spine between her shoulder blades with one broad hand, he urged her to lean back. This position gave him access to her breasts.

Leaning his head over, he pulled one beaded peak into his mouth and teased her with his tongue. She half expected him to be careless with those sharp teeth, but they only gently grazed her flesh. Heat flashed through her body as he sucked on her nipple, making her back arch. Wrapping one hand around the back of his head, she held his mouth there.

It was as if her nipple was linked directly to her pussy, and every time he tugged with his mouth, a bolt of electricity shot down her spine all the way to between her legs. She wanted him to keep doing this, but she also wanted him to put his mouth everywhere else. The competing needs made her undulate her hips. That's when she realized, if she moved her legs a little, she could rub her core against his muscled belly.

With her hand pressing tight to the back of his head, she maneuvered her legs until she could press her wet, throbbing pussy against his keratin-plated skin. Any worry that it might be too rough was dismissed as the crotch of her panties gave the soft shielding she needed.

She pushed her core hard against his muscled abdomen "Please!" she begged, feeling lightheaded from the pleasure and not sure what she was pleading for.

It was hard to believe this was the same body that didn't even urge her to masturbate! Now her body was twisting and shuddering under Hes's touch.

Lifting his head up so he could meet her eyes, he licked his lips with a slow, deliberate swipe of his long, textured tongue. "You taste good, Rain," he said, silencing his rumble so he could whisper to her in that deep voice. "I want to taste all of you. Run my tongue over every part of this delicious body."

"Hes!" she cried, lifting her chest and inviting him to give her other breast the same treatment. "Don't stop. Please, don't stop!"

Although he could've easily resisted her hand on the back of his neck, he let her guide his hot mouth. He started up his sexy rumble, which made his abdominal muscles vibrate against her clit. To her shock, she started cresting. Pressing her clit down hard, she went still and let his rumble push her over the edge.

"Oh! Hes!" she cried out, her body going stiff.

Pleasure flooded her body and she finally understood. Now she got it! This was why people liked sex so much. It was a little sad she'd had to wait until she was twenty-six to really experience it, but she couldn't complain. This was too spectacular to have regrets!

As the orgasm slowly faded, Rain came back to herself. Hes had rearranged her so he could cradle her on his lap. He was alternatively kissing her face and hair and rubbing his oil onto her.

"You're the most beautiful creature," he murmured, his sexy rumble quieting to a purr.

"You make me feel beautiful," she answered, then became aware of something hard pressing against her thigh.

Looking down, she saw the clear outline of a rigid cock straining to get free of Hes's pants.

"Let me make you feel good too," she said, sitting up. She was about to reach down when a voice from behind them made her freeze.

"You might want to put yourself to rights," Auntie said with a soft laugh as she finished descending the ladder. "Everyone is going to be filing down here soon for breakfast."

"Rot!" Rain cursed as she scrambled off Hes and searched for her shirt. Hes got up as well. She had just finished tugging on her sleeping shirt when Hes wrapped the blanket around her shoulders.

"It's chilly," he said gruffly. She glanced down and saw he must have deflated because there was no obvious outline at the crotch of his pants. As soon as it was feasible, she was determined to see what that fabric had been hiding.

Despite almost being caught by her siblings, Rain felt lighthearted. "Let's revisit this conversation later."

"Yes, I'd be eager to do that," he agreed.

"As long as you two do your *talking* somewhere private and not in the living room," Auntie called out from the kitchen area. "And after the buying proposals have been done. We need to get those sent out today, Rain!"

"Yes, Auntie. I won't disappear on you," Rain promised with a laugh. Standing on tiptoe, she pressed her lips to Hes's for a last quick kiss, then she headed for the ladder. The sooner she got dressed and started her day, the sooner she could sneak off. She was already calculating how long it would take for her and Auntie to finish the proposals.

She was determined to get some *Hes time* in today because there was no way she was going an entire day before experiencing all that again!

CHAPTER 7

Hesarium

With Rain and Auntie busy putting together and sending out inquiries to seedpod buyers, Hesarium agreed to accompany the children on a field check. Wind had explained that, once every few rotations, they all loaded up into one of the crawlers and traveled to the outside perimeter of the community's farmland, looking for trouble spots. Usually it was the bog expanding or a new underground cavity developing. The spots were geo-marked and then repair groups were organized and sent out to deal with it.

"Anyway, there isn't much we can do except make everyone aware of a new area of spreading bog," Sunny explained to him as they walked to the crawler.

By the way the siblings cheerfully talked about the day's chores during first meal, it was obvious field check was a favorite task. They were all in cheerful moods as they climbed onto the slowest and most problematic crawler on the settlement. Even he could see it was in poor repair, with gaping holes and an odd slant to the back end.

"I wanna come!" Royal shouted, running up to the side of the crawler with his multi-tech clutched in his hand as Sunny and Hesarium finished climbing up.

Wind, still on the ground, regarded his youngest sibling. "Are you sure you don't want to hang out with Auntie and Rain?"

Royal shook his head, his expression stubborn. "They don't needs my helps. Hes needs me 'cus he doesn't know all the fields likes I do."

"You can come along, but tell me the rules first," Wind requested.

"I can'ts runs off, I can'ts be loud if you guys are concentrating, and I cans sleep if I wants to," Royal answered dutifully.

"You got them all, good job, Roy-roy," Wind enthused, then looked up to where both Hesarium and Cherish were standing on the top of the crawler.

"We've got plenty of blankets," Cherish answered before Wind said anything.

"Then we're good to go," Wind said and grabbed Royal under the arms and lifted so he could grab the handholds halfway up the crawler's side. Leaning over the side of the crawler, Hesarium reached down and easily lifted Royal the rest of the way before the little boy had a chance to try climbing up.

"I'm flying!" Royal giggled, kicking his legs a little in the air. "Zoooom!"

Hesarium sounded an amused rumble. "If you can wait for me, I'll fly you in and out of the crawler each time."

"I can waits for you," Royal promised as Hesarium set him down. The moment Hesarium let go, the little boy wrapped his arms around Hesarium's leg in a hug. Then he let go and skipped to the front to demand Sunny let him pilot the crawler.

The unexpected show of affection from Royal made Hesarium freeze. He remained still even after Royal let go and scampered away. It was only when Cherish came into his field of vision that he broke out of the stunned stillness.

"Royal likes you," Cherish whispered with a frown. "Don't hurt him or I'll figure out some way to kill you and then I'll feed your body to a tweshi."

She probably expected him to react badly to her threat, but Hesarium felt nothing but respect for the fierce girl.

"I'd deserve it," he agreed simply. His words shocked her into a smile before she wrestled her expression back into one of disapproval. Then she moved to the back of the crawler, facing away from everyone else.

Wind had climbed up and was perched on the edge of the crawler for the brief exchange between him and Cherish. After she walked off, the young man gave him a quick smile before joining his twin. He sat next to her and whispered something. She shrugged and went back to staring out at nothing.

Cherish reminded him of Sapurian, who'd lost his entire squad on the first assignment. It had taken Sapurian a while before he'd join them for communal meals. Eventually, Hesarium had realized it wasn't that Sapurian was unfriendly. The warrior was terrified of losing his squad again. He'd survived the death of his fellow soldiers, but the experience had left him with scars inside and out.

With the death of a mother, a father, and a stepmother happening within a few years, it was no wonder Cherish was hesitant to get attached.

"Hey, Hes! Want to join me up here?" Sunny called out as the crawler's engine wound up under them. She was looking over her shoulder and pointing to the seat next to her. On her lap, Royal bobbed his head up and down.

"Comes on, Hes. I gots to point out the places we're going," Royal called out.

"That would be very educational," Hesarium agreed and joined Sunny and Royal at the front. Without asking, Royal climbed from Sunny's lap to his. Hes didn't have to worry about entertaining Royal. The little boy kept up a steady stream of explanations and pointed out every last plant or divot as they traveled.

As the morning progressed, Hesarium understood why this was the siblings' favorite task—it was easy. All they did was drive and occasionally stop to check a spot more closely.

They rarely even climbed down because the spots could be tagged on the community's interactive map from the top of the crawler. So far, they'd found two minor issues that Sunny explained probably wouldn't be addressed until it was time to replant that field.

Sunny and Royal kept up a cheerful conversation but Wind and Cherish were mostly quiet as they kept lookout from the rear of the crawler. With a life full of physical labor, this job probably allowed them the rare opportunity to rest without guilt.

"Is it time for lunch yet?" Wind yelled from the back.

Sunny shouted back without even looking over her shoulder. "Always!"

That got a chuckle from Wind and an exaggerated laugh from Royal. "It can't be lunch all the time," Royal admonished. "That would be weird. There has to be breakfasts and dinners too."

"What if it was always dinner time?" Sunny asked as she tapped on the crawler's control panel. The thing came to a slow stop with a slight shudder, then a loud cluck as the wheel gears locked in place.

"Sunny, don't be a podhead!" Royal exclaimed, doing a good impression of Cherish's eye roll. Sunny froze for a second then roared with laughter. Hesarium sounded a rumble of amusement at the child's dramatics.

"What's so funny?" Wind asked as he grabbed the storage box with the food Auntie had packed for them.

"You had to be there," Sunny said with a small shake of her head. "Come on, let's eat. I'm starving."

"You'd constantly eat if you could," Cherish grumbled from behind them as she swung a leg over the side of the crawler and climbed down. Wind handed her the food and climbed down himself.

Sunny's smile didn't diminish. "Yup! Food and sleep are my favorites, and in that order."

Hiding a smile, Cherish let out a heavy sigh of disdain. Sunny ignored her sister and climbed down after Wind and the food. Cherish followed, and Hesarium stood up with Royal in his arms and walked to the side of the crawler. Wind was looking up at him from the ground, ready to take Royal, but Hesarium didn't hand him down. The distance to the ground was well within his capabilities and made him want to give Royal a fun experience.

"Do you want to fly?" he asked Royal.

"Fly? Yes!" Royal answered.

"Hold onto me," Hesarium instructed. Royal wrapped his little arms around Hesarium's neck, his multi-tech clicking against one of Hesarium's neck plates. Taking several steps back, Hesarium took a few running steps then lengthened his stride to place a foot on the rail of the crawler. With a powerful push, he leaped high into the air.

He heard Wind gasp and Sunny shout a wordless exclamation as he hit the apex of the leap. Tucking his body around Royal, he somersaulted in the air and got his legs under him in plenty of time to land lightly on his feet.

"Wooweee!" Royal screamed and wiggled excitedly in his arms. "Again! Again, again, again!"

Wind hurried to them, his expression interested. "Could you teach me how to do that?"

Cherish stalked up to him, her scowl extra fierce. "That was dumb. You could've gotten Royal hurt!"

Sunny stayed where she was, sitting down next to the open food box. When she spoke, her voice was gentle but commanding. "Royal, quiet down. If you're good, maybe Hes could do that again, but not right now."

"Sunny!" Cherish protested. "You can't decide that! You're not a real adult."

"I'm close enough for this," Sunny responded, her ever-present smile disappearing. It looked like Cherish had finally managed to irritate her sibling.

Cherish scowled fiercely. "Well I say he can't, and Wind sides with me. That's two against one."

"Don't drag me into this," Wind said quickly.

"Let it go," Sunny told Cherish. "Royal had fun and it's obvious Hes knew what he was doing. Until he actually does something wrong, we don't get angry with him. I know that's hard for you to understand because your default is pissed off, but give it a try sometimes. You might like being happy instead of angry."

"Fine," Cherish snarled and stomped over to the food box. Grabbing something out of it, she walked away with long, angry strides. He could hear her angry mutterings, "Stupid Hes shows up and everybody loves him. Can't do anything wrong. Fine then. They can trust him for all I care. Don't come crying to me when he gets someone hurt or killed."

Hesarium felt guilty. He hadn't meant to cause concern or start a fight between the siblings. Lowering himself to a seated position across from Sunny, he met her eyes. "I apologize. I didn't mean to upset anyone."

Sunny waved off his words, her perpetual smile back in place. "It's fine."

Wind settled down on the other side of the food box and reached in for a container. "Cherish will calm down. It's just that she worries a lot."

Multi-tech tucked in his belt, Royal accepted the package of food Wind handed him and danced from foot to foot as he tore into it. His little body had too much energy to sit still while he ate.

Hesarium turned down the offer of food from Wind. "More for us," Wind commented before greedily eating his food.

"Can I ask why there is such a large age difference between you and Rain?" Hesarium asked Sunny. "She seems far older than you, or am I inaccurately judging human ages?"

"You're not wrong," Sunny answered between bites. "Rain's nine years older than me. Mom got pregnant with her really young."

"How young?" Hesarium pressed.

"My age," Sunny admitted. "Mom and Dad had Rain when she was sixteen and Dad was seventeen. After Rain was born, the medic didn't think Mom could have any more kids, then nine years later, I happened. Mom says I refused to be alone, so I did magic as a toddler, and she got pregnant with the twins."

"Dad always said those were the best years," Wind commented. "This place was thriving. We had almost double the number of people and triple the land. We still have a few of the luxury items Mom and Dad bought then." He pointed to the multi-tech Royal was holding. "Dad splurged on that, even though he didn't strictly need it for farming."

Now Hes understood why Royal treasured the multi-tech. It had belonged to a father the little boy probably barely remembered.

Hesarium wasn't sure he wanted to know, but he asked anyway. "What happened between then and now?"

"The poorly done terraforming caught up with itself," Sunny answered for Wind. "There was an earthquake that forced a bunch of water around under the crust. It caused new bogs to develop and existing bogs to spread. Fixing it would've been easy, but expensive. No one here, human or Dorinc, could afford it. The Massoc who own the planet wouldn't fix it either. A lot of Dorinc left after the Massoc refused to do anything."

That explained the sudden decline of the planet. "Why didn't the humans leave then?"

"We could've," Wind answered. "Dad said there was enough funds saved up at that point to start fresh somewhere else. But the community voted to stay here."

When Wind didn't elaborate, Hes pushed. "Why?"

"Because they were lazy, stupid bastards," Cherish said as she stomped back over to them. Her food box was open, and as she flopped down to sit next to Wind, Hes noticed she couldn't have eaten more than a few bites.

Once she was seated, Wind bumped her with his shoulder, and she glared at him but bumped him back gently.

"They weren't stupid or lazy," Sunny argued. Cherish narrowed her eyes at Sunny and opened her mouth to talk, but Wind spoke before she could.

"It was a hard choice to make," Wind told him. "Even though we lost a lot of land to the bog, so many other farmers left that we submitted claims for the empty land. We ended up with as much as we had before the earthquake. If we'd moved to some other planet, we would've had to start from scratch."

"You could have moved to an established farming planet," Hesarium suggested.

Sunny shook her head. "We'd simply end up on another unstable terraformed planet. It's the only place we'd have been able to afford, even at our wealthiest."

"Are all terraformed planets this dangerous?" Hes asked.

Sunny, Wind, and Cherish all nodded.

Sunny pointed to the bog behind her. "They're like this place, still settling and changing. You could go from living in a rainforest to a desert in a couple of years. You never know with terraforming."

"What happened to the land you claimed from the Dorinc who left?" Hes asked. "Did it turn out to not be enough to make up for the land you lost?"

Cherish let out a harsh laugh. "We had all the land we could want for an entire month, then the bog took it away. It won't be long until this whole place is nothing but bog." Her voice dropped to a quiet, bitter murmur. "Everything will be water and mud, and we'll all get to drown in it."

Hes wanted to ask more questions, but a herd of some kind of six-legged animal emerged from the nearby bog at a rapid pace. In twos and threes they leapt high in the air to clear the area at the edge of the bog, all six legs pulled tight against their body before one set of legs impacted the ground. Once on solid earth the three sets of legs moved fast, making them appear to fly over the ground.

Hes jumped up and put himself between the creatures and the children. Bristling his quills and letting his claws emerge from his fingers, he took a strong stance, ready to hold off these animals for as long as he could.

"Run!" he shouted. "Get in the crawler!"

Sounding a deafening war rattle, he braced himself for impact. It was hard to count, but he was sure there were at least twenty animals coming at them. Each one looked about double his size. Against such odds it was unlikely he'd win, but maybe he could give the children time to get away.

"Hes, they're—" Before Wind could finish his sentence, the creatures were on them. Or more accurately, over them. The things jumped over and around the little group without much effort and continued on their way.

Stunned, Hes quieted his war rattle, straightened up, and flattened his quills back down against his forearm. He turned to find no one had moved, and all of them were grinning at him. Even Cherish was smiling.

"Those are enticts," Sunny explained with a little giggle. "They're harmless."

Feeling embarrassed over his dramatic actions, Hes sat back down. It was hard, but he tried to calm his fight and protect instincts. "I see. I'm sorry if I startled any of you."

"You made a sound like a bunch of feet stomping on hard ground!" Wind burst out, jumping to his feet and walking around Hes to look at his back. "That was amazing. Do it again!"

Surprised at Wind's enthusiasm, Hes sounded another war rattle. As Wind watched his backplates move, Hes noticed Cherish staring at him with an expression other than a scowl.

"You were going to fight the enticts," she stated. "You didn't even know how dangerous they might be, and you tried to shield us. You barely know us. No one does that, at least not for humans."

Hes considered her statements before responding. "I will stand between all of you and danger at every opportunity. That is why I'm here."

Cherish tilted her head, as if considering his words. "We'll see."

"No, you'll know," he insisted, then made eye contact with each of them in turn. "As long as there is breath in my body, you will be protected. Let the Ancestors hear my vow."

"We'll see," Cherish repeated in a muted voice then focused back on her food. "Hurry up, guys. We need to see if the enticts messed up any of the ground-minders. They're always stepping on them."

Although she didn't say anything else, Hes got the impression he'd passed some test, and perhaps the perpetually angry Cherish would start to trust him more now.

CHAPTER 8

Hesarium

Everyone was helping to clean up after the evening meal and talking about who would get to use the cleansing room first when there was a chime at the door. It was Zuri, the human in the closest domicile, there to inform them that an emergency meeting had been called by a human named David. It was about Hes, and if they didn't hurry, there might be a vote without Rain or Auntie present.

Rain had told her siblings not to wait up and put Sunny in charge of Royal's bedtime routine. Then they hurried off with Zuri to find out what this human, David, was planning.

The meeting had started as they walked in. Most of the humans in the room refused to meet his gaze. Those that did look over at him were sneering or had other expressions of hostility. On the walk over, Rain had warned him this might happen. Her idea hadn't been popular. The other humans had reluctantly agreed only because Rain promised to house and feed whoever answered her posting for protection.

At the beginning of the meeting, a male named David had raised concerns that Hesarium might be a criminal, someone waiting to gain the trust of the community, and when everyone was relaxed, planned to murder and pillage their resources. It took a great deal of discipline to keep from rattling in anger and threatening David.

Now Rain was busy defending Hesarium with a passion and loyalty that made Hesarium's scent glands ache.

"…besides, he works as hard as any of us. Even after he was wounded by a tweshi," Rain continued. "I didn't require him to labor, he insisted. I tried to hand him the easiest of tasks, he demanded the most difficult. He continues to—"

"None of that matters!" David shouted, cutting Rain off. "We don't know anything about him or his species. He could enjoy eating humans for all we know. Maybe he's being good right now because he's waiting for an opportunity to murder us all and take our things."

"As if we have anything of value," Auntie scoffed.

"We have our seedpod crop," Devon pointed out. Their expression was worried and a little afraid. "What if he steals the crop?"

"It might be a little hard for him to smuggle the entire crop out in his only bag," Rain pointed out with a forced smile. "Come on, Devon, don't let David's dramatics get to you."

"I'm not being dramatic," David thundered, then he realized how he sounded and worked on composing himself. "I'm not being dramatic," he repeated in a more reasonable tone. "I'm being cautious, something Rain doesn't seem to understand. Keeping this Talin in our community is an extra danger we don't need."

"What about protection from the Gorlag?" Auntie protested. "He's so damn intimidating all he has to do is look in the direction of a Gorlag on a Rast. The Gorlag will be so scared he'll probably crash, and Hes won't have to lift a quill."

There were some chuckles and murmurs, but they were silenced by David's glare. Once the room was quiet, David spoke. "You've all heard me say the violence was going to calm down, and it has, right?"

There were some murmurs of agreement, making David smile widely before continuing. "The Gorlag Gang isn't stupid. Destroying us by demanding too much means they ruin their own livelihoods."

"Rain said they're demanding even more now," Gris said, stepping up behind his partner Devon and wrapping his arm around their shoulders.

"She exaggerates," David assured him. "What's happening now is a natural governing evolution. The farmers and the gang are finding an equilibrium. They'll see that settling for a little less is better in the long run. We didn't need this," David gestured at Hesarium as if he was a stupid beast without a name, "Talin to begin with. We certainly don't need him any longer."

Rain looked deceptively calm as she leaned back against the wall and crossed her arms over her chest. Hesarium could see the tension in her shoulders even as she smiled at David.

"Maybe you're right and the Gorlag Gang will back off," she allowed. "Maybe we won't have to pay them as much as they said last month. But I've got one question for you."

"What could you possibly want to ask me?" David demanded with scorn. "How to get rid of your pet?"

"He spent yesterday working side by side with me," Rain announced loudly so everyone could hear. "In the morning, we harvested the entire south field, and in the afternoon, we processed all the seedpods. While we were doing that, Denise, Jenni, and Tam were taking care of the greenhouses."

David spread his arms with the palms up in an exaggerated questioning stance. "Was there a question somewhere in that little story?"

"If he's working hard, why make him leave?" she asked simply. David opened his mouth, but Rain continued speaking. "I didn't see your ass out there helping me."

David's sneer disappeared. "I hurt my foot, remember?" His voice lost the authoritative push and sounded whiny.

Rain pointed at Hesarium's leg. "He's still healing from a tweshi attack. I changed his dressing after dinner and had to apply more bonding gel because he won't take it easy on that leg." She cast him a look of irritation. "But he's going to start listening to me and not reopen his wound. Right?"

Charmed by Rain's commanding tone, Hesarium couldn't stop his rumble of amusement. Otherwise he remained silent. In truth, after a good night's sleep, his leg wasn't bothering him at all. He'd ripped the very end of it open by somersaulting in the air with Royal earlier that day, not because he'd been laboring. Wisely, he kept his mouth shut.

Rain turned her attention back to David. "Not only does he work as hard as any of the rest of us, but we need to be prepared in case the current calm doesn't last."

David recovered his confidence to challenge Rain's statement. "How do we know he could even do anything if the Gorlag Gang attacked?" Then David started shouting at her, far louder than the small space needed. It was clear he was trying to use a loud voice to intimidate the other humans. "He could have no fighting skills at all. You could have let a coward or a criminal into our community."

Hesarium recognized this type of male; he'd dealt with them before. The kind that was all bluster and no blaster. They were generally cowards, but that made them more dangerous when in positions of authority.

Within the Talin Empire, it was hard to maintain any position of significance without wisdom and skill, but there was the rare occasion someone managed it. Apparently Talins weren't the only species that could produce dangerously unqualified, overconfident individuals.

He needed to keep an eye on David or risk the man putting everyone else in jeopardy.

"Be nice to Hes!"

Everyone turned to find Sunny holding Royal on her hip. The little boy looked close to tears and was staring at David. Next to Sunny were Wind and Cherish—all three were glaring daggers at David.

"What are you guys doing here?" Rain asked, straightening away from the wall and striding over to them. Hesarium followed, wanting to stay close to both Rain and her siblings. "I told you to get some extra sleep."

Cherish rolled her eyes, a gesture Hesarium had found meant impatience, annoyance, exasperation, or a combination of all three.

After the eyeroll, Cherish glowered at Rain. "The four of us held our own meeting and decided we were going to stand up for Hes." The implication was clear, the teenager didn't believe Rain was up to the task.

Hesarium felt a strange tightness in his chest. It only got worse when Royal held out his arms, demanding Hesarium take him from Sunny. Rumbling out the soothing sound, Hesarium took Royal and mimicked the way Sunny had held him.

Royal folded himself against Hesarium, the familiar multi-tech clutched in his little hand. "Don't be afraid," he whispered loudly. "We won't let them send you away."

He couldn't think of what to say to the little human. No words would effectively communicate his affection for Royal. Then, Sunny and Wind took up positions on either side of him. It appeared Royal wasn't the only one who wanted to make sure he stayed.

"None of you should be here." David pointed at the door behind them. "Go home. This meeting is for the adults."

"There's no such thing as adults or children in this place," Cherish declared, stepping in front of them to face David. "Only workers. And because of your injury," she cast her eyes down at David's food mockingly, "even Royal is working harder than you right now."

"You don't know what you're talking about," David spat.

"No, David," Rain said, stepping up to stand with Cherish. "You don't know what you're talking about." Her tone was harsh and tears sparkled in her eyes. For a moment, Hesarium worried it meant Rain was upset at her siblings, but then a smile broke across her face as she looked over her shoulder at them. "You guys have amazing timing."

Wind spoke up. "Dad always said, if you want to talk to one of us, you get to talk to all of us. Our family won't be divided or undermined." All the kids nodded, a united front against David and anyone who agreed with him.

Rain gave them all an approving smile before turning her attention back to David. "We can put Hesarium's presence here to a vote."

David's eyes sparked with malice. "Yes, the adults should vote."

Cherish put fisted hands on her hips. "Stop with the adult shit you stupid m—"

Wind was quick to step up and slap a hand over Cherish's mouth before she could finish her sentence. "If there's a vote, we get to be included."

There were some grumblings, but most were willing to give the kids a vote. David became visibly frustrated as he realized this meeting wasn't going his way. Hesarium began to realize why Rain wasn't very worried earlier. David wasn't as respected as he believed himself to be.

"I guess you're wrong and I'm right," Cherish taunted, holding Wind's hand away from her mouth. "How does it feel to be useless and dumb?"

"How dare you!" David snarled, snapping his hand out to slap Cherish. Unprepared for David' violence, Rain was slow to react.

Hesarium saw the intent behind the movement and caught David's arm by the wrist before he could make contact with Cherish's face. It wasn't hard to keep Royal secured to his body with one arm and restrain David with the other.

Fear registered on the human's face, and he started tugging frantically, trying to get his wrist out of Hesarium's hold.

Cherish's eyes were wide as she stepped back, standing close to her twin. "You were going to hit me."

"Of course not," David lied, still pulling at his arm. David looked up at Hesarium and tried to mask his fear with bravado. "Is your INT broken or are you deaf? I order you to let go of me!"

Disgusted, Hesarium gave David a shove as he released the man's arm. David stumbled back but didn't fall. "I'd challenge you if you were Talin. But I see now you aren't even as worthy as the younglings."

"Damn right!" Cherish crowed, regaining her confidence.

"You little bastard!" David screeched and stepped forward as if to charge at Cherish. Hesarium calmly set Royal down behind him so he could face David without worrying about hurting the little boy. In the submarks it took him to complete this action, Rain had moved so she was chest to chest with the angry man.

"If you ever even think about touching a member of my family again, I'll end you," she hissed. Rain might be smaller than David, but she stood with such strength and menace that the bigger male stepped back in surprise.

"D-d-did you just threaten to kill me?" David stuttered.

"Yes, she did," Auntie assured him. "And I'd help her."

"Rain!" David exclaimed, obviously shocked by this turn of events. "I didn't even touch Cherish."

"But you wanted to," Rain stated, anger sparking in her eyes even as her voice remained deceptively calm. "We're a small community. If we're going to survive, we need everyone to get along. That means I'm willing to listen to you bitch, complain, and make speeches about how you would do things if you were in charge. But I will not stand by and let you attack a member of my family."

"Yeah," Cherish said from behind Rain. "You attack one of us, then you're attacking all of us. That includes Hes."

"He's only been here for two and half days!" David shouted. "And he's not even human!"

Rain didn't flinch, despite David's volume. "Doesn't matter. It could be a few days or four years; the answer will be the same. He's family."

From birth to his youngling years, Hesarium had been raised in a cresh by highly trained Talins. They'd been competent and kind but never affectionate. When he was old enough, he'd left the cresh to live with his parents and applied to join the military. It was only now that he realized that at no point during his childhood and adulthood had he ever experienced what family truly meant.

Before, he wouldn't have hesitated to die for the honor of the Talin Empire. Maybe even looked forward to an honorable death in battle. Now, for the first time, he had something he wanted to *live* for instead.

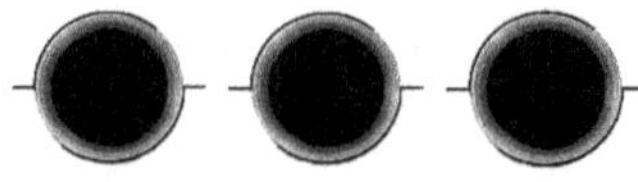

Rain

"His foot isn't even hurt anymore," Sunny grumbled as they walked back to the house. "He forgets to limp sometimes."

Cherish nodded. "I've seen that too. And where does he get off saying that stuff to Hes when he's the laziest person here?"

"Super lazy!" Wind chimed in. "Last time I worked one of the vertical fields with him, I had to do everything because he said he had to pilot the crawler."

"Why would he say that?" Auntie burst out. "We set the fields up so the crawlers can autopilot during harvest."

"He claimed the field hadn't been set up right and we shouldn't risk the crawler hitting one of the verticals," Wind explained.

"You worked with him three weeks ago," Rain exclaimed. "Why didn't you tell me about it?"

"It was right after the slow crawler broke down and you were trying to get parts," Wind explained, refusing to meet her gaze. "You were so stressed; I didn't want to make it worse. Besides, it was fine. I got it done without that lazy ass's help."

Guilt hit Rain hard, and she leaned close to Wind. "You can always tell me stuff like that. Always." Before Wind could answer, Sunny started shouting.

"Lazy ass is the best description for David!" Sunny started waving her arms in the air and jumping a little as if she was trying to announce the words to the entire colony. "David is a lazy ass."

"And he's a podhead," Royal added, making them all laugh. Their laughter only encouraged him. "Podhead, podhead, David's nothing but a podhead!" he sang, secure in Hes's arms.

The moment the meeting was officially over, Hes had scooped up the little boy to carry him home. He only reluctantly set Royal down when the little boy insisted he wanted to walk like everyone else.

With Royal skipping around the group and everyone talking over each other, they were a little band of controlled chaos. Hes constantly monitored everyone and if anyone got a little too far away as they walked, he moved the group until they were all together again. It was cute to watch this big, tough Talin trying to herd a bunch of distracted humans.

As all the kids joined Royal in his improvised song, Rain walked close to Hes. "Thanks for protecting Cherish," she murmured. "If David ever does something like that again, you have my permission to break his wrist."

Hes looked down at her, his purring briefly overwhelmed by a rattle that sounded like hard projectiles being rapidly fired. That had to be the sound of anger. "If he dares try to touch any of you, it's not his wrist I'll break."

"You say the nicest things," she murmured.

His rumble went from purring to sounding like a poorly running engine. His next words told her that was the rumble of confusion. "Perhaps you misunderstood me, I have no intention of being nice. I won't break his wrist because I'm going to break his neck instead."

"Declaring that you're willing to hurt or kill someone in our defense is nice," she explained to the adorable Talin. "This family is a loyal bunch, and we appreciate violence as a solution to bullies."

They walked in silence until he abruptly stopped, using a tug on her sleeve to halt her progress. Turning to face him, she tilted her head inquiringly. "Yes?"

"I also understand loyalty," he announced, his rumbles and rattles completely silent. "And no matter what happens in the future, I need you to know I'll always protect you and your siblings. Do you believe me?"

Rain blinked, a little confused. "You already proved that when you jumped between the kids and a threat."

"It turned out not to be a threat," he muttered.

"You didn't know that, and a herd of entict running at you is an intimidating sight," she insisted. "You couldn't have known they weren't attacking. Every one of the kids, including Royal, pulled me aside to tell me what you'd done. Even Cherish wanted to make sure I knew how brave you were."

"We can discuss that later," he said. "If something was to occur, you might not wish to trust me any longer."

The level of vagueness in that statement didn't sit right with Rain. "Are you planning to betray us by joining the Gorlag Gang?"

Hes's entire body jerked as if she'd hit him. "By the Ancestors, never!"

"Then there's nothing to worry about," she dismissed with a reassuring pat on his arm. His hard, plated skin felt warm, and she fought the urge to snuggle up against his body. The scent of sugar cookies grew stronger, making her smile.

Suddenly she needed another taste of Hes.

Putting both hands on his arm, she went up on her toes, intending to put her lips to his. He stopped walking and turned to start speaking. "If the humans here are to survive, you will all have to leave this place."

His words froze her, making a cold sense of dread wash over her body. Giving up on the kiss, she rolled off the balls of her feet and tightened her hands on his arm.

"What do you know?"

He hesitated, probably trying not to scare her.

"Tell me," she insisted.

"It's more than leaving tracks at the side of the road. They're riding deeper onto the land at night and even during the day at least once. They've gotten bold, and it's a bad sign."

Rain wasn't prepared for things to escalate before the pod sales. She'd fixed that date in her head as when she needed to be prepared for everything to go to hell. If the Gorlag Gang were already patrolling their farms, she didn't have as much time as she thought.

She sighed. "I wish you'd told me before the meeting. Not that it would've made a difference."

Suddenly, she was beyond tired. Worry and work were pressing on her constantly, wearing her down. She was desperate for everyone to be safe, where her concerns could reduce to mundane things like keeping Sunny and Cherish from fighting or making sure Royal ate enough.

Most of all, she wanted to sleep without being pushed awake in the middle of the night by worry or being forced to stay up late to work. She'd never thought of sleep as a luxury, but a full night of rest sounded like an impossible dream to her.

"Rain?" Hes's voice pulled her out of her thoughts.

"Let's go home," she murmured. "I'm tired."

CHAPTER 9

Rain

Once again, Rain should be asleep, but instead she lay there looking up at the dark ceiling of her room. This time was different from all the other sleepless nights. It wasn't worry and anxiety keeping her awake. It was thoughts of Hes. In the bed across the room, Auntie slept peacefully, unaware of Rain's lust-induced insomnia.

After her amazing make-out session and surprise orgasm that morning, Rain had hoped to find a quiet moment in the day to drag Hes off and do it again. That never happened. As was common this time of year, the day was filled with nothing but going from task to task. When the day's chores were done and dinner was eaten, Rain had been delighted to see her siblings and even Auntie yawning.

Then, of course, Zuri had come to the house to drag them to the meeting. After that whole drama was over, she'd been exhausted and decided she'd try to waylay Hes tomorrow.

Except now she lay there, wide awake, feeling a strange combination of horny and anxious about trying to be intimate with Hes again. They might've gotten hot and heavy that morning, but did Hes even want to do it again? He hadn't even gotten to come, or least she didn't think he had.

That brought the fact that she didn't know anything about Talin sexuality to the forefront of her whirling thoughts. Within Talin society, what they did could've been something as mild as a morning greeting or as binding as a marriage ceremony.

Wait, could they be married?

Visions of being married to Hes filled her head. He was patient with the kids, especially Cherish who managed to get on everyone's bad side at least once a day. He was gentle with Royal, and he never interrupted Auntie, no matter how much she rambled on. On top of all that, he worked as hard as the rest of them, even though she'd told him he didn't need to.

He would be the perfect husband.

Except she didn't even know if Talins did marriages. They could have complicated lineage marriages or no pairing-off practices at all. It would be expensive to send out a Unibase information request to the Hub and it would be weeks or even months to get information back, depending on where the Hub was in its figure-eight pattern around two separate stars.

Or she could also simply ask Hes himself.

Right, like that wouldn't be awkward at all, she thought with a grimace. What would she even say? *Hey, Hes, I was wondering if you wanted to sleep with me and get married and spend the rest of our lives together?*

That sounded horrible. Who would want to spend the rest of their life here?

If she wasn't going to sleep or get laid, there was only one thing left to do, she needed a drink. Time for some late night, warmed-up pod-milk with a splash of moonshine. Considering how wound up she felt, several splashes might be called for.

More familiar with sleeping in Auntie's room now, it was easier to pull on a warm outer covering and find her house shoes. Moving quietly to keep from waking up Auntie, she shuffled out of the room and down the ladder. Frowning, she took in the empty lower room.

No, that wasn't her hoping Hes might be up and about so she could casually run into him again, late at night, when everyone was asleep. Nothing else had gone to plan that day, so why would this be any different?

As usual, she didn't turn on any lights except for one in the kitchen area. She almost burned the pod-milk because she kept looking around, hoping to find Hes climbing down the ladder or coming in the front door.

There was nothing but silence and stillness, even after she *accidently* banged her mug on the counter. What did a girl have to do to wake up the sexy Talin upstairs?

When the drink was ready, she sat in her usual chair but couldn't settle. After only a single sip, she gave up. Abandoning the drink, she got up and headed for the ladder. Determined to at least talk to Hes, she climbed back up, only to make a startling discovery the moment her head cleared the second floor.

Hes was silently sitting on the floor next to the ladder. Unsure, she froze in place. "Hes, are you okay?" He didn't answer right away, making her anxiety flare. "Hes?"

It was only then that he finally spoke. "I wanted to go downstairs."

"Um, let me get out of your way," she offered and started to climb down.

His hand snaked out and covered hers, gently trapping her hand against the rung. "I've been here since you got up. Nothing is blocking my egress except my own doubts."

She understood what he was saying despite the unfamiliar, flowery language. "I've thought myself into a circle too," she admitted. "Do you want some spiked pod-milk? I didn't finish mine and you can drink it and tell me what's going on. Maybe we can work it out together."

Images of getting to cuddle while talking filled her head. She really wanted him to say yes, but when he went silent again, her hope dimmed. Then she became acutely aware of his hand still covering hers. He felt warmer than before, and his sugar-cookie smell was getting stronger by the minute.

"Are you sick?" she asked, worry making her tug her hand out from under his grip to finish her ascent. Instead of moving back to give her room to get off the ladder, Hes grabbed her. Unprepared for the move, she made a soft, startled sound and flailed her arms and legs out. One hand smacked Hes across the head before she found herself snuggled securely against his chest.

"Warn a person next time!" she snapped, then felt bad. "Did I hurt your face with my hand?"

"Not at all," Hes said as he started purring. "I'm sorry for my sudden movement. I belatedly became aware of how precarious your position on the ladder was. I shouldn't have let you stay there for so long."

Rain had never felt both agitated and soothed at the same time. "I guess we're both on edge a little bit." The light in the upstairs hall was dim and it took Rain a moment to realize there was something dripping down Hes's face.

"Are you crying?" Worry made her question come out louder than she meant. Before he had a chance to answer, she asked more questions. "What hurts? Are you injured, or is it an infection?"

The purring didn't stop as Hes spoke. "I'm uninjured. What you feel is oil from my scent glands," he reminded her.

Memories of how good his bonding oil had felt on her skin exploded in her mind, making her breath hitch. "I didn't ask before because you seemed to be in control, but does the oil mean you're in rut?"

"Talins don't go into rut, but we do produce oil when we're aroused," he explained. His voice was quiet, as if he was afraid of rejection.

"Oh, Hes," Rain breathed out. Maybe things were finally working out for her today. "I'll make you feel good, even if we aren't biologically compatible."

His purring changed for a few seconds, becoming lower in pitch with a longer beat—oh, she loved his sexy rumble!

"I know we are compatible. Bazium, my Advanced Squad Leader, scent-bonded with a human named Ari. I heard her speaking to another human about the experience. She found it rewarding and not at all uncomfortable."

His quick answer made her smile. Rain put her arms around Hes's neck to make it easier for her to put her lips against his cheek. The oil warmed her lips as she feathered them across the gland, noticing a slight bump under the hard keratin plating of his face. The smell of sugar cookies saturated her nose, throat, and lungs.

Her skin got hot, and her heart sped up as Hes's scent warmed her from the inside out. She spent a few moments with her lips resting on his skin, pulling lungfuls of him in through her nose.

"Yes," she whispered against his skin. "I've wanted you all day."

His arms tightened around her slightly and his sexy rumble vibrated through his chest and into her body.

"I wasn't sure if you would. I feared you might regret what we did this morning the more you thought about it," he admitted to her.

"Never," she assured him.

"I'll make you feel good, like I did before," he promised. The next thing she knew he was holding her tightly to his chest while striding down the hall to his room. His steps were sure despite the lack of light, and soon she was being laid down on Hes's perfectly made bed. It seemed he hadn't even tried to go to sleep that evening. Like her, he'd been awake thinking, but he hadn't even pretended to try to go to sleep.

When he drew back and reached for her robe, she grabbed his hands. Worry replaced her sensual haze with a moment of clarity. "Um, I know you said we're compatible, but does that mean you can get me pregnant? I'm not on any kind of birth control or anything."

Hes's sexy rumble changed back to a purr as he talked. "Initial DNA analysis indicates that our species can interbreed, but you don't have to worry. A childhood illness made me sterile."

Rain's heart went out to the big Talin. "Oh, Hes, I'm sorry!" She scrambled to her knees and wrapped her arms around his neck in a strong hug.

"I don't mourn the loss," he assured, even as he put his arms around her to embrace her back. "Talins don't give natural birth anymore. We all use artificial wombs. My fertility, or lack thereof, would've never been an issue." There was a moment of silence while she digested this new information before Hes asked a question. "Are you upset that I'm not fertile?"

"No way," she assured him, feeling both guilty and relieved that she didn't need to worry about birth control. "I love my siblings, but I've basically been helping raise them since before I was Sunny's age. And because my stepmom wasn't good at paying attention, I did most of Royal's care even as a baby. It feels like I've already had kids. I'm not interested in having any more."

"Then we are perfect together," he concluded, the sexy rumble coming back. "Teach me how to pleasure you, Rain. I want to know everything."

Rain pulled away from their hug and grinned up at him. "Lesson one," she drawled, grabbing hold of his belt and giving it a tug. "Naked is better."

CHAPTER 10

Hesarium

Hesarium had trained under some of the strictest instructors in the military. He'd learned to put on and take off full battle gear in a matter of submarks. Not once during his training or military career did he unlatch something faster than he did his belt at that moment. He was so fast, the belt, with his Ident and pouch still attached, went flying across the room to bang against a wall before dropping noisily to the floor.

Embarrassed, he froze, staring in horror at his discarded belt.

Rain was quiet also, staring at the discarded item with a surprised expression. Then she let loose with a peal of laughter. "I'm going to assume that means you're eager too."

Sounding an amused rumble, he moved his eyes to take her in. The outer garment she wore had slipped off her shoulders and pooled at the tie around her waist, revealing the old and worn shirt underneath. In the soft light of his room, it was easy to make out her full breasts pressing against the thin fabric. Memories of the feel and taste of those turgid peaks in his mouth made him switch from an amused rumble to one of arousal.

The scent glands in his face were inflamed and his mating shaft was already growing large enough to strain the flesh pouch covering it. Standing up, he pulled off his pants and remained on his feet so Rain could look him over. Bazium had said Ari was intrigued by his body despite how Talin males differed from humans. He hoped Rain wouldn't be bothered by the differences, but he worried she might find him too foreign to be attractive.

He was standing next to the bed so Rain was within reach of him. She lifted her hand as if to place it on his abdomen, but stopped with her palm hovering over his keratin-plated skin.

"Where is your cock—uh, mating organ?" she asked.

Placing his hand against the back of hers, he guided her hand over the tight flesh pouch. "I'm under here," he explained, then urged her fingers higher to feel the lip of his flesh pouch. "As my mating shaft becomes engorged, it will force the pouch back. My mating shaft and seed sac will spring free."

He dropped his hand to his side and let her fingers explore him. Her touch was soft and gentle as she ran her hand along the seam of his flesh pouch.

"Your flesh pouch is covered in the same hard plating as the rest of you," she murmured, flattening her palm against it. "Is your—"

The feel of her entire hand on him, pressing against his straining shaft, was the last nudge he needed. The flesh pouch retracted, filling her hand with his hard and throbbing mating shaft. His heavy seed sac dangled under, swinging slightly from how violently his pouch drew back.

He moaned as she squeezed his mating shaft with her soft hand. "That answered my question. Your dick doesn't have any hard plating," she murmured. "It's so soft. I didn't expect that. And no hooks or barbs."

"N-no hooks or barbs," he agreed. "I would've warned you."

Rain ran one hand up and down his cock and brought her other hand up to palm his full seed sac. It was delightful torture.

Bringing up both hands to wrap around his mating shaft, she stilled all movement and held him firmly. "Your cock vibrates."

Thinking was difficult, but he needed to speak. She should know he wasn't a perfectly fit Talin.

"I'm a throwback," he explained, then was forced to suck in a harsh breath when she ran a thumb over the head of his mating shaft.

"Throwback?"

"There are a few things that we can be born with that make us throwbacks. I have extra tendons going from my chestbox to my mating shaft," he explained, tapping his chest over the organ that allowed Talins to rumble, then tracing a line straight down to his mating shaft. "They do nothing useful, so healers have attempted to breed them out of us. It's considered a vestigial anomaly. I would've been terminated if they'd caught it while I was growing in the artificial womb."

Rain gripped him a little harder. It didn't hurt and he had to concentrate on not moving his hips so his mating shaft could glide back and forth in her delicate hands.

"Are you telling me you have a vibrating dick, and your society doesn't think that's useful?" Rain asked, her voice incredulous.

Her squeezing had felt so good it took a moment for her words to sink in. "You like this?"

"Hes, this is the stuff of dreams," she said with a chuckle. Then she let go of him and backed up a little. He greedily watched her strip off her robe and shirt, revealing her dark, gorgeous skin and voluptuous body. He was torn. Part of him wanted to stand there and take in every curve of her human shape. The other part wanted to run his tongue over her skin and taste the most intimate places on her body.

"Come here," she urged, falling back on the bed and opening her legs in invitation. "I've got to know what you feel like. And whatever you do, don't stop rumbling!"

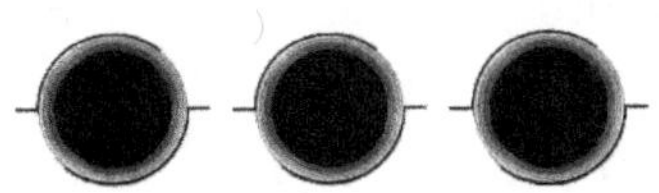

Rain

Could Hes be any more perfect? Protective of her and her family, check. Patient and thoughtful, check. Big, strong, and skilled, check. And now she finds out he has a vibrating dick? Check, check, and check!

If she didn't know better, she'd think he was straight out of her imagination. But no, he was here and very real.

When she'd stretched out, being deliberately provocative, she'd expected him to jump on her. After getting to touch and fondle him, she was hot as hell and ready to go. Although her experience with males and sex was extremely limited, she'd heard enough talk to know guys tended to hurry toward the finish line. That was fine; she was part way there already!

To her surprise, Hes didn't simply drop between her legs and shove his shaft inside her. He lowered his body to the bed and kept going lower. Soon his head was between her legs, his mouth close to her aching core.

"I need to taste you," he whispered, his breath fanning across her dark curls. As much as she wanted to feel his cock inside her, there was only one answer she could give to his request.

"Yes."

Her single word answer made him sound a sudden burst of excited rattling. The rattle was over almost as soon as it began and a second later, his long, textured tongue delved between her labia, lapping at her pussy. He must have studied human female anatomy because after teasing her for a few licks, he found her clit and sucked.

Electricity flashed up her spine, making her gasp and tighten her thighs around Hes's head. "There," she urged. "Right there!"

He didn't seem to mind the pressure of her legs. His only response was to moan against her. Without breaking contact with his mouth, he maneuvered a little, bringing an arm up and around her thighs. His right hand groped up her body until he found her breast and started squeezing, kneading, and playing with the nipple.

He was playing her body like a skillful musician. Where had this man learned all this? Were Talin women similar to human ones? It didn't take long until her orgasm was looming close.

No, she wasn't going to do this again. She felt guilty about being greedy last time and neglecting him. She wasn't going to let that happen again.

"Stop," she gasped, placing a gentle hand on the top of his head.

She expected him to protest or ignore her, but he obeyed her request with speed. Pulling his mouth off her, he withdrew and sat back.

He was panting and stopped rumbling, but he didn't sound angry when he spoke. "What have I done? Did I hurt you?"

"No," she assured him, sitting up and grabbing one of his hands. "I want to change positions."

"Indicate where you want me," he agreed and started up that sexy rumble again.

"On top of me," she explained, laying back down and pulling him with her. He unfurled his body over hers, his hard cock nudging at her entrance.

"Are you sure, Rain?" he whispered. "I don't want to hurt you."

"Start slow and you won't," she promised. She felt primed and desperate for him to slide inside her. Wrapping her legs around his hips, she urged him forward.

As she'd instructed, he slid into her with excruciating slowness. It was probably for the best because she wasn't used to any penetration, let alone anything his size. Then he was fully inside of her, and she felt nothing but pleasure.

Oh good god, the vibrations! How dumb was his entire species that they wanted to breed this out of their males? And how lucky was she that no Talin woman had snatched up Hes before he found his way to her!

"Move, please," she begged.

"I'm challenged," he answered, voice tight and body tense. "I'm not going to last long, sweet human."

"I won't need long either," she promised, undulating her hips against him. He gasped and his sexy rumble got stronger. That vibrating rumble did all the right things to her.

"Hes, that feels so good!" she cried out, desperate. With the bulk of his weight on top of her, there wasn't much room for her to move that delicious cock the way she needed it.

"The desire in your voice is pushing me past my endurance," he growled. "Your body is beyond beautiful. Your taste is exquisite, and your skin is the softest thing I've ever felt. I don't want to find my finish and leave you wanting."

"You won't, now stop with the poetry and move!" Rain demanded, feeling torn between unquenched desire and amusement.

With his sexy rumble still going strong, Hes pulled his hips back and then pushed them forward. It was all still too slow for Rain. Reaching up, she cupped his cheek. Her palm was quickly slathered in his oil, and the smell of sugar cookies thickened. He gasped at her touch and shuddered, telling her his scent glands were probably an erogenous zone.

"Faster," she urged, running her fingers over the weeping scent glands. Hes let out a growl and started pistoning himself in and out of her. The position and pace were perfect and every slide of his cock dragged against her throbbing clit.

Her orgasm hit her like a tidal wave, washing over her and sucking her under. The pleasure was so intense that for a few seconds she couldn't pull air into her lungs.

"I'm releasing!" Hes warned her in a low growl of desperation.

She couldn't talk, so with her hand on his face, she guided his mouth to hers. He opened his mouth against hers, and his entire body shuddered. His rhythm stuttered, and warmth filled her as he moaned into her mouth.

He went still and they stayed like that for an endless moment, connected in a more intimate way than Rain had ever been with anyone else. It wasn't only that his cock was buried deep inside her and their tongues touched and stroked each other, but in that moment, her heart longed to reach out of her chest and bind with his.

She would forever remember this evening as both the most frightening and beautiful moment she'd ever experienced.

CHAPTER 11

Rain

Sitting up in bed, Rain found she was alone. Touching the depression where Hes's big body had lay told her he hadn't left long ago—the sheets were still warm. Yawning, she rubbed the sleep out of her eyes, noticing that her body felt loose-limbed and relaxed.

Dropping her hands to her lap, she blearily took in the room and debated going back to sleep. A chime from the timekeeping unit on the wall pushed her out of bed. The kids would all be getting up soon, and she should get cleaned up and go downstairs to help prepare food before they started stumbling down for breakfast.

When she stepped into the hall clutching a sheet around her naked body, she could hear the soft sounds of Auntie singing in the kitchen. Guilt made her rush through her morning routine and hurry down the ladder.

"Good morning my favorite Rain cloud," Auntie called out, her musical voice turning the single sentence into a melody.

Rain smiled at her aunt. "Morning, sorry I'm late." She grabbed a reconstitutor tray and started emptying rehydration packs onto it.

"I thought you'd sleep later," Auntie answered, turning to lean against the counter she'd been working at. "After the workout you had last night."

Rain's hands froze, holding onto the packet she'd been trying to open. "What?" In retrospect, her surprise was stupid. She shared a room with Auntie, of course the woman had noticed she was missing from her bed. If she wasn't outside or downstairs, the only other logical place was Hes's room. Besides, she'd already caught Rain and Hes making out. "Did we make too much noise?"

"I didn't hear a thing," Auntie assured her with a wide grin. "And I don't mind fixing breakfast by myself to give you a little extra cuddle time with Hes. I bet all the purring he does is nice to snuggle up against."

Putting down the packet, Rain turned to face Auntie. She opened her mouth and the words started tumbling out.

"It's dumb to get attached to him, isn't it? He's going to get fed up with this lifestyle and leave and then I'm going to be a mess. I'm going to cry a lot, and I might never get over him. I've never liked anyone this much before. Not in this way. It would've been better if I hadn't touched him. But he smelled so good and—"

Auntie took Rain's hands in her own and made a gentle shushing sound, stopping Rain's emotional spiral. "Easy, Rain. First things first, was it good?" she asked while rubbing the back of Rain's hands with her thumbs. It was both familiar and soothing.

Even though tears were threatening to fall, Rain nodded her head. "Yeah, it was good. I didn't know it could be like that."

Auntie smiled wide with approval. "That's good. That's real good."

Rain's smile flattened as she thought about the future. "What will I do when he leaves?"

"Has he said he's going to leave?" Auntie asked.

"Not exactly," Rain admitted. "Still, he can't like it here. No one likes it here. Almost every farmer on Omanal is here because we couldn't get land anywhere else. This is a last step before selling ourselves into indentured contracts."

"That's true for the whole, but not the individual," Auntie argued.

Rain frowned. "That doesn't make sense."

Auntie leveled her with a hard look. "We both know you could've gotten an off-world job. Back when the ships came here regularly, there were several times when they needed crew, and you could've signed up. You're smart and those ships value the fact that we humans are small. Instead of leaving, you stayed with us because no ship was going to hire all of us. Do you understand what I'm saying?"

Rain pulled in a deep breath before answering. "What if I'm not enough to make him stay?"

"You're probably not," Auntie agreed then laughed when Rain gave her a sour look. "But you along with Sunny, Wind, Royal, and even Cherish are enough to make him stay. He's gotten attached to all of us."

Rain thought of the way Royal followed Hes around. "Probably not as attached as we are to him."

"I don't think that's true," Auntie objected. "You know how I get a feeling about things?"

"Dad called it your magic intuition," Rain answered with a small smile. "I remember him telling the story about you as a toddler telling everyone to hold onto something because they were going to get the *shakes* and then an earthquake happened."

"I'm pretty sure he made that story up," Auntie murmured. "But I do know something about Hes. I've got a strong feeling that leaving you would kill him."

Rain's eyes went wide. Auntie didn't exaggerate when she described one of her *feelings*. If she said Hes wouldn't survive leaving Rain, then that's exactly what she meant.

"I don't suppose your feeling gave you more details," Rain pushed.

Auntie let go of Rain's hands to rub her temples. Suddenly Auntie looked tired. "No, sweetie. All I know is that he can't be away from you for too long. That his health and happiness are now in your hands."

Suspicion made Rain cross her arms over her chest. "When did you get this feeling?"

"The moment I met him," Auntie admitted. "When I touched his hand, I knew his life was linked to you in an inextricable way. Maybe not at the time, but soon. I don't think you two could have slept together without binding that link."

Rain's shoulders slumped a little. "That makes me feel better and worse all at the same time."

Auntie tilted her head, confused. "How so?"

"It's reassuring to know he has to be with me or he'll die," Rain explained. "Then I start thinking that I might have done something to take away his choices and that's not fair."

"Whatever has happened, he allowed," Auntie argued. "However this link works, he let it happen. Don't let him bind you up in guilt, Rain. That's not how love should be, not with humans at least."

When Rain had come downstairs, she'd felt loose-limbed and happy from the night before. Now she felt the familiar tension in her neck and a headache brewing behind her eyes. "What do I say to him? Auntie told me she thinks you've bound your life to mine; let's talk about it. That sounds insane."

Auntie shook her head with a slight sigh. "I didn't mean to cause drama. I wanted you to know he was stable, that he wouldn't disappear on us. Leave it to you to take a romantic idea and turn it into a trap of certain death!"

The sound of shouting filtered down from upstairs.

"I get to use it first!" Cherish yelled.

"It's my turn to be first, you podhead!" Sunny screamed, then yowled in pain. "Let go of my hair!"

"Hey, both of you stop," Wind said in a loud but reasonable voice.

"Shut up!" the girls yelled at him in unison. Then the distinct sound of slaps hit Rain's ears.

Auntie shooed her out of the kitchen. "Go break them up before someone gets really hurt."

Rain was already in motion, hurrying across the room and up the ladder. In the second-floor hallway, Sunny was sitting on Cherish. The younger sibling was screaming insults and slapping at her older sister while Wind cuddled the youngest child. Royal was crying big fat tears while Wind tried to soothe him.

Rain sighed as she scrambled down the hall to separate the girls. "Sunny, get off Cherish and both of you calm down!"

She reached down to try and pull Sunny away from Cherish and got kicked in the face for her efforts. The blow knocked her on her ass and she saw stars for a moment. Gasping, she hunched over, pain blossoming across her cheek and eye.

Cherish and Sunny stopped fighting and gathered around her.

"Rain? Are you okay?" Sunny asked.

"I'm sorry! I didn't mean to kick you!" Cherish wailed. When Rain lowered her hands to look at Cherish, both girls recoiled when they saw her face.

"Why am I like this?" Cherish said before bursting into sobs and running off to her room, closing and latching the door behind her.

"Rain, are you going to die?" Royal asked, and then he, too, started sobbing.

"It's not my fault!" Sunny declared as angry tears streamed down her face. She stood up and stomped to the ladder, descending quickly.

"Um, I need to use the elimination room, like now," Wind said with a grimace and handed the sobbing Royal to Rain before hotfooting it down the hall.

Face throbbing and Royal crying loudly against her neck, Rain wondered how the day had gone so badly so quickly.

Hesarium

When Hesarium left that morning, he'd hoped to finish a quick survey of the farmlands and be back before Rain woke up. To his disappointment, he'd been forced to attend to an entict. The poor creature had gotten a leg caught on a support strut and it had taken patience and a great deal of strength to set the animal free. By the time he was able to return to the domicile, the sun had risen.

He knew everyone would be up and probably already sitting down for their first meal of the day. Expecting to walk in on a lively group, he was startled to find everyone silently gathered around the table eating. They were subdued, and when they looked up to him, he noticed Cherish was missing.

"What's happened?" he asked as an anxious rattle sounded from his back plates.

"You sound like a bunch of angry bugs when you make that noise," Sunny commented. She tried to smile, but it didn't reach her eyes.

He looked to Rain for an answer to his question and the sight of her face caused an aggressive rattle of anger to fill the room. All the humans flinched, pushing him to quiet his loud rattle.

They were all asking questions about the noise, but he ignored them as he covered the distance between him and Rain with only a few strides. Going down to his knees, he leaned forward to examine her damaged face more closely.

There were patches of discolored skin around the outside of her left eye and high on her cheek bone. The area was also swollen and the eye looked red and irritated. It appeared that Rain had suffered a substantial blow to the head. Everything he knew about human's delicate anatomy flooded his mind. She could have a retinal detachment, a concussion, or even a brain hemorrhage.

"First I'll see to your health," he assured her. "But after you are well, I need to know who did this to you. I'll relish in tearing each limb from their body. I'll make a necklace from their bones so you can wear it as a warning to anyone who would dare hurt you again."

Rain's mouth dropped open and she didn't speak. After a few moments of silence, he worried she'd suffered brain damage. His poor human must have been attacked while he was gone and might be suffering significant head trauma!

He wanted to yell at Auntie for sitting everyone down to eat when Rain was so obviously hurt. Forcing his anger and fear down, he started up a soothing rumble.

"I'm going to take you off planet and find you medical care," he explained, hoping she understood him. "It might hurt when I carry you, but I promise it will get better. When you're healed, we'll come back and I'll execute whoever did this. After we've had vengeance, I'm taking all of you away from this place. Don't be scared, I won't let anything bad happen to you, your siblings, or Auntie ever again."

Rain had closed her mouth by the time he finished talking, but she still looked stunned. Although he wanted to grab her and run to the port to demand passage to the nearest space station, he knew he had to plan his actions out.

"Concentrate on breathing," he urged her as he gently took both her hands in his. He was going to have to carry her, but first he needed to wrap her up to keep from making her injuries worse. "Keep your heartbeat and breathing steady."

"Hes," Auntie said. "Rain isn't—"

Turning his gaze on Auntie, he cut off her words with orders. "Go up and get my smaller case, it's on the floor at the foot of my bed. While you're up there, gather up Rain's preferred sleeping garments and anything else she might need. We might be at the healer's for several days."

Focusing on Sunny, he issued more orders. "Go get the tall crawler and maneuver it as close to the door of the domicile as you can. I'll try to be gentle as I lift her in, but it would be best if we could minimize how much she's jostled."

Neither Auntie nor Sunny moved, despite his clear instructions. All of them were watching him with wide eyes and shocked expressions. They weren't soldiers, he reminded himself. They weren't trained to act quickly under duress.

"I know all of you are scared," he said to them, working on keeping his voice gentle. "I vow that, when we return, she'll be as she was."

Despite his comforting words, no one moved. Frustrated, he looked back at Rain to explain that he had to leave her for a moment to gather their things and move the crawler. To his shock he found she was smiling at him which was completely at odds with the tears streaming down her face.

Was this a sign that he was too late? That the damage was irreversible and terminal? Fear made his comforting rumble dip into the slower and lower tones of desolation. He'd only just found Rain. How could the Ancestors have torn her from his life already?

"Hes," she whispered with a delicate sniff. She parted her legs around his body and moved to the edge of her seat. That put her almost flush with him. Letting go of his hands, she wrapped her arms around his neck, put her lips to his earhole, and whispered.

"I love you too."

CHAPTER 12

Hesarium

"You can talk," Hesarium announced, relief filling him. In other circumstances, Rain's declaration of strong human feelings would make Hesarium ecstatic. His concern tempered his reaction and kept his focus on Rain's health. He fought the urge to hug her to his chest and rub his scent glands all over her hair. Pushing her back onto the seat, he critically examined her face. "How badly are you injured?"

"It looks worse than it is," she assured him. "I don't need a medic or healer. It's some swelling and bruises, that's all."

"Humans are delicate," he responded, planning to push her into being examined. "You could be more injured than you realize."

"Not as delicate as you think," she retorted, then held up a hand to stop him from talking. "I'd know if I needed medical attention. This," she pointed to her face, "doesn't need more than some cooling gel and pain suppressant tabs. If I start having dizzy spells, I promise to tell you."

"I believe you, but I will also be at your side all day today," he informed her. "If I see any signs of decline, I'm going to take action."

She smiled at him, then winced when the expression put pressure on her swollen face. "No action will be needed, I swear."

"We'll see," he responded, then rattled out an angry sound again. "Now I ask, who did this to you?"

Rain pulled his hands from her shoulders and brought them to her lap. "No one is to blame, Hes. It was an accident."

Hesarium forced his back plates to lay flat and started up a strong soothing rumble. It was a struggle but he kept his voice gentle instead of demanding. "You're far too graceful and athletic to have fallen or bumped into something. This damage could only have been caused by someone. Don't protect your attacker, they must face my wrath."

"Then I guess you should kick my ass," Cherish announced as she climbed down the ladder. Once her feet were on the floor, she faced them with downcast eyes, her arms wrapped around her waist. "I kicked Rain in the face. You should hit me back."

A glance at Rain told him Cherish was telling the truth, and now he understood Rain's reluctance. Hesarium finally realized there was a dynamic going on among the siblings he didn't understand.

Rain tightened her grip on his hands, as if to keep him from getting up and hurting Cherish. He had no such intention. Keeping his hands in Rain's lap, he sat back on his heels, hoping to present a less intimidating figure.

"Can you explain to me why you'd kick Rain in the face?" he asked, still sounding his soothing rumble.

Cherish didn't look up from the floor, but he could see that her eyes were red and swollen from crying. "I was angry and wanted to kick Sunny and got Rain by accident."

"Your kick wasn't aimed at Rain, but your intent was to harm one of your siblings?" Hesarium questioned.

Cherish's lower lip trembled, and tears pooled in her eyes. "No. I mean, yeah, but not really."

"Cherish can't help that she's a bitch," Sunny commented. "She was born that way."

To Hesarium's surprise, Cherish didn't lash out at Sunny. Her shoulders slumped a little more and the tears started rolling down her face.

"Not helping," Wind grumbled, getting up from his spot to stand next to his twin. "Rain's not mad at you. Why don't you come eat something?"

Cherish let Wind guide her to the spot next to his. She sat stiffly and didn't accept the food he tried to give her.

Sunny rolled her eyes and reached for a piece of bread. "Stop being so dramatic. You're just trying to make us feel sorry for you so you won't get punished."

Cherish flinched as if Sunny had hit her. Rain saw the flinch and tried to pull away from Hesarium, probably to go to Cherish and comfort her. Hesarium let her tug her hands free, then stood and lifted her up off the chair and cradled her against his chest. Pivoting in place, he sat in her chair. Once seated, he arranged her in his lap so she was facing Cherish across the table.

"I'm not mad at you, Cherish," Rain told her. "I know you didn't mean to hurt me."

"Her intent was still to do harm to a member of her family. Someone she should be protecting above all others," Hesarium pointed out, deeply disturbed by the events.

"Human siblings get into fights sometimes," Auntie explained.

"To the point of damage?" Hesarium asked and gestured at Rain's face. "What if she'd been near the ladder and had tumbled down? Or if the blow had landed on her neck and crushed her trachea? The humans I know would have verbal altercations, but they never hit each other. I don't understand this violence. If it is common, then perhaps this isn't the family I thought it was."

He'd meant for his words to have an impact, but most of the faces around him looked pained, as if he'd delivered an actual blow.

"Ouch," Wind muttered under his breath. "You make it sound like we're abusing each other."

"I might have started it," Sunny announced, staring at the piece of bread in her hand. So far she'd only held it, not tried to take a bite out of it. That's when Hes noticed she hadn't eaten any of her food. "I was really upset and pulled her hair."

"I shouldn't have yelled and shoved you," Cherish whispered without looking up. "I just wanted to use the elimination room really quick. I wasn't going to use the cleansing unit. It made me mad when you started saying no and wouldn't let me talk."

This exchange made him realize that the tight living quarters were part of the reason for the altercation. Having limited resources would naturally cause tension when so many were forced to share.

Sunny tried to offer her the piece of bread in her hand. "I'm sorry I yelled. I needed to go too."

Wind took the bread because Cherish still hadn't looked up. He tried to hand it to her, but Cherish shook her head.

Auntie smiled at the girls. "There, now, all better."

Hesarium might not be an expert at human body language, but he could tell Cherish didn't feel relieved or settled. Rain must have noticed it too.

"What's going on, Cherish?" Rain asked.

"Hesarium's right," Cherish said to the floor. "I could've accidently really hurt you. And at the time, I didn't even care. I wanted to burn the whole house down. I wanted to set fire to our fields and everything. I wanted it all to burn."

"As if I haven't thought the same thing," Rain scoffed.

Cherish looked up with wide, startled eyes. "What?"

Rain's tone softened as she held Cherish's gaze. "If you didn't think about wanting to burn the whole thing down at least once then you're not human. Sometimes I dream of the bog taking over everything and I'd just lay down and let it wash over me."

"I knew you were tired, but I didn't think you were that tired," Auntie said. Her joke was met with a few halfhearted laughs.

"We're all that tired," Rain said with a sad little smile that made Hesarium's chest ache. He never wanted to see that expression on her face ever again. Coupled with the swelling, her expression was that of someone on the verge of giving up.

"My fault?" Royal asked, looking like he was going to cry now. "I know you didn't want me, but I try to help."

"We always wanted you!" Rain assured him, reaching over to pull him off Auntie's lap and cuddle him in her own. Now Hesarium had Rain and Royal perched on him. "Even before you were born, we wanted you. We just didn't know it yet."

"And you're super helpful," Wind added.

"You do so much to help," Auntie agreed. "None of this is anyone's fault."

"It is though," Cherish said, her voice a little louder now. "It's my fault. I'm the one who's always causing trouble. I just feel angry all the time. Angry at Mom for dying and angry at Dad for letting Debra live with us. And then they both died, and I felt sad, but also rage. I'm angry at this planet for the bog." She put both her hands on her chest, as if holding something in. "All of that anger builds inside me until I feel like I can't breathe. I don't know what to do."

She sounded like one of the recruits Hesarium had trained with. She hadn't wanted to be in the military, but family pressure and social obligation forced her into it. One of his trainers had taken her aside and Hesarium had overheard what was said. Now seemed like a good time to repeat it.

"You can't stop the feelings of anger from occurring, but how you handle that emotion is entirely within your control."

Everyone was looking at him now. Even Rain was craning her neck back so she could see his face.

"What do you mean?" Cherish asked.

"Emotions happen. I drop something and it makes me feel embarrassed. That can't be helped. What I can do is then release myself from that embarrassment and reassess the situation. My emotion doesn't help me clean up my mess or figure out how to keep from doing the same thing again. Cherish feels anger then gives into it."

"You make it sound easy, but it's not," Cherish said, finally looking up at him. Her eyes implored him to help her. "How do I control it? I can't even think when I'm that angry."

"You do the same thing you'd do to develop any skill—you practice," Hesarium explained. "It's a simple yet profoundly challenging task."

"No shit," Wind muttered.

"That's not a bad idea," Rain agreed. "I'm not angry about you accidentally kicking me, but what if it had been Royal?"

For a brief moment Cherish looked angry, like she was going to fly into a rage again. Then she pulled in a deep breath and turned her gaze on Sunny. "I'm not the only one with a temper."

Sunny frowned and Hesarium was sure she was about to say something that would push Cherish into a bad emotional state. He was done with discussions. It was time to treat these siblings like raw recruits who needed a clear goal and path to achieving it.

He sounded a demanding rattle that brought everyone's attention to him.

"That sounded like you banged a long-handled uni-wrench against the side of a crawler," Wind said. "How can you sound like metal?"

Hesarium ignored his comment and pinned Cherish with his gaze. "You have to count out loud to twenty before you're allowed to talk to anyone. For every day you are able to keep your temper in check, that number is reduced by five units. Five units are added every time you lose control. Do you understand the assignment and the consequences?"

Cherish frowned at him, but it was more out of confusion than anger. "I have to count to twenty every time I want to say something even if I'm having a conversation with someone?"

"No, only for the first two times you speak in the same conversation," Hesarium said. "This training will require the patience of your siblings, but I'm sure they want to support you."

"I bet she's going to need to count to a hundred by the end of the day," Sunny said with a forced laugh. No one laughed with her.

"Sunny, don't bait Cherish," Rain admonished before Hesarium could say anything. "I didn't realize how bad it was until now, but you poke at her. Why?"

Sunny's triumphant expression turned defiant. "I don't."

"It's been worse lately, ever since Rain and I asked you girls to do each other's hair some mornings," Auntie commented softly.

"That's not it," Sunny argued, but by the way Rain jerked in his lap a little, Hesarium guessed that Auntie had announced a revelation.

"We can go back to doing your hair," Auntie offered. "I didn't mean to make you feel less loved."

Sunny gave up on her denials. "It's not just the hair. I have to share my room, my clothes, and all my stuff with Cherish. Wind doesn't have to share his stuff with Royal. Well, his room, but not his clothes or anything else. Why can't I have anything of my own?"

Again, it came down to scarcity. He wrapped his arms around Rain and Royal as the family talked about how to share what few resources they had more equitably so neither girl felt left out. He applauded the way Rain and Auntie spoke to the siblings, but no matter how kind and practical they were, there was only so much to go around.

Hesarium could give these humans everything. Domiciles with room for privacy, leisure time, access to healers, and above all, safety. He could solve all their problems.

The time wasn't right yet, but he felt he'd be able to confide in them soon. The major worry was that they wouldn't believe him until it was too late. He'd never been to a place that was both geologically and politically unstable like Omanal.

Hopefully he'd convince them all to leave before the planet swallowed everything whole.

CHAPTER 13

Rain

     "Your face is almost healed," Sunny commented as she handed Rain the battered computator. It was an old piece of tech and several sections of the screen no longer worked, but it could still function well enough for them to keep track of crops and machinery. To Rain's relief, it was someone else's job to keep track of job assignments and resource distribution.

     "It really wasn't that bad," Rain said absently as she looked down the row of numbers. As she'd expected, the amount of produce in the final numbers was lower than it had been from last year by a solid ten percent.

     Sunny was silent for a moment then began talking again. "You know, you and Hes sounded like Mom and Dad that day."

     That got Rain's full attention. "We did?"

     "Sunny's right. You sounded just like Jackson, but not Dawn," Auntie commented with a chuckle as she sat down next to Rain to look over her shoulder at the computator's screen. "Are those the final numbers?"

     Rain nodded, feeling a headache building behind her eyes. She set the computator down and sat back to look at Auntie. The older woman was smiling but it wasn't reaching her eyes. There was worry that mirrored Rain's. Only one of them needed to be this stressed, so she focused on Auntie's earlier comment.

"Why do you say I sounded like Dad but not Mom?" she asked.

"You father was a gentle soul; he would've reacted just like you did. Dawn had a temper though. She would've yelled the house down if Cherish had landed a kick to her face," Auntie explained with a chuckle.

Rain's smile became real as she thought of her parents. "Yeah, Mom had a temper. She didn't lose it often, but when she did, it was a sight to see. That's probably where Cherish got her attitude."

"What about me?" Sunny asked, drawing both women's focus to the teenager.

"What about you?" Rain asked, confused.

"Am I like Mom or Dad?" Sunny pushed.

Rain went silent, trying to think of how Sunny was like their parents. In truth, she didn't see much in common between Sunny's cheerful loudness and her parents' usually quiet diligence.

"No, honey, you're not like either of them," Auntie said.

Sunny looked hurt. "I guess I'm the stupid one then."

"Not at all!" Auntie argued. "You're like my mom, your grandmother, Katherine," she explained. "Your dad and I had an amazing woman for a mother. She was pregnant when she and your grandfather left earth. It takes a tough and determined woman to do that. Remember, ours was the first family here and paved the way for other families to join us. She was the one who organized and ran this community until the day she died. After she was gone, it took three people to fill her shoes, that's how much she did."

"I don't know if I'm like that," Sunny hedged with a frown. "I don't think I could run this place."

"Not right now," Auntie agreed with a grin. "You're only sixteen, but in a few years, you might be in charge."

Sunny tried not to look elated. "You think?"

Auntie nodded. "There's one of the ways you're like Katherine—her default was to be happy. I think one of the reasons she was so damn successful was she made everyone smile when they were around her. Could you say no to someone who made you smile all the time? You're like that too."

Sunny looked a little happier, but there was still doubt in her eyes. "You really think I'm like Grandma Katherine?"

"Absolutely," Auntie trilled.

"Without a doubt," Rain said at the same time.

A brilliant smile unfurled across Sunny's face. "Then I guess I'll be running this place next!"

"Hurry it up, I want a break," Rain teased. The computator chimed. Looking down, Rain realized it finished all the predictions for next year based on the data from the current year. The bleak number staring back made her want to toss the piece of tech and cuss.

Instead she set it down and forced a smile on her face. "It's almost time for you guys to use the teaching-station. Could you get everybody together and head over? Wind and Cherish are working with Jenni on the greenhouse and Royal is playing with Mia at Iris's place."

Sunny jumped up. "Of course. See you at dinner." She was humming when she left.

Rain and Auntie didn't speak until Sunny had pulled on her outside boots and left. The moment the front door shut behind her, Auntie spoke up.

"How bad?"

Rain pushed the computator over to her. "Very."

Auntie hissed as she looked at the numbers. "And we still have to pay the Gorlag Gang their percentage. We can't live like this."

Placing her elbows on the table, Rain dropped her face into her hands. "You don't think I know that?"

"What about Hes?" Auntie pushed. "Remember, he said there are humans living on his homeworld. Let's talk to him about going there. "

"He says the humans don't work but are taken care of anyway," Rain said without lifting her face from her hands.

"The humans don't work?" Auntie questioned, tugging at one of Rain's hands until she dropped them to meet Auntie's gaze. "That doesn't make any sense."

"And that's why I dropped the subject," Rain snapped. She regretted her harsh tone immediately. "Sorry."

Auntie waved off her apology. "Even if it's odd, it's worth talking to him more about it. We could be performing tasks that are work but the Talins label them differently. There are really only two things we need to know: would it be indentured labor and can we all stay together? Otherwise we're good at making things work out even if they're not perfect."

Rain shook her head. "I'm scared of leading everyone into a worse situation."

Auntie raised an eyebrow and pursed her lips. "Worse? In what way? That we'd be struggling to make ends meet or that we'd be living each day under threat of violence and bodily harm? Because that would be *so* much different from what we're dealing with right now. Asking questions doesn't create a binding contract."

"Sarcasm isn't a good look for you," Rain shot back. "But you have a point. I'll talk to him some more and try to figure out what's going on there."

"Good," Auntie pointed out as she stood up. "I'm off to help Zuri. You're in charge of putting dinner together."

"Got it," Rain said. "Ask questions and make dinner."

"We'll figure something out. I know this place isn't where it all ends," Auntie declared then leaned over and gave her a quick hug before leaving.

Sitting back in the chair, Rain rubbed her temples. There was a long list of tasks she should be doing, but her head hurt, and she wanted to indulge in a moment of quiet. There might have been a little wallowing in self-pity included.

She was so involved in her thoughts that she didn't know anyone else was in the room with her until she felt a warm presence and heard the sound of purring.

"Hes," she breathed out, opening her eyes and sitting up. He was kneeling next to her chair, watching her intently.

"Your head hurts again."

It was a statement, not a question, but she answered anyway. "Only a little bit."

"Are there any chores that can't wait?" he asked.

Her brows furrowed in confusion. "Nothing really important, why?"

"There are marks left before the last meal of the day will draw everyone back to the domicile. May I take care of you during this time?"

She'd spent every night for the last week in Hes's bed. She'd sneak over after everyone else was asleep and wake up before them. So far, only Auntie knew about the change in their relationship, but Sunny was probably suspicious. As much as she enjoyed everything they did at night, she didn't feel up to that right now. "In what way do you want to take care of me?"

"I've never done it before, but I think the humans are fond of it," Hes said.

Now she was curious. "Whatever it is better not have anything to do with processing seedpods," she warned with a tired smile.

"No seedpods," he promised. "Remain down here, I'll return when I've gotten things ready."

With that, he got to his feet and rushed to the ladder and up to the second floor. Rain remained where she was and listened to him moving around upstairs. Whatever he was doing required some effort, and there was the sound of metal on metal and some banging. By the time he came back downstairs, the need to know what he was doing was killing her.

"It's ready," he announced and picked her up. "Wrap your arms and legs around me."

She did as he instructed and even snuggled her face against his neck. He easily held her to him with an arm under her butt. It felt good to be carried and cuddled but she knew he'd have to let go of her to climb the ladder.

"Oh!" she breathed as he climbed using only one arm while the other continued to support her. Trusting him, she closed her eyes and felt his powerful body moving with his trademark fluid grace.

Once on the second floor, he strode down the hall to the bathing and elimination room. The house had two elimination rooms, one per floor, but only one bathing facility. Theirs was one of the older domiciles and had been built by her grandparents when they were first getting the colony going.

He set her down in the hall with her back to the bathing room. "May I take your clothes off, Rain?" he asked.

She sighed, feeling disappointed that all this had been about sex. "I'd rather not."

His purring stopped abruptly, and he retreated back half a step. Rain felt guilty, but there was also fatigue. Moving forward, she caught his hand and tried for a smile despite the nagging headache.

"Maybe we can have sex later," she offered.

The purring started up again. Pulling his hand free of hers, he sank to his knees then gripped her hips. "You're mistaken," he said, urging her to turn around.

Rain sucked in a startled breath. Hes had pulled down the old bathing tub they'd stopped using when she was a child. The large tub was designed to fold up flat against the wall and stay out of the way when not in use. With the birth of Wind and Cherish, the house had gotten too crowded to allow for much time spent on daily ablutions.

He must have thoroughly cleaned the tub earlier because the last time she'd pulled it down to work on the plumbing behind it, the thing had been nothing but dust and grime. Now it shone like perfectly polished silver. When had he done this?

The tub was full of steaming water and a wave of warm, moist air wafted across her face when she leaned over. A soft floral scent hit her nose.

Hes was pushing in behind her and shutting the room's door to help keep the warmth in. "Now that you know my intentions, are you willing to be disrobed?"

"How did you do all this?" she asked.

"I noticed the tub the first day, and I was told that many humans enjoyed bathing in hot water when given a chance. As you know, I don't require much sleep so I would spend a mark or two each night restoring the tub and fixing the aging joints. At first it didn't hold water, but a conversation with Auntie helped me figure out how to fix it."

"No wonder Auntie was so quick to leave," Rain murmured. "She knew you were planning this. You're a good guy, Hes."

Rain reached down and pulled off her bulky sweater and tossed it into a dry corner. It was followed by her overshirt, shirt, then finally she stripped off her thermals. She only had to pull a layer of pants and thermals off her legs before pulling off her underwear. As usual, by the time she was done, there was a small mountain of clothing, and she was cold despite the warm air of the bathroom.

Shivering slightly, she hurried into the bath, letting out a big sigh of pleasure at the luxurious feel of the warm water over her. Stretching her legs out, she rested her head on the edge of the tub.

Hes sat on a small stool and was quick to tuck a rolled-up drying cloth under her head and neck. Opening her eyes, she looked up at him leaning over her. He held up a square of cleansing cloth. "I'd like to bathe you. I'll be gentle with your skin."

"Sure," she whispered, letting her eyes fall closed again. "That sounds nice."

Starting with her shoulders, Hes rubbed her skin in small, slow circles. The cleansing cloth had a slight abrasive quality to it and felt marvelous. He didn't miss a single spot, even getting between her fingers and toes.

His purring never stopped, and between his gentle ministrations, the warm water, and the soothing sound of his purring, Rain drifted off into a place somewhere between awake and asleep. Her headache disappeared by degrees as the tightness in her neck and shoulders eased.

The water would never cool as long as the tub had power, and Rain wished she could spend the night soaking in the warm water. Unfortunately, she couldn't hold the only bathing room in the house hostage for the night. Eventually, the siblings would be home, and most of them would probably want to take quick showers before dinner.

"It's time to remove you from the water," Hes announced as he submerged both arms to pick her up.

Resisting the urge to protest, she sleepily opened her eyes and swayed a bit as Hes set her feet on the cold floor. He was quick to use a drying cloth on her, starting at her shoulders and working his way down.

She expected that to be the end of his spa treatment, but after he finished drying her, he pulled out a bottle. Uncapping it, he poured some of the contents into his hands and rubbed it across her body. The substance didn't have a scent, but made her skin feel soft and pampered.

"Where did that come from?" she asked lazily.

"I brought it with me," Hes answered.

"You guys need to moisturize your skin?" she asked, surprised.

"Not unless we have an injury or condition," he answered, focused on the task at hand which was working the lotion into the skin of her left leg. "I brought several things suitable for humans, including this. I don't have enough for everyone, so I hadn't unpacked it until now."

There was something about him packing around human-specific products that should have raised alarm bells, but she was too content to think deeply about it.

When Hes was done, he picked her up and cradled her naked body against his chest. Bumping the door open with his foot, he carried her to his room. The air was cold, but between being warm from the bath and being held against Hes's hot skin, she didn't feel chilled.

"I need clothes," she murmured. Her words were slurred, and her eyelids refused to stay open.

"I'll fetch you some later," he promised.

"I should get up and check on the progress of the soil bots," she mumbled. "And it's my turn to do dinner."

"The soil bots will be fine for one afternoon and I'll help with dinner," Hes answered, setting her in the bed and then shedding his own clothes to cuddle in behind her. "Let me hold you while you rest."

She was asleep before she could say yes or thank him.

CHAPTER 14

Hesarium

Dinner was unusually loud and chaotic that evening, or at least it felt that way. This meal was a sharp contrast to the quiet marks he spent bathing and holding Rain while she slept. He knew it would only be another few marks before everyone would retire to their rooms again and he could hold Rain without interruption, but the time seemed to flow far slower than normal.

"What about you?"

It took Hesarium a moment to realize Wind was talking to him. "I'm unsure."

"You're unsure because you don't know or because you didn't hear what I said?" Wind asked with a grin. "I was asking if you've ever been on one of those giant warships. The kind that are floating cities and can be set up as satellite-fortresses around a planet."

Surprised that the conversation had turned to this topic, Hesarium sounded a rattle of agreement. "We call those stronghold class ships, and I was stationed on one for a short time."

All eyes focused on him as Wind demanded more details. "Tell me about it. What did you do? Where was the ship? Were you on it when it set up orbit? I heard that can be scary."

"I was only there for fifty rotations, then I joined the Advanced Squad I would serve with for the rest of my time in the military," he explained. "I wasn't part of the ship's crew."

Wind looked disappointed but Sunny was quick with the next question. "Have you seen a black hole?"

"Only on a technical display," Hesarium answered. "The data I saw was impressive."

Even before he finished speaking, Wind had another question for him. "Have you ever seen a supernova?"

The siblings were full of inquiries about everything space related and asked one question after another without giving him a break in between. There was even a question from Rain about how ships docked to space stations. It took a full mark of questions and answers before Hesarium realized why they were so curious—none of them had ever been to space. Every human currently on Omanal had been born here and had spent their life as seedpod farmers with their feet firmly planted on the fertile soil. It seemed a few Omanal humans might have their feet on the ground but their eyes and dreams on the stars.

Some of the things they asked made it very clear they had an excellent grasp of the inequity of the universe, but much less understanding of practical day-to-day items. None of them realized that not all stations could sustain humans, as the species running the station set it up for their own comfort thereby making it inhospitable to other lifeforms. They were also fascinated by the idea of working on a ship or space station and rarely placing a foot planetside.

"Your species has an empire, right?" Cherish asked when there was a break in questions. "Do you guys enslave other nations?"

Her question caused him a visceral reaction and he sounded an angry rattle before he could stop himself. "Never," he spat out. "We don't believe in slavery."

Cherish wasn't intimidated by his rattle or answer. "Then if you go to war with another civilization and win, what do you do with them?"

"It depends," he answered, feeling a little out of his depth. "I believe they usually pay tribute for a period, and we claim a portion of their colonized worlds. These are the type of questions you should be asking someone like my sister. She joined the Department for War Re-allocation and could give you an entire lecture on how defeated species are treated and why."

"You have a sister?" Royal asked from Auntie's lap. "Why isn't she here with you?" The little boy looked around as if she was going to appear out of thin air to join their conversation.

"I haven't seen Sularium in many solars," Hesarium explained. "Not since we were in cresh together."

There was a beat of silence as everyone, including Rain, regarded him with incredulous expressions.

"Solars means years?" Royal asked, his voice high with worry.

Hesarium sounded a soft rumble of agreement. "I haven't seen my parents in that long as well. It's common among Talins. Our families aren't as close as human families."

He thought to soothe Royal with his explanation but after a beat of silence, Royal burst into tears and lunged for him. Hesarium caught him in the air when Auntie wasn't quick enough to stop the impetuous movement. He drew Royal onto his lap, and the little boy wrapped his arms around Hesarium's neck.

"It's okay, Hes," Royal said, sobbing against his neck. "We won't let anyone hurt you. My family is a really good family, and they'll protect you too."

Startled and confused, Hesarium patted Royal's back as he met Rain's gaze. She was smiling but her eyes were swimming with unshed tears. She leaned close and whispered to him as Sunny got up to speak gently to Royal and help calm him down.

"When Dad and Royal's mom died, the community decided I couldn't take care of him because he was so young. A childless couple took him in, and I didn't say anything. It was tough because we were all mourning Dad's death. Anyway, it took a little while, but I finally got myself back together and realized Royal was being abused. Then it took months to get him away from the family and back with us. There was a lot of negotiating, and Auntie had to give up her place to get it done, forcing her to move in here with us."

"Who are these people that abused Royal?" Hesarium growled.

Rain shook her head and gave him a little kiss next to his earhole. "They died shortly after it all happened. They drowned when the bog spread under their domicile."

"Good," Hesarium declared. By now, Sunny had gotten Royal to calm down, but the little boy wouldn't let go of Hesarium.

"No! Hes needs to know I love him, just like all of you love me. If you think no one loves you, then it hurts a lot. I don't want him to hurt."

At Royal's words, Rain rested her forehead against Hesarium's head. He could feel her tears drip between the plates near his earhole. Holding Royal with one arm, he wrapped another arm around Rain and started up a comforting rumble.

"Leaving my sister and parents was nothing to me. We'd never been a family as you are to each other," he said loudly enough for everyone to hear him. "Now that I've experienced this, leaving any of you would be as if I'd left a vital part of myself behind."

He expected his words to comfort Royal, but instead it drew the rest of the family around him. Sunny, Auntie, and even Cherish circled him and huddled in, wrapping arms around each other.

Lacking the vocabulary to describe what he was feeling, all he could think of was the word *safe*.

"We've got you," Rain murmured in his earhole. He didn't understand the term, but he understood the intent, and it filled him with a warmth he'd never experienced before. If he thought he adored this family before, it was nothing like what he felt now. Forget about fighting the Gorlag Gang, he'd destroy entire solar systems to defend them!

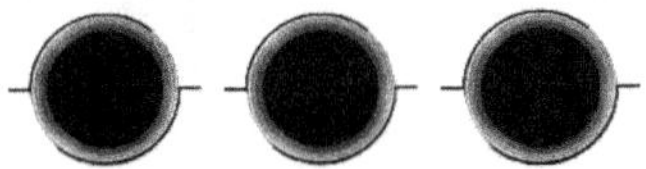

Rain

After dinner, everyone settled in the living room to play a game of seedpod flip. It was half luck and half strategy, and Rain had neither tonight. After getting eliminated early, she sat back in her favorite chair and watched everyone else play.

"Are you fatigued?"

Opening her eyes to answer Hes's question, she found everyone was looking at her.

"You snored!" Royal giggled.

Rain grinned at the little boy and then made an exaggerated snoring sound. "Like that?"

Her antics made Royal dissolve into peals of laughter, pulling chuckles out of everyone else. Playing up to his audience, Royal started making different snoring sounds and invited everyone to do it as well.

"He is easily amused," Hes noted.

"Royal is a gentle soul who feels everything strongly," Rain murmured. "He is willing to be sad or happy with you in equal measures. He'll probably be like Mom, attuned to everyone's emotional state."

"Like you as well," Hes commented.

Rain shook her head, feeling sad. "I try to pay attention, but I miss stuff. Royal's always quick with a hug or questions. Part of it might be from his trauma, but I think most of it is part of his basic personality."

Hes's arms tightened around her briefly. "You're all good humans."

She gave him a little kiss on the cheek, and her lips stretched into a wide smile. "Yes we are, and you're a good Talin."

"I will do my best for all of you," he promised in a solemn tone. "You did seem like you were falling asleep earlier, is it time to retire for the night?"

As Hes talked, Rain watched Sunny yawn, then Wind. "I think it's time for all of us to go to bed."

Hes suddenly tensed and turned his head to the front of the domicile. Before Rain could say anything, a loud bang from outside made all of them jump. Wind knocked over the stack of seedpod cards he'd collected, Royal cried out in startlement, and Cherish nearly fell out of her chair.

"Everyone, stay here," Hes ordered, jumping to his feet and rushing through the front door and into the night beyond.

Rain sat frozen for a few seconds as her brain caught up to what had happened. Standing up, she looked over at Auntie with a questioning expression. "Auntie?"

A look of angry determination replaced the woman's normally friendly, open expression. "Move!" she ordered, already making her way to the front door. Rain didn't need any further urging.

"Sunny, you're in charge," Rain commanded as she followed Auntie to the front door.

"What's going on?" Sunny asked as Rain joined Auntie in shoving feet into boots.

"Probably nothing," Rain answered. "Don't go outside unless we call for you."

Sunny mutely nodded, tightly holding the game card she'd been about to set down between her fingers. Rain gave all her siblings a reassuring smile and then followed Auntie out the door. She grabbed a pod hook laying on the ground next to the single step down before catching up to Auntie.

"I think it came from the greenhouses," Auntie explained as she half walked, half ran in that direction. Even though they were only a few minutes behind Hes, Rain didn't see him anywhere.

Before they got to the greenhouses, Rain could see the damage. Omanal's seven small moons were all full and shining that night, giving her a clear view of a ruined building. One side had completely collapsed, breaking the other load bearing walls and bringing the roof down like a felled tree.

Shock froze her in place. How could this happen? Not even a giant herd of entict crashing into the side of the greenhouse at the same time would be able to do this much damage. Taking a stumbling step forward, Rain felt broken bits of polymer poke at the bottom of her boot. The ground was covered in broken bits of ruined panels.

Each greenhouse represented years of saving to afford and a community-wide effort to set up. Now one of them was gone, and Rain felt it like a blow to her body.

"Maybe the bog extended," Auntie said as she grabbed Rain's arm and tugged her back. "If it was only under one side, then it could've caused the collapse like this."

Rain shook her head. "The side isn't sunk into the ground at all. It's not the bog."

Hes appeared to Rain's right as if summoned by magic. "Rain? Auntie? What are you doing out here?"

Auntie's hands shot to her hips. "We weren't going to let you go off on your own. My turn for questions, where did you run off to?"

Hes moved in close to Rain's side. He purred as he put an arm around her shoulders. "You shouldn't be out in the cold."

"Answer first," Rain insisted, looking back at the greenhouse. "You knew something was going on before we heard the crash. How?"

Although his rumble didn't change, she felt his body tense up a little. He didn't speak right away, and she got the impression he was trying to decide what to tell her.

"You might as well explain," Auntie pushed when he still didn't answer. "Rain and I can stand out here all night if we need to."

Hes sounded the angry wasps rattle of annoyance. "That would be disastrous for your health."

"Then I guess you better talk," Rain said. The angry wasp rattle changed, it became softer and more muted as if she were hearing it through several thick walls. It was the sound of anxiety.

"I heard Rast engines," he explained.

Confused, Rain stared up at Hes. "There was a Rast out here at this time of night?"

Auntie put it together before she could. "They did this, didn't they?" she asked Hes, pointing at the greenhouse. "They ran one of those damn Rasts into the side and destroyed the building."

"Yes," Hes answered simply. "There were three Rasts. They were pulling one of the Rast out from the rubble. They were able to mount up and ride away before I was able to get to them."

Rain felt cold and it had nothing to do with the frigid night air. "They came out here to terrorize us. We haven't even gotten quotes back, and they already wanted to scare us into paying."

"I'm not sure that's entirely correct. I think the three riders came out to assess your harvest." He pointed to a track of disturbed dirt Rain wouldn't have noticed if not for him. "I believe the rider of this Rast lost control and crashed."

Auntie squinted at the track, then looked at the ruined building. "Crashed into the greenhouse?"

"Yes, exactly," Hes agreed. "He didn't mean to do damage, but that doesn't negate the fact that the greenhouse was destroyed."

Rain went silent as she tried to comprehend the damage. At least the seedpod storage building beyond the greenhouses hadn't been touched. Still, this was a significant blow to their livelihood.

"There's nothing to be done tonight," Auntie declared, hugging herself and shivering from the cold. "Let's go to bed and deal with all this in the morning."

"Tomorrow," Rain agreed, already feeling a new headache blossoming.

"And don't bother coming into my room tonight," Auntie warned. "Go straight to Hes's room and stay there 'til morning. There's no need for you to be sneaking around like a teenager with a curfew. Besides, your siblings all know. Well, except for Royal of course."

That bit of news made Rain smile as she turned to begin the trek back to their domicile. "One less thing to worry about, I guess."

Rain didn't get very far. Purring, Hes scooped her up and held her close to his chest all the way home. "No more worrying," he declared as if he could make it stop by simply announcing it.

If only it was that easy.

CHAPTER 15

Rain

It was midmorning, and Rain and Sunny were in the tall crawler crowded with the second load of boxes to fill the proto-plant hoppers on the tops of the vertical fields. If they had Hes to help, they'd probably be done by now, but she and Sunny only had half the south field finished.

"We could be finished already if Hes was here," Sunny complained, sitting heavily on the last box she'd loaded.

"He needed to visit the port," Rain reminded her, leaning heavily on a nearby strut. Even with the lifters and bots to help, filling hoppers was one of the most strenuous tasks they had.

"But why?" Sunny whined, tugging on the edge of her knit hat. "If he waited until tomorrow, we could've all gone to the port with him."

Rain raised an eyebrow at Sunny. "What's so interesting at the port? All Hes is doing is buying time on their comms array to send a message."

"The port isn't here," Sunny said, gesturing to the land around them. "At least we get to look at ships and talk about where they've been and where they're going."

It was a game she and Sunny had played when Mom and Dad had been alive. Sunny had been closer to Royal's age then, and life had been a little easier. They'd sneak off and find a comfortable place to watch the port. Rain would make up all kinds of stories about the ships and their crews. It was so long ago, she was surprised Sunny remembered.

"That's true," Rain agreed, surprising Sunny. "It's dangerous to go into town, but we could pilot one of the tall crawlers to the edge of the bog on the north side of the port and watch from there."

"Could we pack food and make it a picnic?" Sunny asked, a wide smile unfurling across her face.

"Sure!" Rain enthused, getting behind the idea. If they got all the hoppers filled today, then they could take all day tomorrow and do whatever they wanted.

Sunny froze, her smile fading. "Do you smell smoke?"

Rain frowned, sniffing. "Yeah, I do."

Fire on Omanal was rare but not unheard of. Getting up, Rain climbed up on the loading support strut and immediately saw smoke. "I think there's a fire over by the long field."

"We should go over there," Sunny urged. "They might need help putting it out."

Rain started to get down when she realized it wasn't the field on fire, it was a domicile. She froze, staring in shock as flames engulfed the rooms of Zuri's domicile. It wasn't until a second domicile began to burn that Rain realized they were under attack.

"No, no, no, no," Sunny repeated, her voice rising in panic. She'd climbed up and was clinging to the strut next to Rain as the second domicile caught fire. Dust clouds moved rapidly in different directions and several groups of Rasts appeared, each one making their way to domiciles.

As she watched, ten Rasts circled an old domicile they couldn't use anymore because it was too close to the bog. They shot firestarters at it until the entire thing was ablaze.

"They're killing us," Sunny whispered.

Sunny's shocked words spurred Rain into action. Jumping down from the strut, she tugged at Sunny until the teenager jumped down too.

"I need you to take this crawler to the edge of the bog near the old grove," Rain ordered, pointing in the opposite direction of the gang. "Wait there for our siblings, then go deep into the bog."

Tears were running down Sunny's face. "Rain, I can't leave—"

Rain gave her a little shake. "I promise I'm going to get everyone to you, but I need to know you'll be there waiting for them. I'm trusting you."

Without waiting for a reply, Rain shoved her toward the crawler's control panel. She could hear Sunny calling out her name, but Rain was already over the side of the crawler and climbing down. The moment she hit the ground, she started running.

Auntie, Cherish, and Wind should be helping with the greenhouse clean up. If Royal was still with them, it would make it easy to get them all to safety. As she got closer to the greenhouses, she saw Auntie climbing up the side of greenhouse two, trying to see what was going on. Wind, Sabrina, Frish, Zuri, and Mandy were all standing around watching her climb.

"The Gorlags are attacking!" she screamed as soon as she was within earshot. Everyone turned to her, and Auntie froze halfway up the ladder and looked over her shoulder. Rain tried to shout again but didn't have the breath. Thankfully Auntie hurried down the ladder and everyone started to rush toward her.

Taking a bad step, Rain stumbled and almost fell to her knees. By the time she recovered her footing, everyone was gathering around her.

"Go!" she panted, pointing to where Sunny was probably almost to the bog with the crawler. If she could get everyone to the bog, they'd be safe. "Sunny has the crawler. Go to Old Grove Bog. Go now."

Gris shook his head. "Devon and the kids are at Carter and Nova's house using the teaching-station. I'm not leaving without them." He didn't wait for Rain to respond; he simply turned and ran. Rain didn't try to stop him.

"Cherish took Royal back to our domicile," Auntie said. Smoke was starting to fill the air, and they could hear the fearful cries of other humans.

"I'll get them," Rain said with a cough. "You need to go." She cast a meaningful glance at Wind, Mandy, and Suri. Mandy was Wind's age and Suri was barely twenty-two. They wouldn't run and hide unless Auntie was there to make them.

Auntie nodded her head and grabbed Mandy's arm. "We need to go!"

As the small, frightened group headed for the safety of Sunny and Old Grove Bog, Rain sprinted to her domicile. As she got closer, she saw the line of Rasts heading in the same direction. It was obvious her domicile was the next one they were going to burn, and they were going to get there before her.

Time seemed to slow down. She watched the door to her domicile open and Cherish stood there, looking around confused. The lead Rast was close and the Gorlag rider was pointing a firestarter weapon at Cherish. Rain opened her mouth to scream, but no sound came out.

Out of nowhere, a body hurtled through the air. Time started moving again as Hes appeared and tackled the lead Gorlag off his Rast. The Rast tipped and rolled sideways as the two of them crashed to the ground next to the road. Two riders couldn't avoid the leader's toppled vehicle and smashed into it. The other five managed to swerve and started large arcs to come back around.

Hes was sounding a rattle loud enough to compete with the sound of so many Rast engines running at the same time. Rain wasn't sure where she should go; to help Hes or get Cherish and Royal. Hes solved the dilemma for her. He popped to his feet and the Gorlag stayed down and unnaturally still.

Both she and Hes ran for Cherish and Royal. The two stayed frozen in place, Royal visibly upset and Cherish trying to take everything in, her mouth gaping.

"What's going on?" Cherish asked the moment Rain got to her.

"Attack," Rain panted. She was breathing so hard it was difficult to get the words out. "Old Grove Bog."

Then Hes was there. He didn't say a single word, simply grabbed Cherish and Royal. His intensely loud rattling had stopped, and the approaching Rasts' overwhelming noise surrounded them.

"Climb on and hold tight," he ordered, presenting her with his back.

She didn't climb on. Instead, Rain put her hands against his back and gave him a shove in the direction of Sunny and the crawler. "Go now!"

She knew he'd argue so she went around him and started running. Even though he was carrying Cherish and Royal, he was still able to catch up with her at the far side of the road. Carrying one child under each arm, he was able to move, but not with any of his normal grace or speed.

The Rasts stopped in the road as they moved past the first row of vertical planters. She couldn't hear them chasing. A glance over her shoulder showed them gathered around their fallen comrades, pulling riders out of the mess of crashed Rasts.

"Rain, watch out—"

Hes's words weren't fast enough. Her foot caught on the edge of a planter, and she tumbled to the ground. She rolled a few times but the moment she came to a stop, Hes appeared at her side and knelt next to her. He shifted both kids so they could wrap their arms and legs around him, reminding her of images she'd seen of an Earth animal called a koala.

"Are you injured?" Hes asked, kneeling down next to her.

Rain got to her knees, then to her feet. Her right ankle hurt, but she could still walk on it. "I'm fine. You go, I'll catch up."

"If you can't move quickly, you're an easy target," Hes argued. "I can't leave you behind."

"I'll stay hidden," Rain promised. "When Cherish and Royal are safe, come back for me."

"I can carry you also," Hes insisted, but she knew better. He was already slowed by having to carry the two kids. Running flat out on the uneven field wouldn't be possible with her on his back also. The smoke around her was getting stronger, and she could hear the Gorlags shouting at each other. She needed her siblings safe more than she needed anything else.

Royal was sobbing in terror, and Cherish was shaking violently with a blank expression on her face. Rain didn't have time to soothe them, but she could give them a chance at survival.

"Save them first," she demanded. "If you don't do as I ask, then you're not the male I thought you were."

Hes jerked as if she'd struck him. A sound came out of him she'd never heard before. It almost sounded like wailing.

"If you join the Ancestors, then I will also," he declared then sprinted off.

They disappeared among the planters within a few strides. Ignoring Hes's comment about being a slow-moving target, Rain got up and found that she could do a hobble-run without her left ankle giving out on her. She was only a few more rows away when an explosion made her duck behind a planter.

Peeking out from around it, she saw half her domicile missing and the other half engulfed in flames. She froze in place, staring at the ruins.

Everything they owned was there. All the things they needed for day-to-day life had been in there, along with useless but meaningful items attached to good memories. The projects Sunny made out of seedpod husks when she'd been a small child. Royal's baby footprints inked into the wall. Cherish and Wind's matching toddler outfits Mom had made into pillows. All their captured images of the family and their meticulously recorded history starting when Grandma Katherine organized an entire community on Earth to migrate to Omanal.

Rain dropped to the ground like a seedpod with the stem cut. Deep, unmitigated sorrow filled her. They might live through this attack, but how would they survive tonight's frigid temperatures or tomorrow's hunger?

"Where are the others hiding?"

The shouted question roused Rain out of her stupor. She rounded the planter to see Iris struggling against a single Gorlag in the middle of a nearby road. Beyond the two in the road, Rain could see growing flames where the rest of the gang had gone to start more fires. Why this individual had stayed behind and how he'd gotten his hands on Iris weren't important. Rain needed to free Iris and get them both to safety.

"I don't know!" Iris cried out, fighting against the Gorlag's hold. "Let go or I'll kill you!"

Her threat made him angrier. "As if you had that ability!" he scoffed. "You humans are nothing but pests. The universe will be a better place after all of you are exterminated." He did something that made Iris cry out in pain. "Now tell me where they are, and I'll make your death a painless one!"

Skirting around several planters, Rain made it to the road. There was only a short distance separating her from the Gorlag holding Iris. Realizing she couldn't go hand to hand with him, Rain looked around for a weapon. A good sized rock was the only thing available.

Picking it up, she dashed across the road at the fastest hobble-run she could manage. Holding it with both hands over her head, she brought it down with a satisfying thud on the back of the Gorlag's head. He squawked once, then crumbled to the ground.

Released from his grip, Iris stumbled back then rushed to grab Rain in a hug. "I don't understand what's going on!"

"Same," Rain said, hugging the girl back. As much as Rain wanted to stand there and give her throbbing ankle a rest, they needed to get moving. "Come on, I know where some people are."

Iris refused to move. "Mia is at home sleeping. We need to get her!"

"I'll find her," Rain said, pushing Iris away.

Iris blinked a few times, then shook her head stubbornly. "No, I'm staying with you."

Rain wanted to argue but knew Iris too well. Even as a little girl, she had a will of iron. She'd gone without speaking for ten days straight once to win an argument with her dad. She'd picked fights with Dorinc kids twice her size and occasionally won. There was no making Iris do anything she didn't want to do, even if it meant saving her life.

"Fine!" Rain screamed, giving up. She looked in the direction of the domicile Iris and Mia shared. Not only were the burning ruins of several other buildings in the way, but the air was rapidly filling with smoke from all the fires.

The domiciles were all set up in a large semi-circle with the fields extending beyond the houses. In the center of the circle and between the houses, they built storage for the equipment and harvested seedpods. As she took in the area, she noticed that none of the storage or equipment buildings were on fire.

In a flash it came to her. This was why they'd run Rasts around the property last night. They'd been mapping it out to best kill off all the humans so they could claim and sell the entire harvest. Rage filled her.

Her community of humans worked hard and didn't cause problems, and this was what they got? The injustice made her see red. Her fury was so strong that when the Gorlag she'd hit with the rock moaned and started to move at her feet, she didn't even think twice. She raised the rock and brought it down on his head with all her strength.

His moan cut off and he went limp again. Rain had never been so violent before and was surprised when she felt no disgust or horror at her actions.

"I think you killed him," Iris observed. When their gazes met, she gave Rain an approving look. "Good."

The sound of something crashing at the far end of the housing circle caught their attention. Rain started limping toward Alex and Sam's domicile but Iris grabbed her. "Wait, let me look at something."

Leaving Rain standing in the road, Iris covered the short distance to a Rast laying on its side. It was the only one that didn't end up in a pile of broken machines all tangled together. With an amazing show of strength, Iris bent down and lifted it back onto the sliders.

With familiarity Raid didn't know Iris possessed, the younger woman threw a leg over and settled on the long seat. It took two tries, but the engine started up with a high-pitched whine. She maneuvered the machine around until it was facing the correct direction, then pulled up even with Rain.

"Hop on," Iris said.

"I didn't know you could pilot one of these things," Rain commented as she got on behind Iris and wrapped her arms around the woman's waist.

"I secretly dated Togal," Iris admitted, naming the son of the prominent Gorlag member. "He gave me lessons and let me ride his dad's."

Rain wanted to voice her surprise at Iris's revelation but was too busy screaming in shock as Iris gunned the Rast into motion. Rain had never been on something that moved so fast, and she hugged Iris tightly in fear as the scenery flashed by. Everything turned into impressions of color with loose delineation of shape as they sped down the road. The wind slapped her in the face, forcing her to duck behind Iris. Neither of them were wearing any protective gear. How was Iris not affected?

Iris leaned the Rast far over in a sharp turn that made the back slider shift and skid around a little. Rain sucked in a breath and closed her eyes tight. If she survived this, she was never going to ride anything faster than a crawler again!

Iris stopped the Rast so abruptly it forced Rain's body into her and almost toppled them over. Rain opened her eyes to find that they were on the section of the circle road around the property where it intersected with a footpath into one of the fields.

Before she could ask Iris why they stopped, Rain saw the small figure huddled next to a turned over planter.

"Mia?" Iris called out. The young girl stood up and ran to them. Her clothing was dirty and ragged, and her hair looked like it had gotten a little singed on one side, but otherwise she looked whole and unharmed.

"Irish!" Mia, the four-year-old, screamed. "There's fiwr! Everything's on fiwr!"

When Mia reached the Rast, Iris grabbed her and tucked the little girl in front of her. Rain scooted back as far as she could to make room, but with the three of them, it was crowded and awkward, and Rain ended up half hanging off the back.

Iris got the Rast moving into a slow circle to turn around. They were halfway through the turn when the sound of shouting made all three of them look over to find seven Gorlags on Rasts barreling down on them.

Rain didn't have to tell Iris to hurry, she was already trying to move faster. The issue was that Rasts didn't do tight turns.

Jumping off the back, Rain pushed hard on the side of the Rast to help get it in position for Iris speed off. Her ankle screamed in pain and gave out just as the Rast was in position. Using her good leg, she hopped back on and managed to get her arms wrapped around Iris only seconds before the Rast shot forward.

They hurtled down the road at a breakneck speed, and Rain realized the Gorlags following were too close. It wasn't that they were catching up. Iris was too good a pilot to allow that, but with them right on their heels, they couldn't head directly to safety. It wouldn't help anyone if they led the Gorlag's right to where everyone was hiding.

Rain was about to shout the problem in Iris's ear when another Rast appeared in front of them, piloted by Hes. He shot by them, and seconds later, Rain heard crashing. Scared for Hes, Rain looked behind them but between the smoke and a cloud of dust in the road she couldn't see anything.

"Stop!" she screamed at Iris.

Bringing the Rast to a skidding stop, Iris looked back at Rain. "What?"

"You go, I need to help Hes," Rain told her, scrambling off the Rast. Iris looked torn then Mia let out a loud sob and Iris's expression shifted into one of determination.

"I'll come back for you," she promised.

"Don't," Rain ordered. Either she made it out with Hes, or she didn't want to make it out at all. She'd lost so much already, she couldn't lose him too.

"You aren't in charge of me," Iris shot back, her mouth set in a stubborn line as she powered up the Rast and sped away. She would probably try to come back but Rain hoped the others would stop her.

Turning in place, Rain hobbled to the area of road still cloaked in smoke and dust. It was easy to distinguish Hes's intimidating rattle sounding like many feet pounding on the ground. A ball of fire appeared out of the area and shot past her, narrowly missing her head and knocking over a planter.

The fall of the tall planter still covered in old growth they hadn't cleared off yet caused a gust of wind to temporarily clear the road, giving Rain an unobstructed view of the fighting. Out of all the Gorlags chasing them, there were only two left. One of them clearly had a broken arm and was attempting to weld the firestarter weapon one-handed. The other one was doing a good job of fending Hes off with large, bladed weapons.

As she drew closer, she could see Hes was wounded. He was bleeding from several places and one of his arms wasn't extending out all the way. Most of the quills on his right arm were broken and blood seeped from his right earhole.

Even hurt, he was still moving fast, and she could see it was only a matter of time before he defeated his opponents. The Gorlag with the bladed weapons was already starting to slow down and his movements were getting sloppy.

She was content to stay back and wait for Hes to finish him off until she saw the broken arm and firestarter weapon start to slowly rise. The Gorlag was clumsy but determined, and it wouldn't be very long before he had it aimed at Hes. At that distance, he wouldn't miss.

Rain skip-hobbled as fast as she could but knew she was too far away. "Hes! Look out!" she screamed with little hope he'd hear her.

Hes's back was to the Gorlag with the firestarter, and Rain was sure she was about to see the love of her life die. Then something miraculous happened. Hes kicked out a leg and turned at the same time. This caused his body to dip and the blade of his opponent to miss him, while at the same time, his foot lashed out and knocked the firestarter out of the other Gorlag's grip.

When the firestarter landed, it went off again but because of the way it bounced, the round hit the Gorlag who'd been trying to aim it in the first place. His body went up in flames, and he flailed and screamed for a second before slumping over and going still.

The one with the blades saw it all happen and faltered, allowing Hes to finish his spinning kick by sweeping the Gorlag's legs out from under him. Hes moved in and executed a sharp motion that ended in a cry of pain and then, nothing. Straightening up, he looked over to her. Their eyes met.

Relief filled her. Hes was safe. Her siblings and Auntie were safe. Everything else could burn to the ground as long as her people were secure.

CHAPTER 16

Hesarium

Even though she was in obvious pain, Rain continued to limp to Hes. Easily jumping over the ruins of several Rasts, he sprinted to her, fearful she was doing more damage by trying to walk.

Sweeping her up in his arms, he held her tight to his chest and started up a comforting rumble. He began walking into a nearby field and away from the pile of crashed Rasts and dead bodies. It wasn't the most efficient path to Old Grove Bog, but it would keep Rain from seeing the bodies of loved ones.

"Have you further injured yourself?" he demanded.

Wrapping her arms around his neck she hugged him tight. "I don't think so."

"I need to get you to a medic, and the other surviving humans also."

"Surviving?" Rain asked in a whisper and Hesarium wished he hadn't used those words. "Did you see some die?"

Hesarium tried to avoid the topic. "We can speak of it later."

"Hes, please tell me," Rain pleaded.

"Marel, Sam, and Alex were all dead before I could get to them," Hesarium told her.

"Do you know if Gris and his family made it out?" Rain asked.

"I don't," he admitted. "I'm sorry I failed you."

"As if you could predict that the one day you went to town they'd attack," Rain scoffed and Hesarium realized she didn't understand.

"They attacked because I went to town," he explained. "They were waiting for me to leave. I should've realized that was their plan. I was the only barrier keeping them from attacking."

"You couldn't have known," she insisted, then lifted her head to look around at the burning buildings. "How many more are still out there?"

"None are left," Hesarium announced with deep satisfaction. "I've dispatched every Gorlag who came onto your land. I'm only sorry it took me so long to get back here."

"You did amazing," Rain praised him. "We'd all probably be dead if you hadn't gotten back so fast."

Hesarium didn't respond because it very well could be the truth. He didn't want to contemplate how much worse it might have been if he hadn't stolen a Rast and rushed back to the settlement. Rain rested her head on his shoulder, her lips near the patch of bare skin on his neck.

They walked in silence, and soon he found a spot where many fresh crawler tracks disappeared into the bog, giving him hope that most of the humans had escaped.

"Rain!" Sunny's shout made him pivot in place. Hesarium let out a sharp rattle of shock; the young woman was walking on the top of the bog without sinking in!

"Don't fall!" Rain shouted back, apparently undisturbed by the sight of Sunny's ability to walk on the thick, dirty water.

"You stay there. I'll get one of the crawlers," she instructed. As she turned, Hesarium understood what he'd missed. Sunny was walking on some kind of stilts that were barely tall enough to keep her feet at water level. Her movements were slow and laborious, but clearly better than trying to swim through the bog water.

Not long after Sunny disappeared into the thick mist, the three crawlers appeared. They all climbed up on solid ground and came to a stop next to him. Humans flooded off the crawlers and circled them. Still held tightly in his arms, Rain engaged with them.

Hesarium took the opportunity to take in the state of the remaining humans and to note who was missing. It seemed that the humans were down to twenty-eight individuals, including Rain, her siblings, and Auntie. Considering the violent nature of the attack, it was amazing they'd lost only four people.

Everyone looked whole with only minor scrapes or bruises. Most of them were coughing so chances were high they had lung damage from the smoke. He hoped everyone's injuries could be easily healed by any decent medic.

"What do we do?" Gris asked after everyone had hugged. "Everything but the harvest is destroyed. Even if we get top dollar, we won't be able to rebuild."

"My family and I are leaving," Rain announced. "You can all come with us or not, but we're leaving."

"What do you mean you're leaving?" Sabrina asked.

"We're going to sell the harvest and split the money among us," Rain explained. "Then my family and I are going to take our share and go with Hes."

Out of all the decisions he expected to happen today, that wasn't one of them! When Rain looked up to meet his gaze, she smiled tentatively. "If your offer is still available."

"Offer?" Gris asked.

"I can give every human a safe place to call home," Hesarium announced. "My homeworld, Talarian, has a place set aside for humans. You're all welcome to live there."

Everyone was shocked into silence before he was hit with a barrage of questions. Rain put her fingers to her lips and let out an ear piercing sound he didn't know humans could make.

"I'm sorry to do this, but no questions. We have to get the harvest to the port and sold today, or we'll have to wait another twenty days for the next trade ship. We won't get as much but we can't risk another attack. After that, you can all decide to come with us or stay here."

There was some grumbling, but everyone agreed on Rain's course of action. In short order, they were on the crawlers and heading to the storage buildings. The humans were quiet as they passed the destruction. Some of the domiciles were still burning but most were nothing but piles of smoldering ruins.

A few of the humans started crying, but none of them did it loudly, and they were quickly quieted and comforted by family and friends. They didn't have time to mourn their losses yet, that would have to come later.

Hesarium was impressed with the mental fortitude of these humans. Even faced with such tragedy, they were making sound decisions and moving forward with resolve. It helped that Rain had a clear and articulate plan and Auntie was quick to back her up.

It took several marks, but they got the harvest loaded up onto two crawlers. It was hard to keep Rain seated during the process but Royal's need to be held and comforted helped. Once everything was loaded, everyone was ready to leave but Hesarium spoke up.

"The Gorlags I killed were only a few of many," he pointed out. "I'm skilled but I'm no match if so many come at us at once."

"We could travel through the bog and try to stay hidden," Gris said. "Like everyone does when they have to go to the port."

"We still need to come out of the bog somewhere near the port and we could be seen," Zuri pointed out.

"It's not like we have a choice," Rain said. Hesarium could see pain was taking its toll on her. His poor human needed care but that couldn't happen until all of this was done.

"I suggest you let me go first and speak with the cargo hauler while remaining in the bog," Hesarium suggested. "Once the hauler is ready to receive, I'll signal. That will limit the amount of time the crawlers will be on dry land and more visible."

"It's a good plan," Sabrina commented. "Safer for everyone."

"Everyone but Hes," Rain argued. "I should be the one going. It's my idea to begin with."

"You said it first, but we all knew this was how it had to go," Gris argued. "Hes is obviously the most skilled of all of us. He's the one who will survive if confronted."

Hesarium could tell Rain wasn't happy, but she gave up arguing. "Fine, but don't get hurt."

"I won't," Hesarium promised. He didn't foresee many problems. The Gorlags had been overconfident in their attack; they shouldn't be watching the port right now.

Sunny drove the crawler near the edge of the bog and Hesarium was able to jump to solid ground. He waited until Sunny reversed the crawler until it was mostly hidden by the dense bog foliage. Then he jogged onto the port.

It didn't take him long to find the captain he'd seen earlier that day when he'd tried to buy time on the comms array. It was easy to negotiate transport of the cargo and spots for him and all the humans.

The seedpod cargo the ship had originally been scheduled to pick up never arrived, and they needed to leave soon or miss their window for landing at the Hub. Hesarium wasn't surprised to find out about the other cargo. It had probably been stolen by the Gorlags. It was likely the gang had attacked many settlements at once.

The captain was glad to fill his hold with product and increase his profit margin. Hesarium warned the captain that once the cargo was loaded, they'd want to leave quickly. The captain didn't appear surprised.

"This is my last trip here," he said. "There's not enough demand to compensate for the danger of this place. I don't know too many who are going to keep coming here.

It's probably good you and your community are leaving now."

Hesarium simply agreed with him and didn't bother telling the captain about the attack on the homesteads and the humans who lost their lives.

A sprint to the end of the port and a waving of his arms brought the crawlers out of the bog and onto dry land. Every moment it took them to slowly make their way to the ship made Hesarium more and more aware of how exposed they were. It would only take one Gorlag spotting them to alert the rest of the gang to their imminent escape.

To Hesarium's relief, the humans were familiar with the loading process. The pilots of the crawlers took turns expertly maneuvering their vehicles under the ship. The automated loaders did the rest. When that was all done, Rain linked the controls of all the crawlers and piloted them to the edge of the port and out of the way, while Hesarium made sure all the humans had boarded.

When the last human was safely on board, Hesarium hurried over to find Rain attempting to climb down the side of a crawler.

"You are the most stubborn and willful human," Hesarium announced as he grabbed her from the side of the crawler and held her gently against his chest.

"I'll take that as a compliment," Rain replied as she snuggled into his chest. He started walking to the ship and Rain looked back at the crawlers over his shoulder. "I've lived my whole life here. Then, in less than a day, everything is gone and I'm leaving."

"Not everything is gone," he argued.

"No, you're right," she agreed and tried to smile. "We could've lost so many more people."

Hesarium's next words were cut off by the sound of someone yelling. Looking around, he was shocked to see David holding one of the firestarters and flanked by several Gorlags.

Rain went stiff in his arms. "David? I thought you'd died in one of the fires!" Her tone went from surprised to angry as she noticed the firestarter in his hands. "What are you doing with that?"

Hesarium stopped moving and looked for a place to set Rain down where she'd be safe while he took care of this new threat. There wasn't much, but a slight depression in the earth next to him was better than leaving her completely exposed.

"You shouldn't be alive!" David screamed as Hesarium put Rain down in a sitting position. "He promised me no one would make it out alive!"

Rain gasped at David's words. "How could you?" she screamed back and tried to get to her feet. Hesarium was forced to push her down.

"Stay," he ordered her and then turned to face his three opponents. All of them held firestarters, but no other weapons. The firestarters were deadly but hard to aim and slow to recharge. It might be easy for him to dodge their fire, but he had to think of the others. To keep Rain and the ship full of humans safe, he needed to take the weapons away before they were discharged.

"You're the one who's been giving Jorc, the Gorlag's leader, information," Hesarium said, clearly seeing the pattern he'd missed earlier. "It's how he knew who I was staying with and when I planned to leave for the day."

David looked at Hesarium with disgust. "Rain was supposed to be my wife, but she turned me down. I was the only single guy in the whole community, and she said no! Then you show up and she lets you fuck her. How is that fair?"

"You're pathetic!" Rain raged. "I'd rather fuck a tweshi than let you touch me."

"I can make that happen!" David shot back, then pointed into the nearby bog. "All of this is your fault. I was going to marry you, then we could've left with half the money from the harvest. I had it all planned out and Jorc agreed to it."

"People died!" Rain half screamed, half sobbed. "How could you?"

Rain didn't try to get up as she and David shouted at each other, allowing Hesarium to slowly edge away. The Gorlags with David kept their weapons aimed at him, but David's attention was still fully on Rain. That wouldn't work, he needed all three of them looking at him.

"I didn't know humans could be evil," he said to David. "Because of you, I've learned your species is capable of horrific acts of dishonor and cowardice. It's disappointing."

David's attention switched from Rain to him. The man blinked and stared at him, as if his INT wasn't working. Then his expression turned enraged, and he brought the firestarter up, aiming at Hesarium's chest.

"I wasn't going to kill you," David announced, tapping the trigger button. "But now I want to see you burn more than the bitch!"

Hesarium waited until he could see the pre-flash of the igniter, then he jumped to the side and ducked down. The round landed far behind him, sizzling and dying in the bog water. David's eyes widened as Hesarium sprinted forward. The human frantically slapped the firing switch repeatedly, but nothing happened. The other two brought their weapons up, but neither had a chance to fire before Hesarium was on them.

He grabbed the two Gorlags by the necks and brought their heads together with a satisfying crack. Both went limp so he dropped the bodies to focus on the human. David had fallen on his ass and was babbling as he crawled backward.

"You don't understand. I was tired of working and never having anything. No one understood that it was hard for me. Even after I killed Sharon, no one would leave me alone. I was a widower—I should've gotten more sympathy. Someone should've moved in and done everything. It wasn't fair!"

Rain gasped behind him. "You killed Sharon? We all believed you when you said she fell into the bog and drowned. You bastard! She was the sweetest woman."

Hesarium had felt a bit of hesitation at killing a human, but that sliver of reluctance disappeared with David's revelation.

"The universe would be a better place without you," Hesarium growled as he reached down to grab David by the throat. Panicked, David rolled on all fours, trying to get away. His foot kicked one of the firestarters past both of them while he reached for a third one that hadn't been fired yet. The firestarter he kicked went off, the shot harmlessly burning a path on the ground.

David got his fingers around the last firestarter and rolled on his back to aim it up, giving Hesarium a perfect view of the badly damaged barrel. Realizing what would happen if David fired it, Hesarium dove away. A submark later, he heard the explosive round come in contact with the damaged barrel, causing the entire thing to explode in David's hands.

"Fitting end," he grunted as he got to his feet, staring at the charred ground where David had been a moment ago. "No Ancestors will be waiting for you, human. You die without access to an afterlife."

That was one of the worst insults he could think of and still it wasn't half as much as this human deserved.

"Hes?"

Rain's weak voice had him turning in place to see her clutching her chest, blood seeping from a wound. Pieces of shrapnel from the exploded firestarter were embedded in the ground around her.

Sounding a loud rattle of alarm and shock, Hesarium covered the distance between them in only a few strides. When he saw the blood seeping into her clothing, he had to work hard to remain detached. Letting fear overtake him wouldn't do his sweet human any good.

"Let me see," he demanded and tugged her hands away from the wound. The hole was small, but blood was seeping out at an alarming rate, and it seemed she was having difficulty breathing. Ripping the sleeve of her garment off, he pushed it hard against the wound, then set both her hands against it.

"Hold here," he demanded. "I'm going to pick you up and run. Try not to faint."

"Sure," she gasped. She whimpered as he lifted her into his arms but didn't let go of the rag.

"You're a strong human," he told her, setting off at the fastest run he could without jostling her too badly. "You will survive this."

As he ran, he saw Rasts flooding the streets around the port. The port employees scrambled for weapons to hold off the Gorlags, but this time it might not be enough.

Hesarium could hear the ship's engines starting up and only one door was still open. He barreled up the short ramp and flew through the door. He heard shouting and many people asking him questions. The ship shuddered around them, lifting off far faster than normal. He heard something bang against the ship, and then the silence of rapid ascent into space.

All of that registered in the back of his head as he focused on Rain. "She's hurt," he told the gathered humans, his mournful rumble filling the hallway. "Help her."

Then Auntie was there, giving orders and demanding things from the ship's crew. In short order, Rain was lying in a bed and the ship's medic was caring for her. There was little he could do for Rain with the ship's limited capabilities.

"If she survives the trip to the Hub, they'll be able to fix her up there," the medic explained.

"She'll survive," Hesarium said, declaring his determination to the universe. "I won't let her join the Ancestors. Not yet."

CHAPTER 17

Rain

"Can you open your mouth for me?" Hesarium asked.

Of course I can open my mouth, Rain thought, then realized she hadn't said that out loud. She tried again. *Of course…* no, that wasn't out loud either. Then she realized her eyes were closed. It took effort, but she managed to get them open only to be faced with lights so bright, pain shot through her head. Moaning, she shut them tight.

What was going on? Why did she hurt so much and couldn't seem to control anything?

"Oh, my sweet human, I'm sorry. I didn't think you'd try to open your eyes," he said with a surprised rattle. "Let me dim the lights."

She felt the bed under her move and the warmth that was pressed to her side disappeared. A sudden feeling of cold made her shiver.

"What are you doing?" a strange voice asked.

"Rain wishes to open her eyes, but the lights are hurting her," Hesarium answered the voice, taking his place at her side again.

"I've told you she shouldn't be awake," the voice said, agitated.

"No, you said she might wake," Hesarium argued. Even though his voice was impatient, he purred for her. His hand wrapped around hers, warm and solid.

"W-w-w-w," Rain tried to talk, then started coughing. Agony ripped through her chest with every cough.

"I told you to inform me if she attempted to wake," the voice was nearly shouting now, which was probably the only reason she could hear him over her coughing. "She can't be conscious during this stage of the healing process. Are you trying to cause her permanent diminished lung capacity?"

Healing? Had she been sick? Was that why her chest hurt so badly that she could barely breathe? Panic made pulling air into her lungs even more difficult. Hes's big hand held on to hers as he purred, but that didn't help her calm down. If only she could open her eyes or say a few words. This feeling of helplessness was foreign and terrifying.

"Then give her something," Hes growled. "She's not breathing right. Fix it!"

"I am," the voice snapped as she felt a slight pressure on the side of her neck. Then all the pain disappeared.

The sensation of floating made her want to giggle, but her body was still coughing. She heard the voice arguing with Hesarium as she floated into blessed unconsciousness.

Rain

"And then he got me new shoes and says I should runs fast. So I runs all the way ups the stairs. All the stairs! They didn't come off!" Royal's cheerful voice urged Rain into wakefulness.

"You climbed up all those stairs? That's amazing," Auntie exclaimed. "Then what did you do?"

"I rans all the way down them all too," Royal explained. Rain could hear little feet tapping and pictured Royal demonstrating his running.

The thought of running brought up images of Hes running while holding Cherish and Royal under his arms. Memories of being attacked flashed through her head in a jumble of sounds, actions, and feelings.

She sucked a deep breath in, and her eyes popped open. The dimly lit room around her wasn't entirely in focus, but she could make out two distinct and familiar shapes.

"Royal? Auntie?" Her voice was weak and hoarse, but she was able to get the words out.

"Rain!" Royal squealed. He flung himself at her, clambering onto the bed she was on and throwing his arms around her. Or at least he *tried* to throw his arms around her. Hesarium appeared and plucked him up mid-motion.

"No, little Royal," he admonished the child gently. "Remember what the med tech said; we must be careful when touching her. She's fragile."

"I'm fine," Rain said, although she couldn't be sure of that. Her body felt oddly detached. She could move her limbs, but they still felt like someone else was moving them. Nothing hurt though, and that was the important part.

"Are you sure you're fine?" Royal asked.

"Absolutely," she assured him and held out her arms. "And I need a Royal hug really bad."

Hesarium set Royal on the bed but kept his big hands around the boy's waist. "Gently hug Rain around the neck. Don't touch her chest."

"I knows," Royal answered and wrapped his thin arms around her neck and gave a little squeeze. "I missed you. And I miss my bed and our food. But this place is neat, and I'm okay with not going home if you're here too."

Rain did her best to hug Royal back, but her arms lacked strength, and halfway through the hug, they started to shake, and she had to drop them back down to her sides.

"I love you, Royal," Rain whispered as Hesarium lifted the little boy away. She remembered now that their domiciles were gone. She remembered her and Hes piloting the crawlers to the edge of the port. Then something happened when they were trying to join everyone else.

Hesarium must have gotten her on the cargo ship after she fell.

No, she hadn't fallen. She'd been hit by something.

"Time for the evening meal," Auntie announced, stepping up to take Royal from Hesarium. She used that moment to lean over and give Rain a quick kiss on the forehead. "It's good to have you back. You scared us there for a minute."

"I want to stay and eats my meal with Rain," Royal argued, wiggling in Auntie's hold.

"No sweetie, she and Hes need to talk," Auntie told him. "And we need to tell everyone else that she's awake. We'll bring her something back from the galley after our meal."

"Yeah! Green cake! She needs to eat green cake. Green cake, green cake," Royal chanted as they left the room.

Rain's sight was improving by the second, and she could make out more details. The room was full of equipment she'd never seen before, and the bed she occupied was configured to keep someone sitting up even while asleep. Although she'd never been in a medical suite before, this must be what they looked like.

"Did one of the firestarters hit me in the chest?" she asked.

Hes pulled up a stool and sat down next to her bed. Reaching out, he took one of her hands in both of his and purred. "A piece of shrapnel hit you. It penetrated your chest and lung. It took a full day for us to travel here and gain access to a med tech. The delay caused you more damage. The med techs running this place weren't sure you were going to survive when we first arrived."

Rain blinked, trying to comprehend everything he was saying. "Where are we?"

"Dolant Trading Hub," he answered. "Or as everyone seems to refer to it, the Hub. This room is part of the Dolant Collective Medical Suites. All the humans are staying in the long-term-temporary housing on the east side of the Hub."

As he talked, he brought her hand to his face and rubbed his scent gland into her palm. The smell of sugar cookies hit her nose, making her feel a little more grounded.

"How long have we been here?" she asked, amazed she didn't remember any of the trip from Omanal to the Hub or her time here.

"Twenty-three rotations," Hes answered.

"Twenty-three rotations," Rain repeated. "You mean days, right? I've been unconscious for twenty-three days?"

"Yes," Hes answered simply. Rain waited for anxiety to hit her, but there was nothing. Whatever drugs they had pumped into her were muting her emotions. That was probably for the best. Hes waited silently for her to react.

"But I'm healed now? Is there anything missing? You know, inside of me?" she asked. "Like a lung?"

"Your lungs are there and healing well," Hes assured her. "You'll have to be careful for the next twenty rotations or so, but the med techs are confident you'll feel as you did before. There's no long term damage."

Rain smiled at Hes. "Then I guess we're all doing better than expected. Did the pod harvest sell?"

"The pods were sold at market value," Hes said. "You'd be proud of Auntie and Iris. They bargained very diligently with the wholesaler. I believe they received the best price available."

"I'm not surprised," Rain said, relieved to find out that at least they had that money to survive on. "Any word on what happened after we left Omanal?"

"The Gorlags weren't able to take the port," Hes said. "And there's been a fallout among the leaders of the gang. Now they're busy fighting each other while the surviving farmers leave the planet."

"And no one else on Omanal had you to defend them so they probably lost a lot more lives," Rain said, a strange kind of relief filling her. "I know I should feel worse for the people we lost, but all I can feel is relief that I didn't lose any of my family."

"I'm sure they would understand if the situation was reversed," Hes murmured. "And I know their souls have found a place among your ancestors. Even now, they're probably happy that the survivors have successfully escaped Omanal and have a promising future to look forward to."

"What promising future?" she demanded, suddenly feeling daunted and overwhelmed. The drugs must be wearing off because stark reality was hitting her in the face.

When Grandma Katherine first came to Omanal and started farming, she'd been able to bring a lot of equipment with her and plenty of supplies to tide the humans over until they were able to produce for themselves. No matter what deal Auntie and Iris got for the last seedpod harvest, there was no way it was as much as their grandparents had when they first left Earth. That meant they'd be starting over with a lot less resources.

There was no Earth to go back to; they had to find a new place. "We're going to end up as contract laborers," Rain moaned. "Trapped in jobs that will eventually kill us."

"No," Hes protested. "You won't."

"How can you say that?" she demanded.

Hes's purring was interrupted for a moment by a rumble that sounded like a bunch of people snapping their fingers. "I didn't think I should speak to you about it so soon after waking, but Auntie told me repeatedly I would need to because you would worry."

"Speak to me about what?" Rain asked.

"Your new home," Hes said, speaking slowly as if choosing his words carefully.

"Is this about going to Talarian?" she guessed. Grudging relief lessened some of her anxiety. "I guess we don't have much of a choice."

Hes dropped his gaze to where his hands held hers. He was purring again, but for some reason, she almost got the impression the rumble was self-soothing. What was her Talin worried about?

"Confess," she teased. "What deep, dark secret are you hiding? Do Talin's eat their dead like the Mokang? Do they have really complicated marriages like the Marshet? The first one won't bother me, but don't expect me to join in. For the second one, you'll have to draw us family maps so we don't accidently insult someone with the wrong title."

She thought he might sound one of the marbles-clinking-in-a-bag rumbles that signaled laughter or amusement, but even his purr went silent. This couldn't be good.

"Hes?"

"I know I shouldn't make you promise anything before I explain, but could you promise to contemplate what I say before reacting?"

Rain brought her free hand up to rub her forehead. This was giving her a headache, or at least making the one she already had worse. She couldn't tell, nothing felt right.

"I'll think before I act," she promised, dropping her hand back down to her lap. "But I get to ask questions or say something if I'm upset."

"That's fair," Hes acknowledged. Rain had gotten so used to hearing Hes at least purr that his utter silence was disarming. "I haven't lied to you. I spoke the truth when I told you that humans aren't expected to work. In fact, they're encouraged to spend their time playing. Humans are so welcome that our sovereign has built an entire area on their royal property for human use. Right now there are only about eighty humans on Talarian, including the recent babies who've been born. Most Talins hope to grow that number into the many thousands. There are even laws set up for the protection of the humans among us."

All of Rain's suspicions spiked. "That sounds too good to be true. No place welcomes humans as anything but cheap labor that's easy to exploit. What aren't you telling me?" Hes refused to meet her eyes, causing dread to build. "Hes, talk to me."

"All the humans who come to Talarian are cared for as if they were one of us, except you aren't," Hes said, then stopped.

Rain waited, but he didn't continue. "We're different species, of course we're not going to be treated exactly the same."

"It's more than being different species. You are considered pets among us." Hes looked up as he spoke those words, his eyes focusing on her face, waiting for her reaction.

She couldn't have heard him correctly. The word had to be a translation glitch. "Did you say pet? For me that word translates to an animal someone might keep in a cage. A creature that's sentient but not sapient."

"The word pet is correct. The Talin government has labeled humans as a low-intelligence species," Hes explained, his voice quiet and toneless. "Humans are considered to be at the less intelligent end of sapient species."

It took Rain a minute to process his words. She should probably feel outrage, or at least some form of betrayal. The truth was, between fatigue and the headache, Rain couldn't muster up much more than curiosity. It wasn't as if they were on Talarian right now. At the moment they weren't in danger of being enslaved.

"I thought you said Talins didn't have slaves," she pointed out, letting her head fall back into the soft pillows behind her.

"We don't," Hes insisted. "Humans aren't slaves, they're pets. We don't expect anything from you except for you to be happy and let us share in your joy."

That sounded so nice, but at the same time it was completely unrealistic. "No one houses, feeds, and cares for another sentient species simply because they like how we laugh."

Hes started purring. "It's more than your laugh. You give affection to each other without reserve. You have no problems hugging, cuddling, and touching. You fall in love with each other and us. All of those things are foreign to Talins."

"You guys don't hug each other?" There were so many more questions she could've asked, but that was the one that made it out of her mouth.

"No," he answered simply.

Her headache suddenly got worse, forcing her to close her eyes. "I'll ask more questions later," she promised, her body relaxing into the pillows.

"Are you in pain?" Hes asked. She could tell that he'd leaned in close—the smell of sugar cookies filled her nose.

"Yeah, my head."

She could sense Hes standing up and turning slightly, but he didn't let go of her hand. "Med tech," he called out. "We are in need of your assistance."

Only seconds later, someone else came in the room, asked a few questions, then pressed something to her neck. The pain disappeared and she fell asleep to the sound of Hes's purring.

"I won't leave," he promised. "No matter what you decide, I won't leave you."

CHAPTER 18

Hesarium

"The Hub's trading director wants to talk to you," Auntie said as she made herself comfortable in a chair on the other side of Rain. "I told him you'd meet him at his office at thrice bell. I think that's in about half an hour. The time keeping around here is one of the most complex I've ever experienced."

The moment Auntie was finished settling into her seat, Royal climbed onto her lap. Then he looked at Hes with an eager smile. "The trading director cames to our room and brought some fruits with him. It mades my lips green! I wanted to rub it on my skin so I could be green all overs, but Auntie said no."

Hesarium sounded a rumble of amusement. "You probably shouldn't turn green. You might confuse Rain when she sees you."

"Maybe," Royal allowed, moving his gaze to Rain. "Why isn't Rain awake? Auntie said she was awakes before."

Hesarium followed the child's gaze. Rain looked better now that she was relaxed in sleep. Hesarium regretted speaking to her about the future so soon after she woke up. In this one instance, he shouldn't have listened to Auntie.

"She'll wake up again soon," Auntie promised Royal. "It's going to be a little while before she will be able to get up though."

"I wants her to plays with me!" Royal wailed.

Cherish ducked her head into the room. "Wind, Sunny, and I are going over to Dock Eleven. Do you want to come with us Royal?"

"Yes!" Royal nearly vibrated out of Auntie's lap in his eagerness to go with Cherish. Dock Eleven was the busiest part of the Hub, with a constant flow of ships and species coming and going. The siblings would spend many marks observing from one of the high walkways then return, full of stories about what they'd seen. To a group of humans who'd never been off planet before, Dock Eleven was a constant source of wonder.

"Thanks, Cherish," Auntie said as she helped Royal slide off her lap.

"We'll swing back by here later," Cherish said as she took Royal by the hand. She flashed Hesarium a big smile before letting Royal drag her away, chattering excitedly about the things he hoped to see.

"I can't get over the change in that girl," Auntie murmured. "You'd think she'd be even more angry and sullen after everything that happened on Omanal, but no. She's the happiest I've ever seen her."

"Perhaps she's pretending," Hesarium offered. "Within Talin politics, it's common to express opinions and ideas that you don't believe to better ingratiate yourself with others or prevent tension."

Auntie snorted out a laugh. "Humans do that too. I don't think she's pretending. I think it has to do with feeling secure. Our life on Omanal was nothing but stress for years. Now that stress is gone and she's allowing herself to be happy for once."

"Do you truly believe she feels no stress with the decisions all of you made?" he questioned.

"None at all," Auntie assured him.

"I wish you'd let me be there while all of you discussed my proposal," Hesarium said. "I would've liked to know who honestly wanted to start a new life on Talarian and who felt they had no choice."

Auntie stared at him for a moment, but Hesarium couldn't tell what she was thinking. Finally, Auntie shook her head. "I know you felt left out, but it had to be that way. As I've told you before, we all agreed. No one has any hidden resentment. We all discussed every option, but the choice was obvious."

Hesarium finally voiced his true objection. "You made the decision without Rain."

"We had to," Auntie responded with a soft, sad sigh. "We were going to miss that window for you to use the comms array to send out a message to Talarian."

"I told all of you we could've stayed there for another forty days before my funds ran out," Hesarium argued.

"We couldn't risk it," Auntie reminded him. "You told us yourself that if we waited and there were any delays, we could end up in financial trouble. The Hub isn't kind to those who can't pay."

"I still believe all of you should've waited for Rain. I could've figured out a way to pay for our extended time here even if we ran past the forty days," Hesarium said, although in truth, he had no idea how he would've gotten funds fast enough to cover them. The Hub wasn't the most expensive place he'd ever been, but it was close, especially having to provide for twenty-seven individuals including one in need of intense medical care.

"We didn't need to wait for Rain," Auntie responded. "Seeing people you know and love die has a strong effect. No one misses David, but we lost wonderful people. We would've lost Rain too if you hadn't had the wealth to pay for her care while we got the seedpods sold. In the end, no one could stomach the thought of losing anyone else. Taking on the title of pet seems like a small sacrifice to be safe and secure for the rest of our lives."

"And all your descendants," Hesarium reminded her. "Your protection is built into our laws now. The humans living on—"

Auntie held up her hand to silence him. "Don't promise things like that," she admonished him. "You can't know what the next generation will do, or the one after that."

"I might not if I was human, but we Talins are different," he argued. "Once we've pledged ourselves to a course of action, there's little that will deter us."

"Which is the whole reason you need us," Auntie declared. "You've lost the loving part of yourself in pursuit of control and power."

Hesarium wished he hadn't told her all about his emotionless upbringing and longing for affection. It had been in the early days on the Hub when Rain looked on the verge of death, despite the med tech's assurances that she was unlikely to die.

Hesarium found himself unable to stop talking and had filled the small medical room with stories about his childhood, family, and days in the military. The only time Auntie spoke was to ask questions. It was only much later that he realized he'd revealed things about himself and Talin culture most Talins never spoke of, even to each other.

His uninhibited words had given Auntie an uncomfortably accurate understanding of Talin culture, politics, and laws. It had led to one of the most awkward conversations Hesarium had ever experienced, which only ended when he refused to answer any more of her questions until he'd spoken to Rain about their relationship.

"Believe what you wish, but we're a mighty empire," Hesarium responded, feeling pushed by Auntie's words. "Humans don't even have a homeworld of their own. The Talin Empire has colonized hundreds of planets. Hundreds! We have a government that's been stable for thousands of years. Show me even five other species that can boast so much."

Auntie held up both her hands palm out and made a soothing sound. "Every species has good and bad traits. I was only pointing out that while you were growing into a big and strong empire, you forgot how to be affectionate. We never left that behind, no matter how many generations ago we left Earth. We have complementary needs and skills."

Feeling mildly ashamed for his harsh reaction, he started up a loud, comforting rumble. "I'm sorry for my unkind words; they were uncalled for."

"You're forgiven," she said easily. "I know you're scared."

He didn't demand she elaborate on what he was afraid of—they both knew perfectly well. He wouldn't survive if Rain decided she didn't want to be with him.

A chime sounded from the bell emblem on the wall, noting the change in time. If he didn't hurry, he'd be late meeting the trading director. "I should leave."

"I'll stay here until you get back," Auntie promised, pulling out the brand new information square he'd bought her. He'd purchased one for each human, and they'd quickly adapted to having the new tech at their disposal.

"I'll be quick," he promised and hurried away. He hoped to get back before Rain woke up. As eager as he felt to speak to her again, he also feared he'd hear words of rejection. How did one face the potentially best or worst moment of their life?

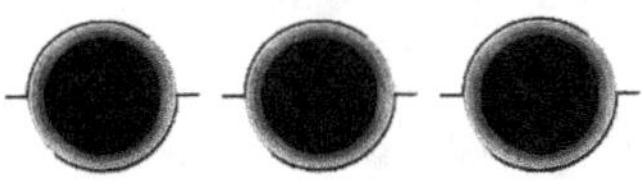

Rain

Rain was relieved to wake up pain free and clear headed. Sitting up, she found the room empty except for Auntie. She was watching something on an information square and only looked up when Rain started talking.

"Can I have some water?"

Auntie jumped a little and almost dropped the information square. "Oh my heart, you damn near scared me to death!"

Rain grinned at her theatrics. "That's what you get for ignoring your patient."

Auntie tried to hide a grin. Setting down the expensive tech, she picked up a sealed canister and handed it to Rain.

"Drink up," she instructed. "The med techs want you to start consuming a couple of these a day."

Rain popped the top off and took a long swallow. She expected it to taste medicinal but there was a pleasant hint of sweetness. She drank the entire bottle greedily.

She felt slightly shaky when she handed the empty container to Auntie and wiped her lips with the back of her other hand. "That wasn't bad at all. I don't think I'm going to have any problems doing what the med techs want."

"How're you feeling?" Auntie asked.

"Good, I think," Rain answered cautiously. "My brain doesn't feel as mushy as before. I want to get out of bed."

Auntie shook her head. "You're not supposed to stand up yet. They said the most you could do was sit up and swing your legs over the side of the bed."

"Fine, let's do that then," Rain agreed, tugging back the thin sheets. She was wearing a soft wrap dress that was gathered around her thighs. It looked unisex, with long sleeves and ties at each hip that held the outfit closed.

Looking up, she noticed Auntie was wearing the same thing but hers was in a deep, burnt orange while Rain's was lavender.

"Did the Hub provide the clothes?" she asked, sitting all the way up with a grunt. "Like a refugee outfit or something?"

"The Hub doesn't take in refugees. If you can't pay, they ship you off to a slave market to recoup any loss," Auntie said, making Rain wince.

"I forgot about that," Rain admitted. It'd been mentioned in the past when they'd talked about leaving—if they fled to the Hub, they'd need to be very careful or end up as debt slaves.

"Hesarium had a bunch of stuff made and delivered to us," Auntie explained. She gripped Rain's forearm and helped her swing around. Rain ended up having to hold tight to Auntie as the room spun around her.

"That was sweet of him," Rain got out after everything settled down. She felt slightly nauseated, but nothing so bad that she was going to vomit. "But I guess that's what good owners do for their pets." She didn't mean for that to sound so bitter, and she was glad Hes wasn't in the room to hear it.

"He doesn't own us yet," Auntie said. "Until we travel into Talin-controlled space, we are still independent entities. He made that very clear to us when he was answering our questions."

"And you told him to fuck off, right?" Rain asked, feeling a strange twisting in her gut at the thought of never seeing Hesarium again.

"We accepted his offer, sweetie. I thought he told you that," Auntie answered. "The only one who hasn't answered yet is you."

Rain jerked at the news. "Are you kidding me? You're all willing to be owned? Just like that?"

Auntie scowled at her and stepped back. Crossing her arms over her ample chest, she looked down at Rain with disapproval. "There was no *just like that* going on. We spent a lot of time talking to Hesarium about the Talin Empire, Talin law, and what our lives would be like. He gave us honest answers, good and bad. We spent days asking him questions, talking with each other, then going back and asking him more questions."

Rain matched Auntie's scowl. "And you guys all just decided without me?"

Auntie gave Rain a disappointed look. "Did I miss the law that says we can't make decisions without consulting you?"

"You can't when it involves me too," Rain shot back. "How can we trust that he's being honest?" she challenged.

"Rain, where else do you think we could go?" Auntie chided gently, her stance softening. "We don't have a future outside of Talarian. It's harsh, but it's the truth."

"We have the money from the pod sale," Rain argued.

Auntie shook her head. "Which isn't nearly enough to establish ourselves anywhere. And you know that. Our choices are to be realistic and survive or idealistic and probably end up in servitude or debt slavery. Rain, the only reason any of us are alive right now is because of Hes. He risked his life during the attack. He paid for our rooms and everything here at the Hub. He got you the best treatment available. And do you know what he kept saying the entire time?"

It was only reluctantly that Rain gave into Auntie's prompt. "What?"

"Everything would be better if we were on Talarian. He feels guilty because he considers everything at the Hub substandard and unsuitable for us," Auntie said, a smile pulling at the corners of her mouth. "We're having the time of our lives, and he's apologizing!"

Rain's shoulders slumped as she realized there was no denying the truth. Hes and the Talins could give them the kind of life they'd never achieve on their own.

"I guess you better tell me everything," she murmured. "I think I'm ready to hear it."

"Let's get you lying down first," Auntie ordered. She guided Rain back down and helped her swing her legs up onto the bed. After the sheet was pulled up, Auntie took a seat and started talking.

An hour later, Auntie finished, and Rain knew what answer she'd give Hesarium, but first she had some very specific questions for him.

CHAPTER 19

Hesarium

It took far too long to get away from the trading director. They'd hoped to get a feel for Talin interest in becoming part of the Hub's permanent trade network. Hesarium explained to them repeatedly that he had no ties to that part of the Talin government and that they needed to go through the proper channels. Still, the trading director wouldn't let him go until they'd shared a meal.

Unwilling to make an enemy, Hesarium was forced to nibble on various colorful foods until enough time had passed that he could make his escape without being rude. The trading director must have thought it was a successful meeting because they sent Hesarium away with several boxes of goods only available at the Hub, a rare feat among trading hubs.

When he got back to the medical room, he didn't go right in. Fear made him hesitate. He hadn't been this scared since his first time in battle. No, that wasn't accurate. During his first taste of war he hadn't been overly concerned. In battle, he only risked a quick, painless death. Here, he risked losing Rain and all the agony that would cause.

Bracing himself, he signaled the door to slide open. Auntie was sitting, reading aloud from her information square. She stopped and looked up at him. "What did you buy?"

"Nothing," he answered, holding out the boxes to her. "The trading director gave all this to me."

"Were they trying to seduce you?" Auntie asked with a laugh as she took the boxes.

"No, our two species aren't sexually compatible," Hesarium explained, confused by Auntie's question. "They were interested in an exclusive trade agreement, but they wouldn't believe me when I said I had no influence within the trade commissions or among the professional traders. I don't know what's in the boxes, but they're probably items the Hub has in abundance this solar."

The entire time he spoke he kept his eyes on Auntie, afraid to look over at Rain.

"The kids will have fun opening them, whatever they are. I'll take them back to our rooms," Auntie said as she stood, and then she turned to Rain. "I know you want to see everyone, but I'm going to hold them off until tomorrow. You and Hes need some time together."

With that, she left the room, the door closing with a soft hiss behind her. Hesarium couldn't hold off looking at Rain any longer. He expected to see anger or outrage in her expression but instead she looked strangely expressionless. He couldn't tell if that was bad or good.

"You're looking well," he murmured, stepping up closer to the bed. He noticed one of the canisters was missing. "And you're drinking. That's good."

"I'm on the mend," she agreed. "One of the med techs came in earlier and said I should be able to leave here in a few days. I'm even allowed to get up and walk tomorrow."

"That's excellent news." He started up a soothing rumble, as much for himself as her. "There's a fascinating Garformin fungus display only a little way from here. You might enjoy viewing it."

"Sounds like fun," Rain responded, but her tone wasn't neutral. He could hear the distinct sound of humor in her voice. "Hes, talk to me."

"What would you wish to speak of?" he asked. He could hear the stiffness in his voice; he sounded like he was attending some formal meeting, not speaking to the female he adored.

Rain sighed a little. "Could you come a little closer please?"

He leaned over, putting his face closer to hers. "Here?"

She rose up to give him a quick lip press. "Yup, right there."

Relief washed through him at her affection. "May I hold you? I've been unable to do so since you've been in this place. I miss your touch more than I miss food."

"I'm not sure if this thing is big enough for cuddling," she said looking up and down the length of her bed.

"Allow me." Working his hands under her, he lifted her off the bed, pivoted so he could lay in her spot, then stretched her out on top of him. The relief at holding Rain was immense, and the tension he'd been holding in his neck plates started to ease.

Rain wiggled around a little until she was comfortable, then sounded a content sigh. "This is nice."

"Almost perfect," he agreed, then gave into temptation and started rubbing his aching scent glands into her hair. Auntie and Sunny had taken great pains to care for Rain's mane, so it was a soft, fluffy mass around her head. The bonnet she'd been wearing was resting on the table next to the bed, along with several full canisters.

Taking his time, he emptied both his scent glands into her mane. He wasn't satisfied until bonding oil was all over it. When he was finally satisfied, he relaxed into the bed, resting his head against one of the pillows behind him.

"You smell so good," she murmured, reaching up to run her fingers through her hair and better distribute his bonding oil. The oil spread and soaked in, making the curls more defined. As the scent of his bonding oil came in contact with Rain's scalp, the scent changed. He pulled in a deep lungful of this slightly different smell, and the rest of the tensions he'd been caring around with him eased.

"Auntie told me about life on Talarian as a pet," she began. "If everything she says is true, it sounds like a kind of paradise. I'm half expecting you to turn red, grow horns, and make us sign a contract in blood."

A rumble of confusion interrupted his comforting rumble. "My species doesn't do any of that. Did someone tell you we did? And why would anyone sign a contract in blood? Are you talking about a biosignature? That's done with simple skin cells, not blood."

His confusion made Rain chuckle. "Ignore what I said. It's an Earth thing."

"I can confirm that Talins won't change in appearance, not to the extent you suggested, and the information Auntie relayed is accurate. Do you have any questions she couldn't answer?"

"There's one thing I didn't ask her about," Rain admitted.

"Present your question to me," Hesarium urged, equally interested in answering her inquiries and fearful it would be a response she wouldn't like.

"Do we have to break up?" The question was asked softly, as if she was afraid to voice it. "I mean, it has to be illegal to be intimate with a human pet, right?"

The thought of never touching Rain again made a shot of pure terror go through Hesarium. He'd never felt this vulnerable in his entire adult life.

Rain moved a little on top of him. "Hes, you okay? You've gone really stiff and you're not purring anymore."

He had to force air into his lungs before he was able to speak. "Ending our relationship would be my death."

Those words made Rain jerk violently. "You'd kill yourself if we had to break up?"

"I might," he admitted. "I've heard that dying from Ending is extremely painful. It'd be less painful to do the deed myself."

"Ending?" Rain questioned.

"The clinical name is Scent Collapse Disease, but everyone refers to it as Ending. It's what happens when we're separated from a scent-bonded partner for too long."

Rain was silent for a moment before asking her next question. "That means you've scent-bonded to me?"

"I have," he agreed and waited for anger or outrage. Among Talins it would be impossible for one partner to scent-bond another without their knowledge and consent. He'd used her lack of knowledge against her and never gave Rain a choice.

"Is that why you're always rubbing your scent glands on me?" she asked, rubbing her fingers through her hair. "Because you bonded with me?"

"Yes."

She twisted around until she was lying on her stomach looking up at him. To his surprise, she was smiling. "So you love me?"

"Love is a human emotion," he answered. "I'm scent-bonded to you."

"I think it might be the same thing," she countered. He was going to argue that scent-bonding was a biological function and love was one of emotions when tears shone in her eyes. "I love you too."

Although he wasn't convinced scent-bonding and human love were equivalent, he was ecstatic to know Rain attached such a significant emotion to their partnership.

"Does that mean you'll go with everyone else to Talarian?" he asked, trying hard to keep his voice from getting too loud with excitement. It was good he was laying on his back plates, or he might have tried to rattle.

"I was planning on going before we started talking," Rain told him. "But I was concerned you were going to break up with me."

"Never!" he assured her.

"Yeah, you're kind of stuck with me," she declared, humor in her tone. "There's that whole 'dying a horrible death' if we part ways."

Going against everything he'd ever been taught, he showed her his weaknesses. "If you weren't in my life, I'd want to die anyway. You give my life meaning, Rain. I never thought to have the kind of contentment and happiness Bazium has with his human, Ari. Then I met you and realized it might be possible. Even before I scent-bonded, I knew you were special. You're the most wonderful human and the entire universe is better for having you in it."

"That's the most beautiful thing anyone's ever said to me," Rain whispered as a lone tear fell from her right eye. She moved up his body until her face was over his and pressed her lips to his.

He opened his mouth, inviting her to deepen the lip press, thrilled to have her initiate this touch. His mating shaft was getting thicker, but he ignored that. Even if Rain wanted intercourse, he would refuse. She needed to heal more before he stressed her body, even if the stress came in the form of pleasure.

They continued the intimate lip presses for a few submarks, then her body started shaking from the effort of holding her face to his. He gently eased her back into lying on him, now on her side. She was quick to snuggle on top of him with a few murmured sounds of contentment.

"Auntie said we're going to have to wear collars," Rain murmured against his chest.

"Yes," he confirmed. "But they'll all be keyed to both me and each person wearing them. You'll have the ability to take them off at any time."

"So they're going to be more like jewelry than restraints," Rain said. "It's going to be hard to keep myself from touching you when we're in public."

In this he could give her assurances. "As long as we don't lip press, no one will care. They believe humans are extremely emotional and needy. Everyone will assume you're easily scared, and that's why you cling to me."

"No more kissing," she said with a soft chuckle. "But hugs are okay? I guess it won't be so bad then. Will we be able to share a bed?"

"Most nights," he confirmed. "Sometimes you might have to sleep in an enclosure if we have an inspection or guest visiting, but otherwise, you'll live with me."

"Enclosure?" she questioned.

He described the place they'd built into a human sanctuary, including the human housing, gardens, and access to the royal residence. He told her all about the humans already there, going into great detail about how they were flourishing. While in the middle of describing the special treatment some of the humans were getting from the monarch, he realized Rain wasn't awake any longer.

"Sleep, my beautiful human," he whispered to her while rumbling out a soothing purr. "We only have a few obstacles left to cross before all our worries are over."

CHAPTER 20

Rain

Although Rain never traveled before the Day of Fire—the name everyone gave the last day on Omanal—even she could tell the Talin space station, Falsof, was an exceptional place. The station wasn't as large as the Hub, but it was still sizable. Unlike the Hub where things were worn and in constant need of repair, this place was nothing but shiny, well-ordered machines and communal spaces.

"Is this place new?" she asked, marveling at the number of bots running around the arrival area. They were shuttling boxes and bags with startling efficiency and never once got in the way of foot traffic.

Hes made a negative rattling sound. "It's a little older than the Hub. I expect they'll replace it soon. It's near our legal limit for a continued-use station."

It was Cherish who spoke up while Rain gaped at him. "This place is considered old?"

Two Talins stepped in front of their group. They were similar in height, but one had a light orange coloring while the other's keratin plating was a dark sand.

"Of course it's old. Look at the shape of the support pads," the dark-sand-colored Talin answered, looking at Cherish and purring. "That style hasn't been used in decades. It's inefficient and the Structures Subcommittee on the Apogee Assembly ruled on it rotations ago."

"Toreum! Varlum!" Hes exclaimed with an excited rattle. All three Talins struck their chests with their fists hard enough to make a loud sound, causing Rain to wince. "What are you two doing here?"

"Traveling through," the light-orange-colored one said. "I don't need to ask what you're doing here. It appears we have the good fortune of meeting on the way back from collecting humans."

Both Talins stepped a little closer, towering over Rain and Cherish. Everyone behind them took small steps back, alarmed by the Talins' sudden interest. Hes had warned them that they might get attention from inquisitive Talins but having these two stare at them with such intensity was intimidating.

"You're very nice-looking humans," the dark-sand-colored one said, leaning over a little. "I'm Toreum of the family Orif within the Delk Clan."

The light-orange one moved in closer. "I'm Varlum of the family Salmik within Delk Clan also. Our clan is famous for producing engineers and builders."

"That's nice," Rain said. "I'm Rain of the family Taylor within, um," she looked back at Cherish for help.

Cherish gave the Talins a closed mouth grin. "We're within Seedpod-Head Clan."

Both Talins sounded rumbles of amusement and turned their attention to Cherish.

"Very clever, little human," Toreum said. "What is your name?"

"I'm Cherish," the teenager said without fear, then she started pointing at everyone with them and naming each one. As she said their names, each person gave a little wave. By the time she was done, a large crowd had gathered around them. The moment she was finished, questions started pouring in from the Talins surrounding them.

"How old are you, Cherish?"

"Are you a female or male, Royal?"

"Do you have a mate, Auntie?"

"Is this your mate and children, Devon?"

"Can you read, Rain?"

"I heard humans need many marks of sleep every rotation, is it like entering a coma each time or can you be awakened before you've finished resting?"

While the questions were coming at them from all directions, they were also being pressed together in a tighter and tighter group. Auntie picked up Royal and Iris grabbed Mia to keep them from getting squished.

"You guys need to back up," Rain called out, but her voice was drowned out by the many Talins purring and rattling in excitement as they talked. Every moment that passed, more and more Talins joined the growing group. It was all happening so quickly, Rain was scared they'd all get crushed under Talin curiosity before anyone could be the voice of sanity.

Then Hes let loose with a war rattle, making it sound like hundreds of feet were pounding the ground around them.

"Everyone back away!" he yelled. "These humans are fragile and new to captivity. All of you are scaring them. I haven't even gotten them to the healers to be assessed."

The change was startling. Every single Talin, except for Toreum and Varlum, moved back as one and went silent.

"You must take them to the healers directly," one Talin whispered loudly. This one had to be a female because she didn't have full quills, only rounded nubs decorated with gold tips. "My cousin works there; I'll rush over and help organize for their arrival." Then she was gone.

"I only see little bag's being clutched in their paws," another Talin said in a hushed voice. "Do they have no other clothes or goods? Poor things. I'll see if there's anything here that can be modified."

In singles, pairs, and groups, Talins rushed off in various directions with one communal goal in mind: to do something for the new humans.

"What just happened?" Auntie asked, clutching a wide-eyed Royal.

"We are going to assure your health and wellbeing," Toreum explained. "There are so few of your kind left in the universe that we fear losing even one of you. Many Talins hope to add a human or entire family unit to their menageries."

"As do we," Varlum added. "We've wanted a human since the moment we saw the first notice and documentary come out about the humans from the Orlok mine that were brought back."

"The demand is great and the resources scarce, so expect a great deal of attention, especially after you've visited the healers," Toreum warned, then looked at Hes. "Varlum and I might not be the highly trained and elite soldiers you are, but we know something about fighting. It would be our honor to help you escort this group to the healers."

"I know of your work building stations in the more dangerous areas of the empire," Hes acknowledged with an agreeing rattle. "If each of you could take either side of our group, that would help."

"I can follow," a Talin volunteered as she walked up.

"Woah," Rain breathed as she took in the latest arrival. She was as big as Hes and wearing full battle armor with weapons strapped all over her body. Only her forearms, hands, and head were uncovered.

"Danisal," Hesarium exclaimed and pounded his chest hard in greeting. "It is good to see you. Have you been assigned to this station?"

"Only for another forty rotations, and then my time in the military is finished," Danisal answered, smacking her chest as well. The sound of her fist striking her chest plate made Rain flinch. Did that hurt?

The warrior turned away from Hes and swept her gaze over Rain and her group. "Don't be frightened. My weapons and skills will be used to protect you, not harm. I will walk behind all of you as added security. If you have any concerns, please voice them to me or Hesarium."

Rain nodded and heard the others murmur words of assent. With that, Danisal sounded a rattle of agreement and strode around them to take her place behind the group. Carter and Nova looked up at her and started to smile, then remembered and quickly covered their mouths.

Danisal sounded a soothing purr. "March on, Hesarium. We must get these humans to the healers."

"I feel like a bunch of entict being herded," Auntie muttered.

"You're not being herded like beasts," Varlum said. He'd moved closer to Auntie without her or Rain noticing. "You're being protected like the precious and rare gems you are. If you're curious, it would be mine and Toreum's pleasure to show you the fascinating parts of this station. It's not very impressive by our standards, but there are a few amenities worth noting."

"You may bring your offspring with you," Toreum added.

Rain watched surprise, pleasure, and embarrassment rapidly flash across Auntie's face.

"I, um, that sounds nice," Auntie answered, stumbling over her words a little. "Royal is my nephew, not my child."

"Does that mean you don't have a mate?" Varlum asked.

Auntie frowned a little. "No, uh, my mate died many years ago."

"If we are able to buy you, we would take good care of you," Toreum offered. "We travel all over, building or retrofitting space stations and hubs. You could come with us and see many interesting things. Varlum and I would be good, attentive masters to a human as gorgeous as yourself."

They were all walking now and Toreum's little speech made Rain stumble. Hes sounded a rumble of worry and snatched her up, holding her against his chest. "Are you feeling unwell?"

"Is the human hurt?" Danisal called out from behind them.

"She's still recovering from a grievous wound she barely survived," Hes explained. Rain wouldn't have told her that, but she had to trust Hes knew what he was doing. "I'm going to carry her the rest of the way."

Danisal echoed Hes's worried rumble. "Do any of the other humans need to be carried?"

"We're fine," Gris called out, trying to hide his grin. "No need to carry anyone else."

"Unless you wish to be carried," Toreum said to Auntie with a purr.

Auntie met his gaze, her expression curious. "There are twenty-eight of us here. You could have your pick. Why are you singling me out?"

Toreum spoke so softly Rain almost didn't hear him. "You are the most beautiful of all the humans. I noticed you right away and hoped to garner your attention."

"Are you sure Varlum agrees?" Auntie shot back. Rain craned her neck so she could see Auntie's face. "He could have a different opinion than you."

"We know each other very well," Toreum answered in a low voice, making Rain think the two Talins might be intimate. "Words don't need to be spoken between us to find an understanding. We are as one in this opinion. Out of all the humans here, you are by far the most beautiful, and your voice is musical."

That's when Auntie giggled, forcing Rain to hide a grin against Hes's neck. "My family calls me Auntie, but I'd rather you called me Georgia. That's my name."

"Auntie isn't your proper name?" Toreum asked.

"It's more of a title," Auntie explained. Then she pronounced it as *aunt* so the Talin's INT could properly translate the word's meaning rather than its sound.

"Ah, I see," Toreum said with a loud purr. "Georgia. A name as lovely as the human who answers to it."

"He's laying it on a little thick, isn't he?" Rain muttered. She wasn't surprised when Hes answered her.

"I've known Varlum and Toreum a long time. They're honorable Talins," he whispered in her ear. "If Auntie wishes to be owned by them, she'll be well taken care of."

"This is weird," Rain murmured, settling down in Hes's arms to watch the station pass by as they walked. "I never thought we'd be interviewing owners."

"Nothing is as straightforward as we'd like to believe," Hes commented. His tone made her remember their conversation about what would happen if they separated. It was only then Rain realized that, in some respects, she owned Hes, not the other way around.

They made rapid progress across the station, aided by Danisal barking at Talins to get out of their way and threatening those that tried to get too close. Soon they were all sitting on beds in a long row, as healers and assistants moved from person to person.

As the human who almost died, Rain got special treatment. Instead of being with everyone else, the healers had Hes carry her to a private room. Rain protested but they wouldn't relent. The best she got was insisting they leave the door open so she could see everyone.

A healer and two assistants were dedicated to her care while the rest of the healers and assistants saw to her friends and family. They asked her lots of questions, scanned every part of her twice, and urged her to drink some nasty vials full of nutrients and medications.

Hes had told her how the humans would be treated, but she hadn't believed him. Now the evidence was irrefutable. The staff even had food delivered from one of the station's eateries. It was bland but filling.

One of the assistants even brought in some colorful swatches of fabric that changed color depending on the temperature. He gave several to each kid and rumbled with amusement when Mia shrieked with joy as her handprint appeared on the fabric.

No other species had ever treated humans so well, even when acknowledging them as intellectual equals. Rain reached up to touch the collar she wore. They'd all put them on the day before getting to the station. At first it felt foreign and heavy. Now, not even a full day later, it was a comforting weight that signified care instead of simple ownership.

Mama, Papa, I think we're safe, she thought and could've sworn she felt a slight rush of love and happiness.

CHAPTER 21

Rain

No one asked Toreum and Varlum to leave, so the two stayed with Auntie, engaging with her constantly. Despite how close together the beds were spaced in the medical suite, the Talins managed to squeeze a stool on either side of Auntie's bed.

The three only stopped talking when one of the healers needed to ask Auntie questions. Rain couldn't hear what they were saying from her room, but Auntie looked like she was having the time of her life.

Rain was relieved to find out the healers discovered only a few problems with everyone besides her. Several people had some lung damage and a few old injuries that had never healed properly. All of it was easy to fix for the highly skilled healers with an abundance of resources. Every Talin taking care of them marveled at their level of health despite having little to no access to medical care over the years.

Danisal took a position outside the doors to keep everyone away. They'd all heard the warrior rattle loudly and use her commanding voice several times. She only let one Talin through because he was suffering from an obvious and severe injury. That poor guy was immediately shuttled into a private room with several healers to attend to him. Other than him, Danisal refused entry to everyone and explained they'd simply have to come back later.

For a while it was quiet, but not any longer.

There must be a lot of Talins out there if the noise was able to get through the well-insulated station walls. Rain worried they were about to get mobbed.

"I'm not interested in wounding," Danisal shouted over the noise. "It's inefficient."

The threat did little to stop the crowd. If anything, they seemed to get louder. Rain was worried a fight might break out when a loud sound issued from the station system. Rain and several others jumped at the sudden noise. There was a beat of silence, and then a voice began talking.

"This is a station-wide announcement from your station director," an official-sounding voice declared. "As many of you know, we have humans on our station. They're all being seen by the healers. To keep from causing them stress, everyone in the halls in that section of the station will disband. I'm in communication with the owner of the humans and will request visitation rights for those interested in meeting and interacting with the humans. That will not happen if the Talins in the halls around the medical suites don't disperse. We must keep in mind, humans are rare and delicate. We can't afford to scare them and potentially cause mental or physical harm."

There was a pause then an audible throat clearing before the voice continued.

"I'm quoting from the Introduction to Humans pamphlet issued by the Committee of Pet Welfare. 'All possible caution must be used when taming wild-caught humans. Not only are their bodies easily damaged, but they can become so frightened they develop nervous system issues or even die. It is best to proceed with an abundance of caution and infinite patience.' Everyone must test your *stellian* for as long as the humans are here. Refer to station announcements for further information."

There was absolute silence for several seconds after the announcement ended, then Rain, along with her friends and family, all roared with laughter.

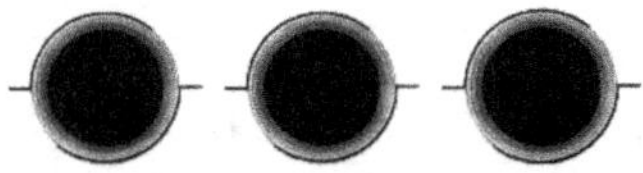

Hesarium

After the station director's announcement, Hesarium had been prepared for Rain to be upset, maybe even angry. When all the humans started laughing, a relieved rumble escaped his chest.

He was well aware that much of the information disseminated by the Committee of Pet Welfare made humans seem hopelessly delicate, both mentally and physically. The Advanced Squad he belonged to was the first to encounter humans and bring them back to Talarian. A complicated series of laws forced them to declare the humans as pets.

There'd been some rocky moments and one escape attempt before his squad and the humans figured out a way to make living on Talarian as pets work. Part of that had been deliberately misleading Talin authorities about how smart and capable humans were. That had snowballed into humans being seen as nearly helpless.

He and his fellow squad members had retired from the military and expected to spend their lives on Talarian with the humans they rescued. What none of them could've known was how popular humans would become even before they reached the planet. No Talin would ever admit it, but they were all hungry for the affection the humans gave and received so easily.

"You weren't exaggerating," Rain said after she finished laughing. "We are popular here."

"I haven't seen our people this universally obsessed about anything since the trisolar eclipse," one of the healers said with an amused rumble, then handed Rain a vial. "Here, drink this please."

Rain accepted the vial but made a face. "How many more of these do I have to drink? The last few were really bitter."

The healer had been turning away, but Rain's words made her snap her focus back to Rain and she started asking rapid-fire questions. "They don't taste good to you? Does the medication hurt your mouth? Is it causing you distress to swallow? Do you taste with your lips or—"

Hesarium sounded a soft rattle of warning to stop the healer. "Slower, Healer. She can't answer if you don't stop asking questions."

The healer sounded a soothing rumble. "I'm sorry, little human. Please explain to me what impact the medication has on you."

"It doesn't hurt," Rain assured her. "I can drink it without a problem. It just doesn't taste very good."

The healer called out for one of the support staff to fetch a canister of sopa. Soon, the healer was pushing the sweet drink into Rain's hands.

"This should offset any unpleasant taste," the healer explained. She waited until Rain took a sip and made an appreciative sound before letting someone else call her away over a dietary question.

"What's *stellian*?" Rain asked.

The question was well timed. They'd been in the medical suite for several marks and Hesarium was finding it more and more difficult to keep from touching Rain.

"I'm practicing it right now," he answered with a humorous rumble. Dipping his head close, he whispered in her ear. "It's a challenge to be so close to you while unable to touch you or rub my bonding oil on you. My restraint is proof of my *stellian*."

"So it means willpower," Rain murmured. She reached out to grab one of his hands, tugging at him while speaking loudly. "Come sit on the bed close to me. I'm cold."

"That won't—" he started to say when one of the staff members ran across the room to Rain, carrying a heavy blanket.

"You poor thing! Let me help you." He draped the blanket over her and tucked it in around her body, sounding a comforting rumble the entire time. Rain was forced to let go of Hesarium's hand because the helpful Talin insisted both arms be under the blanket. "These are infused with nanos so they'll keep you warm. We're working on getting every human one of these blankets and an omni. It's the minimum all of you should have."

After the male left, Rain looked up at Hesarium with a little smile. "That didn't go as planned. I thought they'd let us cuddle."

A humorous rumble sounded from Hesarium's chest. "I tried to warn you."

Rain's eyes looked left then right before she focused back on him. "Come close," she whispered.

Curious, Hesarium stood so he could put his earhole near Rain's lips. Instead of speaking, Rain kissed gently over his earhole. Heat washed through him, and his scent glands ached fiercely.

"Was that a lip press?" one of the healers asked, her voice loud from excitement. Hesarium straightened up to see five healers all staring at them through the open door with avid interest.

"Lip press?" Rain questioned.

"Humans press their lips to each other to comfort or show affection," another healer said, stepping closer. "Especially to the face and lips of another human. But you lip pressed Hesarium. Do you see him as an honorary human?"

"I've read that humans will lip press any individual they feel affection toward, independent of species," a third healer interjected. "I know the Ari human owned by Bazium presses her lips to his face often. I've seen images of it from when they've been in public."

"Yes, that's true!" the healer next to her agreed. "I've seen that also. We should make note of this in Rain's records."

"I feel like a celebrity," Rain murmured, her attention bouncing from healer to healer as they talked.

"You are," Hesarium told her.

"The Ari human was badly traumatized and needed constant comfort from her owner," another healer pointed out.

A third healer sounded a rattle of agreement. "Just so! Rain is like her, in need of far more attention due to past events. We're lucky most of them are fine being in separate beds. It's only Rain that requires more reassurance."

"It's not simply a matter of mental strain. Rain was also the most ill," the first healer pointed out. "She probably needs constant reassurance of his affection. I'm sure all the humans worry about being abandoned, but given her weakened state, she'd be more fearful."

"Oh, dear lord!" Rain exclaimed under her breath, but Hesarium could tell she was more amused than upset by the healers' conversation.

"Yes, I believe you're correct, Joyleum. Seeking comfort from her owner probably makes her feel much more secure. All these humans should really be owned individually or risk neglect," the healer said, then set their eyes on Hesarium. He'd been waiting for that kind of mild accusation and had a reply ready, but Rain responded first.

"*She* is right here and can hear you," Rain said loud enough to be heard by almost everyone. "All of us are staying with Hesarium. He's our Talin. We don't want another one, right everyone?"

There was a quick series of whispered conversations between beds before everyone started shouting their replies.

"Hesarium is our Talin!" Gris called out.

"You can't take him away from us!" Iris called, little Mia on her lap.

"Yeah!" Mia said, although she looked confused as to what they were talking about.

"Can they really take Hes away?" Cherish asked, making a production of sniffling loudly and pretending to wipe away a tear.

"Don't cry, my delicate sibling," Wind said with a dramatic flair. Hesarium could see the male was biting his lip to keep from smiling. "I'm sure they wouldn't take away our Hes. He's the only one who really loves us. The only one we trust. No one could be that cruel."

Sunny put a hand to her chest and threw back her head. "My heart couldn't take being separated from Hes. He's like another sibling to me. The older brother I've always wanted."

"They are all very attached to you," the healer said, sounding a surprised rattle as he moved closer to Hesarium. "I hadn't realized they'd bond so quickly."

"Hes saved our lives," Rain said. "That's a quick way to win our affection."

None of the healers were familiar with human tone or facial expressions, so they couldn't perceive the wry nature of Rain's words and expression.

"Yes, yes," the healer said with a rumble of comprehension. "I understand now. This aspect of human nature must be covered in great detail for my report to the Committee for Pet Welfare. This is vital knowledge." With that, he turned and rushed away, probably to record everything while it was fresh in his mind.

"I need to lip press you again," Rain said, her eyes dancing with humor.

"You're trouble," he murmured, leaning in close again. Rain brushed her lips against his cheek, over his scent gland. A shock of pleasure shot down his spine.

"Careful," he whispered before moving his head a safe distance from those tempting lips.

"Hesarium?"

Turning his head, he found a female Talin standing at the open door to the room. She wasn't wearing a healer's green tunic or any identifying badges on her belt, but she had to be important for Danisal to have let her pass.

"Yes?"

"I'm Auxiliary Director Miehlum," she explained. "Station Director Lakorum sent me here to discuss registering your humans and help you deal with the counterclaims."

Hesarium stood up to face Miehlum. "Counterclaims?"

"There are three Talins on the station who are putting in claims for your humans," she explained, sounding a soothing rumble. "You didn't file any records or requests before you arrived, only the permissions permits. Several members of the station's crew are attempting to take advantage. We're obliged to take allegations seriously. If you will come with me, I can explain everything, and we can start the process to legitimize your ownership."

It never occurred to Hesarium that someone would try to usurp his claim on the humans. Anger made him want to rattle out a sound of challenge, but Miehlum was quick to stop him.

"It's unlikely they will be able to take any of the humans," she assured him. "However, it's imperative we establish your ownership quickly."

The last thing he wanted to do was leave, but it seemed as if both Miehlum and the station director were on his side. He needed to take advantage of their goodwill.

Standing up, he took Rain's hand in his and gave it a little squeeze. "I'll return as soon as I'm able."

"Don't be afraid, human," Miehlum said to Rain with a comforting rumble. "We won't keep your owner away from you for any longer than necessary."

A few others shouted questions and concerns as he started to leave, but Rain was quick to call out for them to quiet down. Danisal stepped aside to let him pass but Hesarium paused and faced her.

"Warrior Danisal, I'm entrusting you with the things most precious to me," he said, slapping his fist hard against the keratin plates of his chest.

"I know my duty, Citizen Hesarium," Danisal answered. "Fear not. No one but those cleared to pass will get by me. You have my word."

"Then I'll owe you a debt of honor," he said, feeling reassured.

Before he could turn away, she spoke up. "You'll pay that debt before you leave."

"What?"

"I wish to speak with them," Danisal said in a low tone, "and interact, especially with the young ones. I'm intrigued beyond comprehension. Do you understand?"

Hesarium understood all too well. "I'll request that you're assigned to escort us back to Talarian."

Danisal sounded a brief rattle of excitement before she remembered decorum and went silent. "That would be an honor. If I'm not assigned as an escort, then I'll resign my position and accompany you as a citizen. Be assured, I will still be well armed."

That almost made Hesarium sound a rumble of amusement. "I'm not worried. You're no doubt dangerous even without weapons."

"Not at range," she answered and Hesarium could hear the subtle humor in her tone. "But within arm's reach, no one stands a chance. Now, be on your way and know your humans are well guarded."

CHAPTER 22

Rain

Hesarium wasn't gone very long when one of the healers broke the bad news to Rain. "All of you will be staying here for the next rotation," he said while looking at his Ident and tapping it a few times.

"I'm sorry, maybe my INT mistranslated," she said. "Did you say we have to sleep here?"

The healer sounded a rattle of agreement without looking up. "All of you need to be observed for at least one full rotation. We'll monitor your sleep state and reassess once you wake again."

Spending the night here meant no privacy for her and Hes. What if Hes started suffering from Ending if he couldn't rub his bonding oil on her soon?

"We'd all really like to have some private rooms," she countered.

"Are you not comfortable?" the healer asked. "Please indicate what is causing you distress so I can alleviate it."

Like with declaring herself cold and getting a blanket instead of snuggles from Hes, this conversation wasn't getting her what she wanted. It was clear the healers were going to insist on keeping them overnight. When Hes got back, they'd simply have to figure something out.

"Are you pining for Hesarium?" the healer asked. "If you're fearful, you can clutch or cling to me." He sat on the end of her bed and opened his arms as if inviting her to hug him.

Rain wrinkled her nose at the offer. "I only clutch and cling to Hesarium."

The healer didn't make a sound as he dropped his arms, but she could tell he was disappointed. "Do you think any of the other humans would want to clutch or cling to me?"

"I don't know," Rain answered. This felt like when she'd been a teenager and Gris kept asking her if Devon was interested in him.

"The Auntie human is very engaged with Varlum and Toreum, so she is well comforted. None of the other humans seem interested in interacting with the healers outside our duties. All of us are ready to provide the comfort humans need." He looked over at Sunny and Royal sharing a bed. Royal was tucked up against Sunny, fast asleep. Sunny was reading on an information square propped up on her knees, but her eyes kept drifting closed. "I suppose there are so many of you that you comfort each other and don't need us."

"You could ask around. Someone might need a hug," Rain suggested even though it was obvious that it was the healer who needed a hug!

"No one is in obvious discomfort, but many prey animals hide their distress for fear of attracting predators," the healer decided, already standing up and moving away. "I'll inquire to see if anyone requires calming."

Rain leaned forward, just enough to grab the edge of the healer's tunic before he moved out of her reach. He stopped and looked down at her with an inquisitive rattle.

Rain let go the moment he looked at her, and she spoke quickly. "Don't make anyone touch you, okay?"

She didn't expect any of these Talins to push a human's boundaries if they said no. They saw the humans as far too delicate to cause distress by ignoring requests, but it was best to make sure.

"Of course not," the Talin responded with a purr. "That would defeat the purpose of trying to comfort them. Don't worry. I'll make sure they know they've successfully hidden their distress if they indicate they wish to clutch or cling. It's important to praise humans so they feel secure."

With that, he strode off. Rain watched with interest as he approached Zuri and inquired if she needed to clutch or cling to him. She looked confused and glanced at Rain.

Rain pantomimed a hug and Zuri's expression turned humorous as she agreed to give the Talin a hug. Rain expected him to sit on Zuri's bed and open his arms as he'd done with her. That wasn't what happened. Instead, the healer picked her up, set her on his lap, and wrapped his arms loosely around her. Zuri gave a little muffled exclamation of surprise then giggled.

"I've watched many vid captures of humans clinging and clutching to their Talins in this manner," the healer explained. "When you're finished clutching and clinging, I can lay you back down on the bed as you were before."

Zuri covered her mouth while she laughed. "You guys are so damn strong. You need to warn a person before you pick them up!"

The Talin sounded the distant-bass-drum rumble of concern. "Have I injured you or caused distress? That was the opposite of my intent!"

Zuri was quick to calm the healer and even wrapped her arms around his neck in a hug, resting her head on his shoulder near his neck. Rain knew from experience it was a pretty comfortable position. It was like Talins were designed with human *clinging* in mind.

"This time it's fine," Zuri reassured him. "You only caught me by surprise."

The Talin started up a purr. "I apologize and promise to ask in the future. My duties for this rotation are complete so you may clutch and cling to me for as long as you require. If you fall asleep, I can arrange my body in a more recumbent position for your comfort. You're safe, human. I pledge to hold you and rumble to you even as you slumber."

Zuri's muffled voice was barely audible. "Um, yeah, I think I might like that."

Rain couldn't see Zuri's face, but she sounded like she might be tearing up. Watching Zuri snuggle up against the healer made Rain realize an additional advantage she hadn't thought of before—potential romantic partners.

With so few humans left on Omanal and no surviving human enclaves close by, individuals like Zuri had assumed they'd live their life without a partner. Now they were heading toward a thriving group of humans none of them were related to and had an entire population of Talins to choose from.

Even with having to be careful who they let in on their secret, there were a lot of options out there. This could all work out even better than she'd expected.

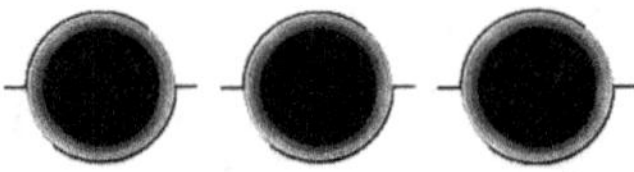

Hesarium

Danisal was still on guard when Hesarium returned many marks later. "I'm back. You can take a break now."

She sounded a negative rattle. "The medical suite only secures in case of structural failure or attack. Otherwise, there is no way to lock these doors. That means I'll remain here until the humans are in rooms that can be properly secured. Don't be concerned about fatigue. I've done multi-rotation duty before; I know my limits."

"I didn't think the healers would want us to stay an entire rotation," Hesarium admitted. While he'd met with the station director, he'd gotten word from the healers that they wanted to monitor all the humans during a rest cycle.

As much as he knew the humans wouldn't like it, it gave him extra marks to file petitions and secure agreements with officials on his ownership of the humans. Now that his position was more secure, he could focus on other important tasks.

Hesarium pulled in a deep breath. "My duty is to find rooms and beds for all the humans. I've heard the station is at capacity right now."

"You don't need to concern yourself with that," she assured him. "With permission from the station director, I reserved the jadik sector for all the humans. I'm surprised the auxiliary director didn't tell you."

Hesarium was surprised and pleased by the news. The jadik sector was reserved for visiting royalty and their staff. There would be plenty of room for the humans, and it had restricted access. If you weren't housed or working in one of the rooms, you couldn't even get into the hallways in that section.

"We were very busy. She probably forgot," Hesarium said, feeling grateful to the soldier. "Thank you for thinking of this when I hadn't. When we're settled in those rooms, you should ask Royal about his multi-tech. He is the second-smallest child among the humans. He'll enjoy explaining everything about the tool to you."

Danisal sounded a rattle of excitement before quashing it. "I'll look for the small human with a multi-tech, then inquire about its uses."

"You should also sit on the floor with your legs in front of you," Hesarium added. "He might take it as an invitation to sit in your lap."

"I will do as you instruct," she promised. Then she resolutely turned to face the hallway with her hands in the relaxed, ready position that was second nature to all soldiers. Danisal wasn't being rude. Hesarium recognized the maneuver for what it was—using cold military formality to cover an excess of emotions.

Knowing she wanted to be alone, Hesarium left her to guard and sought out Rain. The inside of the medical suite was dim with the lights set low. All the healers were speaking in hushed tones and were walking with careful, controlled steps to minimize sound.

A look around told him almost all the humans were asleep. Cherish and Wind were awake and had an information square set on a stool between their two beds. They were taking turns tapping it, leading Hesarium to guess they were playing a game.

Farther down the wall of beds, Gris and Devon were curled up in the same bed. As he watched, one of the healers passed by and tucked Devon's arm under the blanket, covering them both. Two of their three children were sharing the bed next to them, with the oldest getting her own bed on their other side.

Iris and Mia were sharing a bed, but Mia had somehow squished her little body at the head of the bed, taking up a great deal of room and forcing Iris to curl up on her side to fit. Both were fully asleep, leading Hesarium to guess this wasn't an unusual sleeping arrangement for the two of them.

"We tried to separate them, but the little human started leaking water out of her eyes," one of the healers whispered, coming to a stop next to Hesarium as he paused next to Mia and Iris's bed. "Then we offered to push two beds together but the Iris human said it wouldn't matter and they'd end up in that position anyway. It appears the humans' level of affection and need for touch and comfort hasn't been exaggerated."

"Not at all," Hesarium agreed. Then he noticed Zuri lying on top of one of the healers. "Did something happen to Zuri?"

"She sought comfort from Kasium," the healer explained. "His work cycle was finished so he was able to soothe the human to sleep. We fear if he moves, she might wake, so it's best he remains where he is."

Zuri was draped across the Talin's chest with a slight smile curving her lips and one hand gripping several of Kasium's fingers. Kasium's RK eyes were closed, but he was awake and sounding a constant soothing rumble while gently petting Zuri's back.

Toreum and Varlum were still there too. Varlum was sitting in the bed with Auntie, his back against the wall and his legs spread on either side of her body. Toreum was sitting next to her, halfway on the bed. Auntie had one of Toreum's arms hugged to her chest and although the position looked awkward in the extreme, Toreum was sounding a constant soothing rumble.

Auntie looked sound asleep and the two Talins were talking over her in hushed tones. Although they were trying to be discreet, he could see both of them were struggling with overfull scent glands. He was surprised the healers hadn't noticed, but then again, they were all so entranced by the humans—why would they bother paying close attention to the Talins in the room?

Talins might be the species with a mighty empire, but the humans had conquered them with clutches, clinging, and lip presses.

CHAPTER 23

Rain

The suite Hesarium carried her into the next day was opulent. Sunny, Cherish, Wind, and Royal were right behind them.

"This place is twice as big as our domicile was!" Wind exclaimed and hurried over to one of many doors and ordered it open. "Wow, each room is huge. Cherish, come look."

Cherish was quick to follow him and gaze through the open door. "Do we each get a room?"

"If you like," Auxiliary Director Miehlum said, stepping into the suite. Behind her were Auntie, Toreum, and Varlum.

Varlum was carrying a sleeping Royal, and Auntie pointed to a large chair that could easily accommodate several humans at once.

"Lay him down there for now," Auntie instructed, then looked at Miehlum. "I didn't realize we'd each get a room. I half expected we'd be living dormitory style, like in the medical center."

Miehlum pointed to the hall beyond the room. "The jadik section is able to accommodate over a hundred individuals, so each human could occupy an entire suite and there would still be plenty of space left empty."

"I don't need a whole suite, but a room sounds good,"
Cherish said then turned and gently shoved her brother away
from the open doorway they'd both been standing in. "This
room is mine!"

Wind pretended to stumble and called her a podhead
as the room's door slid shut. Smiling, he turned to Rain.

"I think this is the highlight of Cherish's life so far."
Then he ran to the next door over. "I'm claiming this one!"
he shouted cheerfully as the doors slid shut behind him.

"I think I'll take this room," Auntie announced and
moved off to the room furthest from the door to the suite.
Toreum and Varlum were right behind her as the door slid
shut behind them.

"This is really nice," Rain said, looking around the
room. "But can you afford it, Hes?"

"There is no charge for these rooms," Miehlum
explained. "The monarch has jadik sectors on every colony
and station in the Talin Empire. Our most gracious monarch
has extended the use of the jadik rooms for the humans so the
cost will fall under the normal operating costs."

"That is generous of the monarch," Hes said. "But I'm
not surprised. He has a family of humans living at the royal
residence. Both he and the queen are fond of humans."

"So I've been informed," Miehlum said with a rattle
of agreement. "These rooms aren't the only kindness the
monarch is showing all of you. In four rotations, the
monarch's personal ship, The Honored, will arrive. It will
only take several marks for the ship to be ready for the return
trip to Talarian."

While Miehlum was talking, a Talin came into the
room. He was operating a hover cart stacked high with boxes
and crates that he started unloading in the middle of the suite.
In the hall beyond, Talins rushed back and forth, carrying
items or operating hover carts. Danisal stood in the center of
the walkway, looking threatening and warning everyone to
leave the humans alone.

Then another Talin came in with a second hover cart
and left it for the first Talin to unload. She saw more hover

carts passing down the hall, one right after another. Rain frowned at the sight. If there was so much free space, why couldn't they use one of the empty suites to store their supplies?

The Talin finished unloading the second cart and hit the controls for both of them to autopilot back from where they'd come. Standing at Miehlum's elbow, the Talin made a soft, inquisitive rumble.

"Do you need to speak to me, Tolvern?" Miehlum asked.

Tolvern spoke quickly. "Each suite has two hover carts worth of gifts now, but there might still be some necessities missing. We might want to set up a credit in the merchant area so anything omitted can be purchased."

The entire time he talked, Tolvern was edging closer to where Sunny was standing. She'd been staring at the boxes curiously instead of going off to explore the rooms with her siblings. When Tolvern got close enough, he started purring and dropped to his knees.

"Do you need to clutch or cling, Sunny human?" he asked, holding his arms out wide. "I'm Tolvern, of the Gal family and Picmor clan. We're a modest family but my clan controls the entire Reforum colony."

"Tolvern!" Miehlum barked, making the young male Talin flinch. "You were explicitly instructed not to engage with the humans. This is grounds for termination of your employment contract. I knew I shouldn't have employed someone from a newly formed clan. None of you from the colonies can be trusted to act with decorum!"

"Don't be mean. He only asked for a hug!" Sunny protested and stepped close to Tolvern. While standing, he towered over Sunny. Now that he was on his knees, her head was at his shoulder, making it easy for her to wrap arms around his neck. "We all need hugs sometimes."

Tolvern purred loudly and carefully wrapped his arms around Sunny's waist. "You can clutch and cling as hard as you need. I'm tough and strong. My family name might be unknown and my clan only two generations old, but I'm as honorable as any Talin."

Miehlum let loose with a loud rattle that sounded like a cloud of angry wasps. "You're being willfully disrespectful. This is unacceptable behavior. I'll have you restrained in the brig until transport back to Reforum colony can be arranged for you."

Sunny jolted at Miehlum's harsh tone, and her arms tightened around Tolvern. Two big fat tears welled up in her eyes then dramatically rolled down her cheeks. "You can't put him in jail for wanting a hug."

Rain watched with fascination as Miehlum went perfectly silent and still, watching those tears wet a path from Sunny's eyes to her jawbone.

"Fluid is leaking from your eyes," Miehlum whispered, horrified. "Have the orbs been punctured?"

Rain put her lips to Hes's earhole. "Do something before we end up back in the medical suite for another day of observation."

Hesarium's response told her very clearly that he'd spent too much time around her and the other humans.

"I can't fix your sister." That statement was followed by a humorous rumble. He was laughing at his own joke!

"Hes!" Rain hissed, trying not to smile. "There's no privacy in medical, remember?"

That reminder pushed Hes into action. He set Rain on her feet and faced the second most powerful Talin on the station. "Auxiliary Director Miehlum, I don't believe the Sunny human is physically hurt. Humans often leak fluid from their eyes when they are deeply, emotionally distressed. Your threat to punish Tolvern is causing Sunny to go into a state of mourning. She might not understand that he wouldn't be harmed."

"What happens to him shouldn't matter to her. He's only been here for half a mark," Miehlum protested. "The human female couldn't possibly have bonded with Tolvern this fast."

"Yes, I can, because he's sweet," Sunny explained, still hugging Tolvern's neck. "And he smells like peaches. He should stay with us."

Rain was startled by Sunny's description. For Rain all the Talin's smelled like soap or something medicinal except Hes with his addictive sugar-cookie scent. Could the smell of a Talin be an indicator of potential attraction? It was an interesting idea, but something to think about later.

"Humans can form bonds with great speed," Hes explained.

"Tolvern can't leave me!" Sunny cried out, still holding onto Tolvern. "If he leaves, I'll cry and cry and cry. I won't be able to stop!"

"Be at ease, Sunny human. Tolvern can stay here until you don't need him anymore," Miehlum said, sounding a purr. Then she turned to address Hes. "Inform me if the young human's attachment dissolves, and I'll deal with him. Otherwise, Tolvern can leave with all of you to Talarian. The Clan Authorities Council there can deal with him once you land."

"Of course, Auxiliary Director Miehlum. Thank you for being so accommodating," Hes said. "Before you go, can you elaborate on where we might take the humans on the station without causing an issue?"

As Hes and Miehlum spoke of a few practical things about the station's schedule and areas appropriate for humans, Rain made her way over to where Sunny was still hugging Tolvern. It was good Talins had armored necks, or she would've been cutting off his oxygen with how tightly she was holding him.

"You can ease back on the dramatics," Rain whispered. "They're not looking anymore."

Sunny turned her head and gave Rain a quick smile. "I'll stop after she leaves," Sunny whispered. "She's got a mean voice. I don't want to give her a chance to pick on Tolvern."

"Fine, but you're going to have to be responsible for Tolvern," Rain teased her. "You'll have to make sure he eats and take him for walks."

Sunny snickered. "I promise to keep him out of trouble."

"I've never been in trouble," Tolvern interjected. "Well, except here. This is the first time I've disobeyed any authority."

Sunny pulled back a little so she could look him in the eyes. "Don't worry, Tolvern, I will teach you the best ways to misbehave."

Tolvern's purring was interrupted by the slow irregular rumble of confusion. "Why would I want to misbehave?"

"Because sweets taste better when you sneak them," Sunny informed him sagely.

"That doesn't make sense," Tolvern answered, going back to purring. "It must be a human thing."

"It totally is," Sunny agreed with a little chuckle.

Miehlum's Ident started to ping, and she had to leave in a hurry to deal with some issue in another section of the station. The moment the doors of the suite shut behind her, Sunny let go of Tolvern and turned her attention to all the boxes he'd brought.

"What's all this?"

When Tolvern rattled, it sounded like a bunch of tools being dropped on a metal floor. At first Rain thought he was surprised but then remembered that this rattle could indicate excitement also.

Jumping to his feet, Tolvern hurried to the boxes. "These are gifts from the station," he explained, tugging one open and pulling out a bright, blue topaz garment. He proudly presented it to Sunny.

"Gifts from the station?" Rain asked as Sunny took the wrap and held it to her front.

"It's so pretty!" Sunny exclaimed.

Rain turned to Hes. "Why are we getting gifts from the station?"

"Everyone wants to meet you," Tolvern explained as he pulled more items from the box and started laying them out on the top of the other boxes. "These gifts are to attract the humans' attention and earn Hesarium's favor."

"What about the counter claims?" Rain asked.

Hesarium purred and drew her close to him. "They're already quashed. The message I sent back when we first arrived at the Hub has reached the monarch. He sent instructions about our treatment and expenses, and that ended any attempts at counter claims."

"Wow. I'm not sure if I'm impressed or worried that the king of your empire knows about us," Rain murmured.

"Monarch, not king," Hes corrected her. "And he doesn't only know that I'm bringing home a group of humans, he knows each of your names. He's also sent his personal ship, The Honored, to collect us, and we'll be traveling back to Talarian with a military escort."

"He's sending one of his back-up ships, right?" Rain asked. "He's the monarch. He must have hundreds of ships."

He sounded a negative rattle. "This is his only ship at the moment. The queen also has a ship, but they don't have a fleet. The fact that he's sending The Honored means a great deal within the empire, Rain. His interest has helped to make humans an obsession among Talins."

There were a lot of things Rain wanted to say, but none of them were fit for mixed company. Not only was Tolvern in the room, but there were still Talins moving through the hall well within earshot.

Rain looked back at the array of clothing, shoes, blankets, belts, pouches, and pillows. Everything was brightly colored and high quality. Sunny had put the blue wrap garment on over the dark gray one and was now sliding her feet into the matching slippers. As Rain watched, Tolvern found a jeweled belt and urged Sunny to take it.

"This will look very fine with your outfit, Sunny human," Tolvern declared.

"You don't have to add the human part after my name," Sunny teased. "Or should I call you Tolvern Talin?"

"You would rather I only used Sunny?" Tolvern asked with the irregular beat of an inquisitive rattle.

The teenager's expression suddenly turned serious. "Call me Sunshine," she murmured, leaning in close to Tolvern and taking a deep breath. "I think I want you to use my full name."

The two were staring deeply into each other's eyes in a meaningful way Rain wasn't comfortable with. Smacking her hands together in one loud clap, she drew Tolvern and Sunny's eyes to her.

"Sunny, you should probably put everything back for now," Rain suggested. "We don't want to make anyone think they have a claim on us."

Tolvern scrambled to his feet and put his body between Rain and Sunny, as if shielding the teenager from her. "The gifts cannot be returned and come with no social or financial obligations," he insisted.

Rain looked at Hes. "Is that true?"

Hes sounded a rattle of affirmation. "It's mostly true. Do you see this?" He pointed to the side of the box where there was a crest-like image. "These are family crests. I'm sure every Talin who wins the lottery will be proudly displaying their crests on their belts in hopes of being recognized as gift givers and gaining the attention of one of the humans. If they can earn your affection, then they can petition the Committee of Pet Welfare for ownership reassignment on the basis of emotional well-being."

Rain stared at him, blinking owlishly as she processed everything he'd said. "Let's start with you explaining what the hell this lottery is, yeah?"

CHAPTER 24

Hesarium

Two days later, Hes carried Rain through empty corridors as Danisal led them and all the humans to the room where the twenty lottery winners would get to meet the humans. To his relief, Rain had been mostly amused by the scheme he and the station director came up with to keep a station full of eager Talins calm. Every Talin interested in interacting with the humans entered their name. Out of three thousand who entered, twenty were chosen at random.

They wouldn't leave until the day after tomorrow, so to keep the Talins on the station who didn't win the lottery content, there was a second lottery available. There would be a single winner and that individual would get to ride back with them on The Honorable.

To keep the peace, the second lottery wouldn't be held until the humans were already on board Honorable and the Talin who won would be given non-penalized personal time for the duration of their trip to Talarian and back. Danisal had told him last night that almost every Talin on the station had packed in case they were the one whose name was called.

It was an exceptional level of preparedness, even among Talins. Hesarium couldn't blame them; he would've done the same thing, because who wouldn't want to spend time with a bunch of adorable humans?

"A lot of people are excited about this meet and greet," Rain murmured as they moved slowly from the secure jadik section of the station to an observation deck picked for the occasion.

Danisal had assured him the deck and surrounding hallways were all cleared, with guards posted at regular intervals. Hes trusted Danisal implicitly but was still tense.

If he was being honest with himself, he was partially tense because he didn't want to share Rain's attention with any other Talin. He didn't want to share his human.

"Are you excited?" Hesarium asked. He and Rain were at the tail end of the line of humans following Danisal. Behind him was another fully armored and armed Talin protecting their flank because Danisal wasn't one to leave anything to chance.

"I wouldn't say I'm excited," Rain answered. "I know everyone else is interested in interacting with more Talins. So far, the only Talin they've really talked to is you, and some with the healers, but our time in medical was all business. I think they're hoping to get a better understanding of your culture here. I know most of them have been reading articles and watching vids available on the station's Unibase. "

"They are?" Hesarium asked, startled by the news.

"You're surprised?" Rain countered with a raised eyebrow. "We're at your mercy, and you don't think we want to know everything we can about you guys?"

"Worded as such, I feel foolish," Hesarium admitted, feeling a little sheepish. If the situation was reversed, he'd be reading and watching every piece of information he could get his claws on. This moment was a good reminder that, unlike the doctrine put forth by the Committee for Pet Welfare, humans were as intelligent as Talins.

"Are you like the others, interested in meeting other Talins?" Hesarium asked.

She shook her head. "I'm not against meeting new people, but I'd much rather explore the station instead."

Hesarium felt a pang of guilt. "I'm sorry I can't take you on a tour. It would cause too much disruption."

"I know," she answered with a little shrug. "At least we're going to a new spot to meet the lottery winners. That's a nice change."

Before Hesarium could ask her another question, Danisal stopped everyone in front of a set of double doors.

"Before I let you in there, I want to remind all of you that we'll be in there watching," she said, pointing to herself and then the three other men she'd brought with her. "The lottery winners were given strict rules. All touching has to be at the invitation of the human. No raised rattles or loud voices. If any of them make you feel uncomfortable, you come to one of us. What do you shout if you're trapped and need one of us?"

"Fail," the humans murmured in unison. Usually when shouted, the word was shorthand for a structural issue on a ship or station, but in this context, it was a general word for distress.

"Very good," Danisal praised them, sounding very much like one of the highly trained professionals that worked with Talin children at the creshes. "We will be in here for three marks. If you become fatigued, there are pallets laid out on the floor against one wall with pillows and blankets. There will also be sustenance if you become hungry. You are to seek out food and drink yourself. The lottery winners are not allowed to move from the spot where they are sitting. Do we all understand?"

Everyone nodded their head with a few voicing affirmations. Danisal sounded a single sharp rattle of agreement and turned to tap the control panel. The large doors slid open to reveal a completely rearranged observation deck.

The original tables and chairs were gone, leaving mostly open space. Along one wall were enough beds to accommodate all the humans and each one was piled high with plush pillows and nano-infused blankets. Along another wall were tables laden with every food the healers had deemed safe for human consumption.

Hesarium had expected nice accommodations for the humans, but he wasn't prepared to see twenty Talins all sitting on the floor in neat rows of four. They'd created as much space as they could between each other without encroaching on the food or bed areas.

Spread out around each Talin was a collection of objects, including educational toys for very young Talins, old fashioned tools, and random items such as glowing namoid crystals or a small terrarium full of udeck beetles. It took a submark for Hesarium to realize these Talins had surrounded themselves with interesting things in an effort to attract a human's attention.

Once all the humans were in the room, there was a moment of silence as the Talins all watched them like predators. The humans froze, unsure and wary. Hesarium wanted to shout at all the Talins to start rumbling out sounds of comfort at least, but he was worried about startling the humans.

It was Mia who broke the stillness. Tugging free of Iris, she ran to a Talin in the second row who had several hoops imbued with iridescent micro-organisms. Their ancestors had used them many thousands of years ago as a way to light rooms, but they'd long since been replaced with far brighter and more efficient methods. While the hoops lacked the power to truly illuminate a room, they made up for it in a random flashing of blue and purple light without a discernible pattern.

"Pretty!" she shouted and reached for one. Iris rushed to follow her while every set of eyes in the room followed her progress.

"Mia, no!" she cried out and managed to catch the girl before she grabbed hold of the hoop.

"I want!" Mia wailed, big tears gathering in her eyes. Every single Talin sitting on the floor started up a comforting rumble and several looked to him and Rain for guidance. The Talin with the light-hoops was quick to pick one up and hold it out, trying to hand it to Mia.

"They are perfectly safe," she assured Iris. "The pup can touch and play with it. They're very hard to break. Even if the outer shell cracks, there's nothing toxic or poisonous inside. The worst it will do is stain her wrap."

Iris dropped to a seated position in front of the Talin and arranged Mia in her lap then took the light-hoop from the Talin and presented it to Mia. That's when Hesarium noticed the young woman looked tired. He made a mental note to speak with Rain about Iris later.

"I'm sorry," Iris murmured to the Talin as Mia took the light-hoop. The little girl's tears instantly disappeared and she brought the light-hoop close to her face, laughing with delight. "I'm so used to everything being dangerous, that I might be a little overprotective."

"You're a good dam to the little pup," the Talin assured her. "My name is Palathum, of the Uriam Family within the Uriam Clan. My family is related to the monarch through marriage and we're one of the shareholders of this station."

Hesarium felt a jolt of surprise hit him. He'd heard of Palathum, but this was the first time he'd ever seen the female in person. She was a powerfully wealthy individual and was said to have a supernatural ability to know where to build stations. In contrast to her wealth, the items she picked to display around her were of minimal monetary value but had managed to attract one of the youngest human children.

"You must be very important," Iris murmured, then moved her head to avoid getting hit by the light-ring as Mia shoved it in her face.

"Look at the pretty! Look, Iris, look!"

"It's really pretty, Mia," Iris agreed with a small smile. "What do we call that color?"

"Blue!" Mia said then the ring changed. "No, purple!"

"That's good. Can you count how many times it changes color for me?"

"I can!" Mia agreed then stared intensely at the light and started counting out loud. "One. Still one. Stilllllll oooooone. Oh, two! It's turning into a two. It's all two now."

Mia kept up her number announcements as Palathum spoke softly to Iris.

"Your pup looks healthy and happy," she complimented the human. "You're doing a fine job raising her."

Among Talins, that was a high compliment because raising children was considered something only highly paid professionals should do. Hesarium knew Iris wouldn't fully understand the extent of Palathum's compliment, but she reacted with pleasure anyway.

"Thanks, Palathum. When Mia's parents died, we almost lost her too," Iris told her, making Hesarium jolt.

"Iris isn't Mia's dam?" Hesarium whispered to Rain.

Rain shook her head. "After Iris lost her parents, she was old enough to live alone but asked to move in with Tish and Juri. It was a good thing too because we lost her old house to the bog a few months later. Anyway, when Tish and Juri had Mia, it was love at first sight for Iris. She's been like a second mom to that girl from the very beginning. Then we lost Tish and Juri, and no one thought twice about Iris taking over Mia's care."

"So much loss," Hesarium murmured. It was rare for a Talin to die of anything but old age, war, or one of the rare diseases with no cure. To hear of so many deaths suffered by the humans in a relatively short time span made him hurt for what they'd endured.

"The worst of it happened during and after the bog expansion," she said. "It got to the point where we all started getting a little numb to loss."

Hesarium wished he could've reached the Omanal humans before tragedy started piling up, but at least he could give the remaining humans a bright future. "That dark period is over now."

"Agreed," Rain said with a grin. "We've left unexpected death behind and moved into unexpected gift territory."

No one else but Mia and Iris had moved yet. The Talins sitting had turned their attention to the group of humans and kept up the comforting rumbles. A few had picked up items and were holding them out in invitation.

"Should we encourage them in some way?" Hesarium asked. As much as he didn't like having to do this, he saw the value in keeping these Talins content with their experiences. The more popular humans became, the easier it would be to get funding to save more of them.

"Let me," Rain said, then pulled a breath and spoke loudly to the group. "Everybody, go meet a Talin. It can't be worse than digging new field guides!"

Everyone chuckled at Rain's words and slowly started moving. Most circled around the Talins before picking one to sit next to. Soon the room was filled with rumbles, conversation, and the clink of items being handled.

Sunny picked a Talin with a small cage and sat down in front of him. "What's in there?" she asked.

"It's a jool lizard," the Talin explained eagerly as he unlatched the cage to pull the colorful creature out. "They're specially bred on Eforn by the Opuro."

"Is it a boy or girl?" Sunny asked, leaning in close.

"Neither. It's the fourth sex: a monisk," the Talin explained. He launched into a quick explanation of the jool lizards' four sexes and their function. Sunny nodded and occasionally asked questions. Soon she was holding the lizard and cooing while the animal tried to climb up her sleeve.

Auntie sat down near a Talin who'd brought several old tools. Hesarium could see she didn't want to be there, but she worked hard on being charming and friendly with the stranger.

Tolvern, Kasium, Toreum, and Varlum had been asked to remain within the jadik section. None of them had been happy about it, but they also knew not to disobey a station director. The Talins assigned to escort and guard the humans circled around, offering to bring humans food and drinks, or carry them to a bed to rest.

"I should probably go talk to someone," Rain murmured and tapped his arm, an indicator she wanted to be put down.

"You don't have to," Hesarium objected even as he lowered her to her feet.

Rain petted his arm above his quills. "Don't worry. You'll always be my favorite Talin. I do want to get a closer look at those beetles though."

Before Rain could take a step toward the only Talin in the room without a human to talk to, Station Director Lakorum walked in. She marched up to him and slapped a fist to her chest plates.

"Rise with the Ancestors, Hesarium," she said.

He voiced out the response to her greeting. "Let their wisdom guide us."

With the formalities over, she looked down at Rain and held her arms out away from her body. "Hello, small human, would you like to clutch or cling to me?"

"Not right now," Rain responded, using the script she and Hes had come up with. "I only like to touch my owner."

"I'm not surprised," Lakorum said with an amused rumble. "The feeling appears mutual. It's quite obvious he favors you out of all the humans."

"I guess it's only fair because he's my favorite Talin," Rain responded.

Auntie's loud laughter caught the station direction's attention. "That is the one named Auntie, correct?" Lakorum asked.

"Yes," Hesarium answered. "It appears Toreum and Varlum will be accompanying us to Talarian to stay close to this human."

"I read in the report she's too old to reproduce," Lakorum commented. "It's a pity because she's such a friendly human. Her offspring would be charming."

"She's only forty-one," Rain started to protest but Hesarium was quick to cut her off.

"Although she'd make a wonderful dam, you're correct, her age puts her at risk," Hesarium said to the station director, hoping Rain would understand what he was doing. "But even if the human can't reproduce, they're important to the group as companions and caretakers for others. Separating any human from their familial groups puts both the group and individual at risk for stress sickness."

"Ah, yes, I remember reading that they use cooperative childcare," Lakorum mused. "For a primitive species, it's a beneficial system."

"Yes, exactly," Hesarium agreed. "We have to let the humans become comfortable with individual Talins before attempting to separate them."

"If Auntie left, I don't know what I'd do. Except cry, a lot!" Rain added, finally figuring out what he was doing. "She's like a mother to me."

"Don't be fearful," Lakorum said with a comforting rumble. "No one's going to force your herd to separate before you're ready. The place you'll be living was set up specifically to care for all of you en masse. There are even humans there already, and I'm sure they're eager to meet you."

Rain pretended to cling to his arm, putting on a show of being a little fearful. "That's good. I'd like to make new friends."

Lakorum looked to him. "Hopefully their familial bonds will diminish once they've lived in a safe environment for a while. We really need to spread the human population out among the Talins more. They're such delightful creatures. Really, everyone should have one."

As the station director continued to drone on about what perfect pets humans were, Hesarium deliberately didn't look down at Rain. He knew her expression would probably be a combination of amusement and annoyance. He couldn't blame her. For as much as his species claimed to have power and prestige in the universe, they were just as likely to be willfully obtuse as any civilization.

CHAPTER 25

Georgia

Although she had fun talking to all the lottery winners, Georgia was eager to get back to Tor and Vee. The moment she'd met them, she'd gotten one of her *feelings*. Not only was she sure that Tor and Vee were trustworthy, but she was also sure the three of them had a future together.

All the time they'd spent with her in the medical suite had only cemented her feelings. Then she'd given them nicknames. She'd expected push back, but far from admonishing her for the lack of formality, they'd seemed pleased.

They continued to call her by her entire first name. Because everyone else called her Auntie, to the point that Royal didn't know her by a different name, it was almost like having a nickname.

"That was a lot more fun than I thought it'd be," Devon said as she, Gris, and their children filed down the empty hall in front of her.

"I thought the Talins would be pushy," Gris admitted. "But they were all really mellow."

"I got to play tweshi and entict!" Ruth, their youngest exclaimed. She was hyper right now, bouncing around her parents and siblings, but Georgia knew from experience the child would be out cold not long after returning to the suite.

"You were the fastest entict there!" Gris praised the little girl. "None of those big Talins could keep up."

Ruth giggled and started in on a long-winded explanation of why she was so fast that included such children's logic as "being closer to the floor means less gravity." No one mentioned that the Talins weren't allowed to chase her, and it was only when she got close to one of them that she could be *caught*.

Georgia still marveled at how indulgent every Talin in the room had been, not only with Ruth. They'd been patient, kind, and generous with all the humans. It was such a novel experience that many in the group had asked to extend the time when Danisal announced the meeting was over.

They were passing an intersection of corridors when a large figure appeared next to her. "Georgia, it's good to see you."

The guard behind her jumped forward to get between her and the figure, but Danisal was quick to call him off. "That's Toreum," she explained to her fellow guard. "Let him approach Auntie human."

Toreum didn't spare either of the other Talins a glance as he held his arms out, inviting Georgia to hug him. She didn't hesitate to wrap her arms around his waist and snuggle in close. She loved her family, but it'd been a long time since anyone sought her out purely to give her affection.

"Where's Vee?" she asked, basking in Toreum's hug.

"He's waiting for us," Toreum explained with a purr. "I promised to show you something special, but if you want to see it, we have to leave now."

"Toreum, you and Auntie need to start walking," Danisal ordered. Georgia let go of Toreum to see everyone else had moved a substantial distance ahead and would soon turn a corner and be out of sight.

"I'd like to take Georgia on an excursion," Toreum explained. "I already have permission from Hesarium. All I need is her to agree."

The rattle that sounded from Danisal clearly said the warrior wasn't happy about this arrangement. "No one informed me, and it's convenient that you've come to take Auntie away while Hesarium isn't here."

"I'm aware he had to take Rain to the Medical Suite because she was coughing. I've communicated with him at length," Toreum assured her. "Check your Ident."

Danisal unclipped her Ident with an aggravated snap. It took a few taps before she paused, then reclipped it to her belt.

"Very well," she said and directed her gaze to Georgia. "Do you wish to accompany Toreum without any of your fellow humans or owner?"

"It's fine," Georgia assured Danisal.

Danisal sounded a rattle of agreement then looked over Georgia's head. "Granthian!"

Granthian had stationed himself halfway between the rest of the group and them. He was quick to jog back and stand next to Georgia, his eyes on Danisal.

"I'm assigning you to this human," Danisal explained. "She will be in the care of Toreum and Varlum. Check in with me about location and activity every quarter mark. You will have her back to the jadik sector for the human's evening meal."

"Yes, Lead Commander Danisal," he responded, body stiff, tone crisp and respectful. Danisal gave a last rattle of acceptance and hurried to catch up with everyone else. Georgia knew Toreum didn't want Granthian coming along, but no one went against Danisal's orders on Falsof Station unless they wanted to spend time in the brig.

"This way," Toreum said without acknowledging Granthian. He held out his hand for Georgia, a practice he'd adopted after seeing Hes and Rain do it. Sliding her hand in his, she let him lead her through a maze of narrow corridors until she was thoroughly confused. She was glad it wouldn't be up to her to find the way back, or they might never return to the jadik suites.

Except for the occasional Talin busy in the distance, they didn't encounter another soul, probably because they were in an area that looked more industrial and likely was only used to access the station's systems.

She was so busy looking around, she managed to trip over her own feet. With a gasp, she tried to catch herself. Strong arms went around her, and the world tilted crazily. When everything settled, she was in Toreum's arms, cradled against this chest.

"Are you hurt?" he asked, sounding the distant-bass-drum rumble of worry.

"I'm fine, only a little clumsy," she explained. As a tall, big-boned woman, she'd rarely been held as an adult, even when she was young and had those two blissful years with her husband. She'd always been so big and strong that as a joke on their wedding day, she'd carried Danny into their domicile. No one could've known that, even then, the cancer that would kill him was growing in his body.

"Do we need to go to medical?" Granthian asked.

"No!" Georgia said quickly. She didn't want to miss whatever Tor and Vee were planning. "I tripped, that's all."

"She might be a little fatigued after spending so much time interacting with the lottery winners," Toreum said to the guard. "I'll carry her the rest of the way."

She should probably object. As a whole, grown-ass woman, she could walk on her two feet just fine. Spending a few hours with the lottery winners wasn't taxing for someone used to spending entire days engaged in hard physical labor. All those thoughts rolled through her head but were dismissed quickly.

Like all the other Talins she'd met so far, Tor was a giant even compared to her larger size. None of them had ever struggled to pick any item up. She'd seen Hes lift things that weighed three or four hundred pounds. If Tor wanted to carry her, she was going to let him and enjoy the ride.

It didn't matter where they were going now that she was snuggled up against Toreum's muscled chest. She pulled in a deep breath, enjoying the basil smell that filled her nose. It took her a moment to realize she didn't like that Vee wasn't there to add his tarragon scent to the mix. She'd gotten so used to both of them always being together that it didn't feel right to only smell one and not the other.

"We're here," Toreum announced with an excited rattle.

Opening her eyes, she looked at the vast empty space around them. In the center of the space was a pile of pillows and blankets in a nest-like arrangement. She didn't know why the Talins thought humans liked nests, but it was a nice, comfy way to lounge around.

Toreum stopped and faced Granthian. "You can stay here and guard the door. The other points of access were all barred during the retrofitting and haven't been returned to original yet. This is the only way in or out."

Granthian was quiet for a moment, taking in the room, the doors, and the hallway behind him before meeting Toreum's gaze. "I can't leave, but I'll stay here," he agreed then looked at her. "Call out if you need me. I'll be able to hear you and I'll respond with appropriate force."

"Sure," she answered. "But Tor and Vee would never do anything to hurt me."

Granthian didn't answer as Toreum turned to carry her to the nest. As they got closer, she saw that Vee was kneeling in the nest, smoothing out blankets and fluffing pillows. The moment they got near, he popped up and started purring.

"You made it! I was worried Danisal wouldn't let you leave the safety of the group," he said, rushing up to take her from Toreum.

"We don't have much time," Toreum told Varlum as they shifted her from one set of arms to another. "Lay her down in the nest and make her comfortable. I'll activate the halos."

With her in his arms, Varlum stepped into the nest and sank to his knees. Georgia expected him to lay her down in the soft bedding but instead he reclined, turning himself into the bed. It almost made her laugh. They went to all this effort to make a soft place and yet here she was, lying on top of a hard Talin.

Not that she was about to complain. He might be covered in keratin plating with dense muscle underneath, but he was still warm and nice to snuggle against.

Toreum tapped on his Ident. The large room which had been well lit when they first walked in, quickly went dark. Then massive halos lit up the entire place, turning it into a field of planets and stars. Georgia sucked in a breath at the beauty of it all rendered in colorful detail. A comet slowly made its way over their head, its long tail brilliantly illuminated by the sun in the distance.

"This is beautiful," she murmured as Toreum settled down in the nest next to her and Varlum.

"It was the best way we could think of to show you what we want to promise you," Toreum explained.

"Promise?" Georgia asked, tearing her eyes away from the images overhead to gaze at Toreum. "What do you mean?"

"We travel for our work," Varlum said. She could feel his words rumbling through his chest against her back as he spoke. "We see sights like this all the time. The last assignment we had was near a system with a red dwarf. Before that, there was a dual star system. If you agree to join us, they would be your experiences too."

Georgia had guessed Vee and Tor were going to ask her to leave with them, but never imagined they'd do it in such a poetic and spectacular way. Like everyone else from Omanal, she'd been born there and never left before the Day of Fire. Unlike everyone else, she'd dreamed of travel and adventure.

"I want to say yes," she admitted. "But I'm not sure I can leave everyone behind."

"We'll return to Talarian to visit at regular intervals," Varlum assured her. "If you find you can't be separated from them, we can settle back on Talarian for good."

"But what about your work?" Georgia asked.

"We own shares in several lucrative stations," Toreum explained. "It's enough for us to live very comfortably for the rest of our lives, even on a planet as expensive as Talarian.

Varlum also has access to family money if we're ever in dire need."

"Aren't you guys required to get married and have a couple of kids?" Georgia pressed.

Toreum and Varlum exchanged a look and both of them stopped purring for a few seconds. Neither spoke for almost a minute.

"What is it?" Georgia pressed, feeling dread building in the pit of her stomach. These two had a secret they didn't want to tell her.

"We were, uh, granted special dispensation," Varlum finally answered. "Most of the successful stations in the Talin Empire have been designed and engineered by someone in our clan. The empire relies on our clan to help with expansion, so the authorities are quick to grant anyone in our clan an exemption from the marriage and child requirements."

"Are you happy about that?" Georgia asked, trying to figure out why Varlum and Toreum would hesitate to tell her this.

"We are," Toreum answered. "If we were to have a child, we would want to raise it ourselves, but that's illegal, so we'd rather have none."

Georgia had forgotten about the cresh system and the strict protocols surrounding birth and child rearing among the Talins. As much as she wanted to ask more questions to fill in her knowledge base, Toreum's use of the word *we* caught her attention.

"Are you two a couple?" she asked.

Varlum sounded the irregular beat of a confused rumble. "A couple of what?"

His question forced her to stifle a laugh. "Let me try again. Are you two romantically involved?"

They both lowered their voices to whispers when they answered in unison. "Yes."

"Why are you whispering?" she asked, her own voice hushed.

"We've scent-bonded to each other," Varlum explained. "It's forbidden and we could be condemned to death by Ending if we're found out."

Georgia sucked in a breath and moved off Varlum. He didn't try to stop her and sat up once she was clear of his body. Sitting cross legged, she faced the two of them, taking one of their hands in each of hers.

"Do you need me as a cover for your relationship?" she asked, her heart going out to these males. "I would think having a human pet would give you all kinds of excuses to always be together. I mean, we need a lot of looking after, don't we?" She said the last in a teasing tone, hoping to convey that she didn't condemn them at all.

"We don't need a cover," Toreum said with a purr. "We want a third."

"A third?" Georgia questioned, hope rising in her chest.

"We are scent-bonded and enjoy each other, but when we met you, something felt right," Varlum explained.

"We wish you to be a partner to us in all the ways that entails," Toreum added. "We know humans are sexually compatible with us. We know you're intelligent beings, and that most of the information the Committee of Pet Welfare publishes is incorrect."

"How do you know this?" Georgia demanded.

"Bazium, one of the Talins that first brought humans to Talarian, is a good friend of mine," Toreum revealed. "We grew up in the same cresh and kept in touch even after leaving. It's through Bazium that we know Hesarium. When I asked him about the humans, he divulged the truth and that he'd bonded with the human Ari. That is how much trust we have with each other."

"Does he know about you two?" Georgia asked.

"He does," Varlum assured her. "We were planning to return to our homeworld to meet the humans when we got word of Hesarium and all of you arriving here. It was a sign from the Ancestors."

"A sign from the Ancestors?" Georgia questioned.

"Yes," Toreum said with an excited rattle. "The Ancestors put us in the right place and time to meet you. Will you be our third, sweet human?"

CHAPTER 26

Rain

When Auntie walked into their suite, followed closely by Toreum and Varlum, she had a strange look on her face. She didn't look upset, but there was something serious going on. It prompted Rain to stand up and go to her before the three of them could reach the communal area where everyone was starting in on the evening meal.

"Auntie, I need your help," Rain explained, taking the woman's hand to lead her away.

"What do you need?" Toreum asked. "We can—"

Rain didn't give him a chance to finish his offer. "We'll be right back," she said, dragging Auntie away into the closest room. The moment the door slid shut behind them, she faced Auntie. "Are you okay?"

"Yes and no." Auntie let out a long breath, and Rain was shocked to see tears in her eyes.

Rain grasped both her hands. "What did they do? Are you hurt? What happened?"

"Lower your voice, Rain," Auntie requested. "No one hurt me."

"Then tell me why you're so upset," Rain demanded. "You look like you're about to cry. You never do that."

"That's not true," Auntie said with a shake of her head. "I do cry."

"Rarely," Rain countered. "What happened, Auntie?"

Auntie's tone was soft. "Tor and Vee want to give me the universe. They're in a relationship together and want me to be a third. They want to scent-bond with me and take me traveling."

Rain suspected the two Talins were interested in Auntie, but she never would've guessed the extent of their intent. "Do you want to go?"

"Yes!" Auntie confirmed, tears starting to drip from her eyes. "But I'm scared. I'm scared to leave all of you. I'm scared to fall in love. I'm scared…" her voice trailed off, heartbroken.

"You're scared of losing someone again," Rain finished for her. Auntie rarely talked about her long-dead husband, but the few times she'd spoken of him had been full of love and loss.

"I was only twenty-two and a widow," Auntie said, pulling one hand free of Rain's grasp to wipe her eyes. "It hurt more than when we lost Mom and Dad. They'd at least had long, full lives, but Danny was young and full of life. Did I ever tell you what happened?"

"I heard he got sick," Rain answered.

Auntie nodded. "Pancreatic cancer. It was horrible, Rain. It took him a year to die. He just kept getting weaker and weaker. He was so sweet. He never wanted to be a burden, but by the end, he couldn't get out of bed without help. He was always in pain, and even if we could've afforded it, there wasn't any medical help for a human on Omanal. I held his hand while he died, and it nearly broke me. He was the love of my life, and he left me."

"And you're afraid of losing Tor or Vee?" Rain guessed.

"Terrified," Auntie murmured.

"I could tell you how unlikely it is for any of these Talins to die," Rain said. "Especially two guys as successful and important to the Talin Empire as Tor and Vee. Hesarium told me they're in constant demand and have political connections everywhere. It was no accident they were here when we arrived."

That got Auntie's attention. "What?"

Rain nodded. "The only one who knew our schedule was Bazium, but somehow it got leaked to them."

"Bazium probably told them," Auntie explained. "Tor is an old friend."

"There go all my conspiracy theories," Rain said with a soft laugh. "I was working on some really good ones too. Anyway, that doesn't change the facts."

"That fact that I'm an idiot?" Auntie asked.

"The fact that you have a chance to love again," Rain argued. "These Talins are so starved for love and affection that when they bond to you, it's a soul-deep connection. I have no regrets about Hes."

"Even if you have to pretend to be his pet instead of his partner for the rest of your lives?" Auntie challenged.

Rain wasn't bothered by her harsh tone. "Even then. We're human, Auntie. We've had to compromise for generations. You and Dad always said that Omanal wasn't the best or worst choice, it was the only choice."

"Your grandmother said that," Auntie said. "She was such a smart woman. It had to be hell knowing that, when she left Earth, she'd never see any of those people ever again."

Rain sighed. "That's what I mean. Everything in the last sixty years of our history has been about survival. Grandma leaving Earth a generation before the Final Cataclysm. You and Dad growing up with such a small human population to pick partners from. Every single one of us waking up every day knowing it would be a struggle. Maybe it's time to live instead of only surviving."

"Rain's right. You should go with Tor and Vee," Cherish said from her bed, startling both Rain and Auntie.

"Cherish!" Rain squeaked, jumping a foot in the air. "What are you doing here?"

Cherish rolled her eyes. "This is my room, you podhead. You guys came in here, remember?"

Rain took a deep breath, trying to get her heartbeat under control. "You could've said something when we first walked in."

"I was asleep," Cherish said with a yawn, sitting up in her bed. "I woke up while you guys were talking. I think I heard most of it though, and I agree with Rain. You should leave with Tor and Vee, Auntie."

"You want me to leave?" Auntie asked, sounding a little hurt.

"I want you to be happy," Cherish countered. "Go out and see all the stuff we only read about. Then come back with lots of stories and gifts. Maybe someday I'll pick a Talin who'll take me on adventures. Or there might be a guy with the humans on Talarian I'll fall in love with and get married to, or whatever. I could have a kid. There are so many possibilities we didn't have even a month ago. So yeah, I say go. Come back if you miss us, but I don't want to be the reason you stay behind."

Rain felt a little shocked at Cherish's speech, the thirteen-year-old sounded far older than her years. She also pushed Rain to say something she'd thought, but never voiced.

"We were never going to make it," Rain murmured, feeling a burden fall from her shoulders. "Even in the beginning, when our grandparents first got to Omanal, the colony was never going to be sustainable."

Auntie made a soft, sad sound. "Grandma always planned for a second and third wave of settlers to join us, but there was only ever the first group. She knew there weren't enough of us to keep the place going for more than a few generations. No one ever said anything because there was always the hope that a bunch of humans would magically find us and we'd have all the help and fresh people we needed."

"It was never going to happen," Rain said, realizing she'd had that magical thinking to a degree also. Even though she'd been grim about their future, she'd also thought that something would come along and solve all their problems.

"The Omanal humans have been lying to ourselves from the beginning."

"Yeah," Cherish agreed. "I heard Gris and Devon talking about it after Ruth was born, but I was too young to really understand what they meant until years later. Then, randomly that conversation popped into my head, and I couldn't stop thinking about it. The whole dying out thing kept circling in my brain, and then everything kept getting worse. No one wanted to talk about it, they just wanted to pretend everything was fine." Cherish's expression turned angry briefly, then dissolved into sadness. "It was frustrating, and I wanted to start screaming at everyone. We didn't have a future, and no one would admit it!"

Her heart breaking for her sibling, Rain hurried to Cherish's side. Sitting on the bed next to her, she wrapped an arm around the girl and hugged her tight. Auntie sat on the other side, making sounds of sympathy.

"We have a future now," Cherish continued, tears streaming down her face. "It's not a perfect future, but it's better than anything we could've done by ourselves. Do I care that we're owned by Hes? Yes, but not as much as I cared when we lost Mom and Dad, or Mia's parents, or Devon's baby, or all the other people who died and didn't have to."

All three of them were crying now.

"I'm scared," Auntie whispered.

"Well, I'm not," Cherish declared, sniffing back her tears and straightening her spine. "I'm not afraid or angry anymore, and you shouldn't be either."

"I'll try," Auntie whispered.

They must have been in the room a little too long because Hes, Vee, and Tor all came in to check on them. There was a flurry of activity when they found the three of them hugging and crying. Thankfully it was quick work to calm the Talins, and soon they were all sitting down for the evening meal.

Surveying the happy faces, Rain wanted to start crying again but only for the best reasons.

CHAPTER 27

Hesarium

With access to their own room in a large, well-appointed suite, Hesarium expected it would be easier to have time alone with Rain. He was wrong.

Life on the station was without days full of intense physical labor and looming violence, leaving the humans with far more free time then they'd ever experienced before. To Hesarium's dismay, it seemed that most of the humans wanted to spend their free time with Rain!

People were constantly visiting their suite or inviting Rain, Auntie, and the siblings to spend time in their suites. At first, Hesarium assumed this constant visiting would die down, but these were humans, not Talins. Spending time with each other wasn't a social or political obligation to them, it was a joy.

Even during their normal rest cycle, privacy wasn't guaranteed. There'd been numerous instances where humans had dropped by the suite at random times to visit. Hesarium had finally realized that the lack of natural day/night indicators was causing the humans to keep odd and inconsistent sleep patterns.

All of it meant that Hesarium was desperate to have a stretch of alone time with Rain. Not only to engage in intimate activities, but to simply hold and cuddle her without the risk of interruption.

Once they boarded the monarch's ship to travel to Talarian, the lack of privacy might get worse. Desperate to take advantage of the last few days they had on Falsof Station, Hesarium requested Toreum's help to make arrangements. The Talin hadn't hesitated, and now all Hesarium needed was Auntie's assistance.

"Vee said you needed to talk to me?" Auntie said. At her back, Vee wrapped his arms loosely around her shoulders and sounded a soft comforting rumble.

"I'm going to sequester Rain away for half a rotation," Hesarium explained. "Barring a true emergency, I'm not going to let anyone disturb us. To do this, I need you to take her place for that time period. Can you please keep the other humans content while she's gone?"

Hesarium didn't understand why his request was met by laughter. Auntie's boisterous humor filled the room for several submarks before she quieted enough to talk.

"Feeling a little needy?" she asked. "You were really patient when Iris and Mia visited last night, but I could tell they'd interrupted you two. And before that it was Gris, Devon, and their kids coming over to show us the new game they'd been gifted."

Now he could see the source of Auntie's amusement. She'd noticed the lack of privacy early on. She'd probably known this would happen.

"Yes, all their visits were ill timed," he said with an annoyed rattle. "I don't require you to remind me."

Varlum was quick with a warning rattle. "Do not make that kind of sound at Georgia," he growled.

She patted him on the arm soothingly. "It's fine, Vee." Then she looked back at him and smiled. "I'll make sure everyone knows Rain isn't available for a while. My only stipulation is that you answer if Vee or Tor try to contact you. I promise I'll only do that if it's a real emergency."

Hesarium sounded a rattle of agreement. "Yes, of course," he agreed.

"Rain is with Zuri and Kasium," Auntie told him. "If everything goes well, I guess I'll see you two tomorrow."

Hesarium sounded a happy, comforting rumble at Auntie's words. "I have one last request to make."

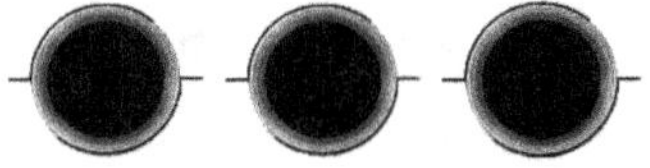

Hesarium

Worry and anticipation hit Hesarium in equal measures as he led Rain into the solarium. Most stations had a solarium set up to mimic Talarian as a way for those working far away from their homeworld to stay connected to the heart of the empire. This particular solarium was in the old style where every surface, even most of the ceiling, was covered in plants. Newer stations imported stone and wood to create a more nuanced environment.

"Oh, wow!" Rain breathed, stopping only a stride into the solarium to take in the green space. Many of the plants were of the flowering variety, so delicate perfumes permeated the air. The room was also kept warmer and more humid than the rest of the station, to better mimic Talarian.

"Do you like it?" Hesarium asked, a wave of anxiety hitting him. He'd thought she'd find the large space full of plants comforting, a vague reminder of Omanal, but now he worried it might be too much. Except for some of the plants being the same green and gray as the seedpod plants, there were no other similarities between this room and the planet Rain grew up on.

"It's beautiful!" Rain assured him, stepping farther down the path, her eyes jumping from spot to spot. "I've never seen so many different types of plants in one place before."

"These are all native to my homeworld," he explained proudly. "Everything here is safe for you to touch but not to eat.

"Don't worry, I'm not an entict," she answered with a chuckle. "I'm not interested in grazing on the greenery."

"I didn't think you would," he assured her, following at a sedate pace as she made her way deeper into the room.

The door behind him slid shut, cutting off the bustling sounds of the station.

"Tell me about this place," Rain demanded, turning around and holding out her hand. Before he could take it, she withdrew and looked around. "Oh, um, maybe we shouldn't hold hands out here in public. Or can we? Sometimes I'm not sure what your species would see as bad or inappropriate. You should make a list. It would be helpful for Auntie and Zuri too."

Rumbling out a comforting sound, Hesarium reached down and wrapped his hand around hers. "There's no one in here, we don't have to worry about being seen by others."

"This place is empty?" Rain asked, looking around. Many of the massive pots had trees growing out of them, making it hard to see all the paths weaving through the green space. "That's lucky then."

"It's not luck. It's deliberate," Hesarium told her. "The solarium is ours alone for the next ten marks."

Instead of looking pleased, Rain's brows knitted in confusion. "Ten marks? That's a long time to wander around a garden. I mean, it's a nice garden, but still."

Sounding a soothing rumble, Hesarium led her down one of the paths. A pattern that simulated cobble stone had been etched in the metal under their feet. Neither the color nor the sound of his boots ringing every time he stepped down did much to create a realistic illusion of a stone path, but it was still nicer than boring metal plating.

Soon they were in the center of the solarium. A round area devoid of plants was ringed with backless benches. It wasn't uncommon for Talins to conduct informal meetings in this space, but when they occupied it, there probably wasn't a nest of pillows and blankets taking up the ground in the center.

"What's going on?" Rain asked with a laugh.

"I arranged for us to have time to ourselves," he explained. "I'm not sure what life on the trip back to Talarian will be like, and the first few days there will probably be busy. I decided we needed to steal a few marks to ourselves while we could."

Rain took in the bed, then looked around the room. "What if someone walks in?"

Hesarium tapped his Ident. "I was given the power to lock the doors for the next rotation. They can only be opened by Danisal or someone of equal or higher rank. The display on the door will inform anyone looking for access that the space is being serviced."

"That must have taken some effort," Rain said, turning to face him. Pulling her hand free of his, she wrapped her arms around his waist and clutched him. "I adore you, Hes!"

Elation filled him at Rain's positive response to his effort. "I was worried you'd be upset by my deceit."

"It's not really deceit," Rain said as she drew away from the hug to turn back to the nest. "It's more like a romantic surprise."

"Would you like to walk around more?" Hesarium asked.

"Maybe later," Rain said, tugging him toward the nest. "You're not the only one who's missing something!"

He paused at the edge of the nest to pull off his Ident and verify the doors to the solarium were locked; then he dropped the Ident to the floor near the nest and reached for his belt.

"Wait," Rain said, facing him. "I want to undress you."

"As you like," Hesarium agreed, his mating shaft already starting to fit tightly in his flesh pouch at the thought of Rain touching him.

She didn't reach for his belt. Instead, she placed her palms high on his chest and slowly ran her hands down his front. The simple touch left a trail of fire on his body, and he was forced to curl his hands into fists.

"Your touch feels good," he said, then cursed himself for using such mundane language. *Good?* That word didn't even begin to cover what she was doing to him! He tried to think of other words, but when her hands unlatched his belt, his ability to think plummeted.

Anticipation of her touch made him waver on his feet a little as her delicate human fingers slid under the waistband of his pants. With deliberately slow movements, she eased the pants over his hips and down his legs, running her fingers over his flesh as she went.

By the time he was kicking his pants out of the way, his mating shaft was straining against his flesh pouch. Rain stared at his groin and licked her lips. Her fingertips danced across the seam of the flesh pouch, then dipped inside.

"I love the feel of this," she murmured. "It's almost like you have a pussy. Like you're both, and as you get turned on, you go from female to male."

Her touch was too distracting for Hesarium to work out what she was saying. All that mattered was the feel of her fingers caressing him. Her finger dipped lower into his flesh pouch, rubbing against the sensitive, unprotected skin.

Moaning filled his ears. It wasn't until he heard Rain make a soft, happy sound that he realized he was the one moaning. That woke him up enough to think of Rain's pleasure.

"You should be naked also," he insisted.

"I will be," she promised, then removed her hand from his pouch. "If you lie down, I could touch you more."

Hesarium might never have moved faster than in that moment as he dove into the bed of pillows and blankets. He rolled over on his back and looked up at her, his rumble slow and sensual. Blood drained from his mating shaft due to the movement, but he was sure it would return rapidly once Rain was touching him again.

Smiling, Rain toed off her slippers and pulled her underwear off from under her wrap. To his disappointment, she didn't remove her wrap before kneeling down next to his supine form. She gazed at him for a minute before changing her position. Throwing one leg over him, she straddled his thighs and sat. Her warm weight made him rumble even louder. Unable to stop himself, he reached down and placed his hands on her knees, pushing the wrap up to mid-thigh.

"You're so beautiful, sweet human," he murmured, his mouth watering at the thought of getting to lick her again. "If you moved up, I could lick the nectar from between your legs."

"I'm not sitting on your face, Hes," she answered with a shake of her head, but he could tell she was intrigued. "Well, maybe later," she amended.

"Any time," he promised, his tone eager. He wanted to take her by the hips and lift her to his face right then, but his human wanted to play with his body—he would display his stellian and let her.

She went back to running her fingers across the seam of his flesh pouch and, very quickly, his mating shaft was engorged enough to allow her to slip her fingers back inside.

With each pass, she pressed her fingers deeper and deeper into his flesh pouch, rubbing against his mating shaft and skin. His sexual rumbling got stronger as his mating shaft thickened.

"Close," he warned with a little gasp. Her clever fingers were rubbing right on the sensitive tip of his mating shaft. It was the most delicious torture he'd ever endured.

There was a slap of flesh against flesh as his flesh pouch fully retracted, revealing his mating shaft and seed sac. By now his scent glands were weeping oil down his face, soaking the pillow under his head.

"Nice," Rain breathed, hunching over and licking the tip of his throbbing shaft.

"Rain!" he cried out, his hips moving slightly with the need to thrust forward. He would never force his mating shaft into her mouth, but any touch right now felt overwhelming.

"I was going to give you a blowjob," Rain murmured, her warm breath wafting across his heated flesh. "But I don't think I have the patience."

"You can blow your breath on me if you like," he urged, unsure why that would please her. Maybe it was something human males liked.

"A blowjob means I put you in my mouth," she said with a huffing laugh. "Let me demonstrate."

Before he had a chance to say anything, she grasped hold of his mating shaft and fit her lips around the end. He was far too large to fit entirely in her delicate human mouth, but when she sucked on the head of his shaft, he realized it didn't matter.

He cried out as a wave of lust rolled over him and he nearly released. "Rain!"

Her hand tightened around him, and she drew her mouth off, scraping her flat teeth delicately across the very tip. "You can perform a blowjob any time you like," he panted, his body rigid with need.

"I will," she promised, letting go of him as she sat up. "But I really need your vibrating cock inside me right now."

Reaching down, she grabbed hold of her wrap and pulled it off over her head. It bunched under her breasts, and with a frustrated sound, she tugged harder. Hesarium heard something rip and she was finally able to pull the garment completely off.

Tossing it aside, she rose up and knee-walked up his body until her hot core was poised over his needy shaft. The temptation to keep his hands on her was too great, but he feared he might press her body down if he did. Lifting his hands off her legs, he tossed them to the sides and dug his claws into the bedding with a growl.

With one hand on his shaft, she had him where she wanted him, slotting the tip of his shaft against her hot core. Her sex was dripping with slick and the sweet smell of it invaded his nose. His only regret was that he hadn't had a chance to rub his bonding oil all over her first. The smell of the two of them when mixed became a powerful aphrodisiac.

"How do I keep forgetting how big you are?" Rain whispered as she wiggled her hips, seating his tip into her entrance but not sinking onto him any further. He should be telling her there were other ways he could pleasure her. That if she lay back, he could use his mouth and hands on her.

The problem was, all ability to use spoken language had fled the moment she'd wrapped her hand around him. The best he could do was moan.

Closing her eyes and throwing her head back, Rain let go of his shaft and sank down agonizingly unhurried. He hadn't realized time could slow down until he watched her lower herself onto him at glacial pace. Her tight sheath slowly enveloped him, driving out all rational thought until he was nothing but need and sensation.

"Yeah, like that! Keep rumbling like that," Rain moaned once he was fully sheathed inside her. Her words spurred him to push out a stronger sexual rumble. He could feel the rumble causing his mating shaft to move inside her as she ground her pelvis down hard against him.

"Don't stop!" she demanded, her movements becoming more frantic. She was grinding herself so hard against him, he worried she might hurt herself.

Concern helped him focus enough to bring his hand back to her hips. He thought to gently calm her movements by gripping her thighs as before. The moment he touched her legs she grabbed his hands with hers and slapped them onto her breasts, never once breaking her rhythm.

"Touch me here," she ordered, her eyes slitted in pleasure.

All his good intentions disappeared as he squeezed and kneaded her soft, voluptuous breasts. Her movements were getting more frantic now, and both of them were moaning and gasping.

The pressure of an oncoming orgasm made his spine stiffen and arch. He opened his mouth to warn her, but he couldn't form words, only deep sounds of pleasure. He was reduced to nothing but his most basic needs.

Suddenly Rain's body went stiff, her back bowing. Her sex convulsed around him as she cried out with pleasure. He couldn't hold back while her body was squeezing his shaft. With a roar, he climaxed, filling her with his seed. Pleasure coursed through his body, making every part of him feel strangely fevered and chilled at the same time.

For a timeless moment, they remained still, drowning in a moment of carnal perfection. Then Rain slowly collapsed forward with a dazed expression.

"Rain?" Hesarium croaked, his voice hoarse from his earlier cries.

"I'm good," she mumbled, stretching out on top of him. She nuzzled his cheek, putting her mouth over his scent gland and giving him a lip press. "Really good."

He had to work at making his brain function as the climax kept ricocheting through his body. "Do you need care, my sweet human?"

"I'm good," she repeated, snuggling on top of him. She seemed content for his mating shaft to remain buried inside of her, and in truth, he was too.

"We have many marks before we need to leave," he reminded her as he wrapped his arms around her back and shifted his rumble from sensual to comfort. "I'm your most willing bed."

It was a long time before either of them moved. Later, when they were back in the suite and Auntie asked Rain about the solarium, she smiled mischievously.

"It was good."

CHAPTER 28

Rain

Rain was suspicious.

It had been a normal day, then things started happening. First Hesarium was called away. Then Danisal took her break to get some sleep and check the charges on her weapons, which wasn't weird at all, but all the guards were called to guard one position. When Rain asked, none of them knew why. She'd suggested they contact Danisal, but the guards had acted like she was a cute child and sent her back to her room.

There'd only been a few times in her life Rain felt this uneasy and each one proved her intuition was correct. All of that meant when a klaxon sounded throughout their section, Rain knew it was a false alarm.

"We must evacuate," Vee announced, rushing out of the room he, Tor, and Auntie had been sharing for the last few days. Behind him, Tor had Auntie in his arms, holding her securely to his chest while sounding a loud purr.

"Fear not, Georgia. We'll get you to safety," Tor assured her.

"Don't worry about me, get the kids!" Auntie protested. Vee and Tor shared a look then spoke at once.

"I'll see to Georgia," Tor said.

"I'll care for the pups," Vee announced at the same time. They both sounded a rattle of agreement and shot off in different directions. Tor headed out the door, carrying an upset Auntie, while Vee started opening the doors to Cherish and Wind's rooms and ordering everyone to dress warmly and come with him. Sunny and Tolvern were sitting on chairs in the living room talking when all this happened, with Royal sitting in Tolvern's lap playing a game on an information square.

"I can see to Sunshine and Royal's safety," Tolvern promised as he stood with Royal held on his hip and hugging his free arm around Sunny.

"Rain, come along," Vee urged as he guided a sleepy Wind and annoyed Cherish out the suite door.

"I'm right behind you," she lied. Cherish was asking a lot of questions and Royal was starting to cry.

The cacophony of humans talking, Talins purring, and the klaxon's shrill warning made it hard to hear any individual voice. As everyone filed out, Rain took a good look at the hall full of confused humans and concerned Talins escorting them. She didn't see Iris or Mia anywhere among them.

Determined to find the two, she headed in the opposite direction as everyone else. A sense of urgency pushed her into a run.

Iris and Mia had ended up in the last suite around the corner, mostly because it was the only suite with a large observation window. Mia could be fussy at night and the window delighted her, meaning no one argued over those two getting the special room. Not that too many of the humans had been eager to have a room with a giant window showing them the cold depths of space. It was a little much for a group that had little or no interaction with space faring before.

Rain was almost to Iris and Mia's door when it slid open and two Talins came out carrying Mia and Iris. Both humans had their eyes closed and were limp. Outrage and fear filled Rain in equal measure.

"Vee! Tor!" she shouted as she ran at the Talins. "Iris and Mia are being kidnapped! They're–"

She didn't get a chance to finish. The Talin carrying Mia tossed the little girl to the other one. "Take the child!" he said as he reached for Rain.

Belatedly, Rain realized that she was an idiot. No one was going to hear her. Why had she run at the abductors instead of away? What was she going to do, take on two fully grown Talins by herself with no weapons?

Stopping mid-step and trying to turn at the same time put Rain in a half-splits position that forced her to fall to the floor to recover. Before she could even sit up, strong hands were grabbing and lifting her into the air. She was unceremoniously thrown over a shoulder.

"Do you think this one's a male?" the Talin holding her asked as he and the other one started jogging down the hall.

"Help!" Rain screamed. She couldn't see anyone in the corridor around them, but there wasn't much else she could do. Slamming her hand down on the Talin's armored back got her nothing but bruises and scrapes on her fist. "Heeeellllpppp!"

"Quiet!" the other Talin growled. He took a step back so she could see his face. "We only need these two, you're extra. If you cause too much trouble, I'll shove you in a disposal unit or airlock."

Ending up dead would be a major disadvantage, so Rain snapped her mouth closed and focused on memorizing the path they were taking. It wasn't surprising the kidnappers stuck to narrow hallways that looked like they were for accessing systems on the station instead of general foot traffic.

It wasn't long before Rain was hopelessly lost. All the hallways looked the same to begin with, but hanging upside down and struggling to hold her head up made it even harder to remember the path. She was also worried about vomiting down the Talin's back. His shoulder was digging into her belly, making it hard to breathe. Fear and discomfort made the snack she'd eaten earlier want to come back up. Would throwing up make him carry through with his threat?

"Wha…"

It took some effort, but Rain was able to twist her body enough to see Iris. She was coming awake but looked groggy and confused. "Rain?"

Iris had a notorious temper and unleashing it on these Talins might get her hurt. "Stay calm, Iris."

"Why is the larger one waking?" the Talin holding Rain asked with an angry rattle.

"I was worried about giving them too much," the one holding Iris and Mia explained. "I might have administered too little sedative."

They both stopped and the one holding Rain turned to face his partner. This deprived her of seeing what was happening. No amount of twisting or lifting gave her a view, but she could hear Iris cussing with perfect clarity.

"Stop thrashing!" one of the Talins growled before Iris cried out and went silent.

"Let me at least check Mia," Iris said in a subdued tone.

"No time," one of them said and then they were moving again. With the two Talins jogging side by side, Rain was able to see Iris. Their gazes met and Rain saw death in her friend's eyes.

No words needed to be spoken between them. Talins might see humans as weak and simple, but none of them knew what humans were truly capable of.

They were carried into a dimly lit room and almost simultaneously dumped on a haphazard pile of pillows and blankets. Iris was quick to grab Mia and cradle the small girl in her lap.

"You stay with them. I'll fetch the buyer," one of them said before leaving the room.

"Remain in your nest," the remaining Talin ordered with a harsh rattle. "You can rest until your new owner gets here. Don't make me punish either of you."

Rain and Iris remained silent as the Talin unclipped his Ident and sat down in a nearby chair. He was soon focused on reading something on the Ident, all but ignoring them.

"I think she's fine," Iris whispered. "Why did they take us?"

"I think they meant to only steal you and Mia," Rain told her. "I was worried because I couldn't find you guys and went looking. I found them carrying you two out of your room."

Iris shook her head. "Let me guess, you charged in instead of running for help."

Rain felt her face heat with embarrassment. "Maybe."

"So no one knows we're missing?" Iris asked.

"By now they've probably noticed," Rain assured her. "The good news is we're on a station. There can't be that many hiding places here, right?"

Iris shot her an annoyed look. "Rain, there are hundreds of ships docked here. They could slip us onto one of them and we'd be gone before they even searched half the station."

Rain cursed under her breath. Waiting for rescue might be the easy plan, but it wasn't going to save them. "What do you think we should do?"

"See that cylinder on the wall?" Iris asked, gazing past Rain's shoulder. Looking in the same direction, Rain saw a dark gray, two-foot-long cylinder that was about as thick as her forearm. "That's a systems monitor. They're only installed on walls on the very outside of the station. If we pull at it hard enough, the station engineers will want to figure out why it's going haywire. They'll probably get here fast to see if there are any structural issues going on."

"How do you know that?" Rain asked, looking back at Iris.

"There's one in our room," Iris said, her eyes lowering to look at the sleeping Mia. "The Talin who showed us the room repeatedly told me not to touch it and to keep

Mia away. Even with all that, he had an engineer come in and mount a box around it so we couldn't bump it by accident."

They couldn't know for certain if the cylinder was that sensitive or if the Talins were simply being overly cautious. Either way, it was the best plan they had at the moment.

Rain rolled her eyes to the seated Talin. "How do we distract him?"

"I could make him angry again," Iris offered, rubbing her shoulder. That was where she must have gotten hit before.

"Let's try something else besides you getting beat on," Rain responded.

Iris gave her an annoyed look. "I'm so sorry I was willing to sacrifice myself for you."

Rain rolled her eyes at Iris's snark. "I'm going to try something. When you get a chance, go for the cylinder. If it doesn't work, then we'll try something else."

"If you get a chance, stab him," Iris requested, eyes gleaming with malice.

Rain ignored her. Training her features into what she hoped was an expression of subservience, she called out. "Sir? I need to use the elimination room. Sir?"

Rattling with annoyance, the Talin met her eyes. "Can't you do anything yourself?"

"You told me not to move from here." she reminded him, lowering her eyes to his feet. "I didn't want to do anything wrong."

The Talin let out a long suffering sigh. "Go on, you can use it."

Rain pretended to look around the room with confusion. "Where is it, sir? I don't see it."

"Your species is even more stupid than I thought." Standing up, he went to the door and pressed the control panel. The moment his back was turned, both women moved—Iris to the cylinder and Rain to the Talin.

"You're magic, sir!" Rain cried out, distracting the Talin by getting close and grabbing the hand that had pressed on the control panel with both of hers. "You made the wall disappear."

To face her, he had to keep his back to Iris. This was working better than she expected.

"I'm not magic," he scoffed, but didn't pull his hand away from her grasp. "It's simply how these rooms work. Can't you open the door in your suite?"

"No, sir," Rain responded, petting his hand. "The door disappears, and we can't get it to open again."

"Your hand is very soft," he said with a purring rumble. "Is the rest of you that soft?"

"I don't know, sir. It all feels the same to me," Rain answered and had to work hard to keep from flinching when he reached up to touch her face.

"You're such a helpless species," he murmured, running a finger down her face. "But I see you can be respectful. I wouldn't squander my wealth on one of you, but I might be tempted if I was wealthier. I read that your kind needs to clutch and cling to each other to feel safe. Is that true?"

"Very often," Rain answered. More and more, she wanted to get away from him. Then she saw Iris back in their nest of pillows and blankets, freeing her from continuing the interaction. "I still need to use the elimination room, sir. Can you use your magic and close the door for me when I'm inside?"

He stopped purring and dropped his hand to her shoulder. With an impatient rattle, he roughly pushed her into the room.

"Hurry up," he ordered. "When you're finished in there, I'll let you clutch and cling to me."

The door slid shut and Rain did a quick check of the room. As with all the other elimination rooms, there was little there and nothing that could be used as a weapon. It was a good thing she didn't need to use the room because the door slid open way too quickly.

"You're done. Good," the Talin said and stepped into the small space. She didn't expect him to pick her up and carry her out.

Going still and stiff, she was able to cast her eyes around the room as he carried her to the chair. The cylinder looked exactly the same and she moved her eyes to Iris. The woman gave her a slight shrug. Maybe the thing wasn't so delicate after all.

Damn, now they needed a new plan.

CHAPTER 29

Rain

Settling back down on the chair, the Talin sat her on his lap. "Now you can clutch and cling," he announced. Rain hesitated, unsure if she wanted to get any closer to the guy. He smelled like bleach to her and being this close was already giving her a headache.

"Like this," he said, grabbing her wrists and pulling her arms around his neck. Biting her tongue, Rain leaned in close and hugged him. Bile rose up in her throat. He smelled disgusting.

"There now, don't you feel more secure?" he asked. He was running one of his hands up and down her back, but it was too rough to be a caress. "Perhaps you should be naked. It is probably better for clutching and clinging."

"No, sir," Rain got out between clenched teeth. She did not want to take her clothes off! "This is perfect, and I'd have to let go to disrobe."

Before the Talin could insist, the door to the room slid open. Pulling her arms free from around his neck, she turned in his lap to see who'd arrived. Her hopes for rescue were dashed when she saw the other kidnapper and the familiar face of Palathum.

"I'm so impressed, Umoran and Yufreum. You two have managed to acquire three!" Palathum said with a happy rumble, taking in Rain, then dropping her gaze to the pile of blankets and pillows in the center of the room.

She hurried to the nest where Iris had moved herself in front of Mia. "Hello, Iris. Don't worry, I won't wake up little Mia. I have your room on my ship ready. It's full of toys and piles of the softest pillows and blankets available."

There was a moment of silence before Iris slid her eyes over to Rain. It looked like Iris wasn't sure what to say either. Did it matter to Palathum that they weren't here of their free will or, more egregious for an average Talin, that they'd been stolen from their rightful owner?

"What about me?" Rain asked, testing the waters.

"Of course you can come with your friends. If you can bear to be parted from Yufreum," Palathum stated, settling on her knees in front of Iris. Yufreum must be the Talin holding her. That meant Umoran was the name of the other Talin. Rain needed to remember those names in case they got a chance to bring these men to justice.

"I can be parted," Rain was quick to tell her, making Yufreum rattle with surprise.

Palathum sounded a pleased rumble. "You can stay in the same room with Iris and Mia, or I can outfit a room of your own. I would have bought all the humans so Mia would have plenty of company, but Hesarium refused all my offers."

"I'm keeping this one," Yufreum declared, wrapping his arms around Rain and hugging her to his chest. The air rushed out of her as he squeezed. "She wasn't part of the bargain so she's mine now."

Gasping, she tapped at his arm. "Can't breathe!"

He eased his grip but didn't let go of her. She sucked in a big breath of air then regretted it when the smell of bleach made her want to gag.

"You want to keep one?" Umoran asked. "I thought you said they're disgusting?"

"I said they're dumb, not disgusting," Yufreum corrected. "They're complete imbeciles, but pets aren't meant to be intelligent."

"Perhaps it would be best if I took her as well," Palathum said, sounding a concerned rumble. "She looks like she might be ill, and I have a healer on staff on my ship. I'll give you a third again as much as we agreed on to include this human."

Mia made a little sound and moved in her sleep. Palathum looked down and started purring. Her fingers were opening and closing on the pillow she was holding, as if she was fighting the urge to touch Iris or Mia. She spoke without looking away from the little girl. "You'll have the funds within two marks."

Umoran stepped closer to Palathum, sounding an angry buzzing rattle. "You owe us more than wealth. We want the position of power you promised."

Standing up, Yufreum set Rain down on the chair with a rough thump. "Stay here, human." Without waiting for her to respond, he moved to stand next to Umoran.

"I want a seat on the Apogee Assembly," Yufreum demanded.

Palathum stopped purring and stood up to face Umoran and Yufreum. "I can't simply give someone a position in the Apogee Assembly. As I told you before, all I can do is declare you my candidate of choice during the next clan selection. That will go a long way in gaining you support from the other families in our clan."

"What if I don't win?" Yufreum asked. "You are the wealthiest member of our clan and your mother is the current Clan Leader. Push a vote of no confidence for the current Apogee Assembly member and have her name me as successor."

A startled rattle came out of Palathum. "She wouldn't do that. Her reluctance to elect anyone who's been a member of the War Council is well known."

"I've heard she owes you a large debt, use that to force her hand," Umoran suggested.

Palathum went silent for a moment and Rain got the impression the woman was shocked at Umoran's words. "What you're asking me to do is reprehensible."

"You'll give us what we want," Yufreum declared, his quills starting to straighten away from his forearm. "We committed a crime on your behalf!"

Palathum let loose with a single hard clap of a challenging rattle. "Crime? What Crime?"

"Getting these humans for you," Umoran said, pointing to Iris and Mia.

Palathum sounded a rattle of surprise. "When I couldn't persuade Hesarium to sell me any of his humans, I thought you would have a better chance. I've been told there is comradery among those who've served in the military. Are you telling me he refused you also?"

"Of course he did," Umoran scoffed. "Why would he sell to us if he wouldn't sell to you?"

Palathum looked over her shoulder at Iris. "Did they steal you, Iris human?"

"Yes," Iris said with relish. "They broke into our room and drugged us."

"They faked some kind of emergency," Rain added, getting off the chair and moving closer to the group of Talins. "I saw them carrying Mia and Iris and tried to stop them. They–"

Rain wasn't prepared for Umoran's hand to fly out and strike her across the face. With a cry of surprise, she fell hard to the floor. It all happened so fast it took a moment for the pain to catch up, but when it did, tears formed in Rain's eyes. Her face was throbbing and she could taste blood in her mouth.

"Rain!" Iris cried out.

She'd fallen right next to the nest. Gentle hands on her shoulders guided her back until she was sitting next to Mia. Iris examined her face and winced, telling Rain it looked as bad as it felt.

"I think I'm okay," Rain offered, but her words were slurred because her lips were having a hard time moving. At least her brain didn't feel rattled, so no concussion.

The sound of scuffling made both women look up to see the three Talins fighting. Palathum had put herself between the humans and their kidnappers. Even though she was outnumbered, she was doing a good job at holding both the men off.

"How dare you strike the Rain human!" Palathum raged, swiping at Umoran with her claws while avoiding a strike by Yufreum. "I'll see you punished. You'll both be declared dishonored by your families and dismissed from your clan!"

"You're the one who's not fulfilling your promises," Umoran shouted. "We have plans for this empire, and we can't do anything until we're in the Apogee Assembly. You promised us that seat!"

"You're both sycophantic, power-hungry males!" Palathum taunted them. "Neither of you deserve to be called Talins! There will be no ancestors to greet you at the Domicile of Souls!"

That must've been one hell of an insult because both Umoran and Yufreum filled the room with enraged rattles. They attacked Palathum at the same time, and although she was managing to hold up under their onslaught, Rain could see she wasn't going to last long. She refused to move away from her spot in front of the nest. Without the ability to move around, it was only a matter of time before the men got the upper hand.

"I'm not letting this happen," Iris muttered darkly and scrambled to her feet.

Rain tried to get to her feet to follow "Iris?"

Iris didn't answer, she was too busy rushing around the battling Talins and out the door. It was the perfect opportunity to escape. No one noticed what was going on until the door was sliding shut behind her.

"Find help!" Palathum managed to shout out before the door was finished closing.

"I'll deal with Palathum, you get the human!" Yufreum ordered. Umoran didn't hesitate to obey and rushed out the door after Iris. Rain was scared for her friend. Iris didn't have much of a head start and Umoran would be running full out to catch up to her. Unless there was help nearby, Iris was in danger of being seriously injured or even killed when Umoran caught up with her!

Rain focused her attention on the battling Talins in front of her. With one opponent gone, Palathum forced Yufreum back several steps. If Rain helped, Palathum could win the battle against this male and then she could run to help Iris.

Getting to her feet was harder than Rain expected, and she felt wobbly and sick to her stomach. Her eyes were watering, making it even harder to see. It took some effort, but Rain managed to pick up the only chair in the room and hurl it at Yufreum. The chair was light and the throw was weak, but hurting him wasn't her aim. She wanted to cause a distraction.

The chair impacted Yufreum with a sad little clink and cluttered harmlessly to the floor. Turning to face Rain, Yufreum roared and swiped at her with his claws. She'd been ready for that and simply gave into gravity, falling heavily backward. It was hard on her ass but saved her face from getting clawed.

Rain's tactic worked and Palathum used the distraction to tackle Yufreum to the floor. The room filled with her deafening war rattle as she grabbed hold of one of his neck plates and ripped it back. Yufreum screamed with pain as the plate was almost completely detached. He tried to buck her off, but Palathum was quick to shove her claws into the vulnerable skin no longer protected by the plate. Yufreum's scream turned to a whimper and his body went limp.

The moment he went still, Palathum was up and running out the door after Iris and Umoran. Rain sat on her aching ass, the room eerily silent around her. She refused to look at Yufreum.

"Rain?" Mia's scared voice gave her something to focus on.

"Hi, bug," Rain murmured, crawling over to the nest. Mia was sitting up and looking around, obviously confused.

"What happened to your face?" Mia asked, tears welling in her eyes. "Where are we? Why is it so cold? My head hurts."

Whatever drug they'd given the little girl was having some side effects. Drawing Mia into her lap, Rain did her best to wrap a blanket around them both. She briefly thought about trying to get them out of the room. No, bad idea. She probably wouldn't make it very far and she couldn't send Mia out to wander the halls alone.

The blanket around Mia helped shield the little girl from seeing Yufreum take his last breaths. Rain wasn't an expert on Talin anatomy, but she knew the sound of someone dying when she heard it.

Rain didn't answer Mia's questions; her face hurt too much. Instead, she hummed to the little girl and hoped help would arrive soon.

CHAPTER 30

Hesarium

The moment Miehlum told him there'd been no request for his presence, Hesarium knew it'd been part of a bigger plan. He didn't stay to talk or find out how a false request had been doctored to look real. Turning on his heels, he sprinted back to the jadik section.

As he got closer, he heard the sound of klaxons and human voices. Soon he could see that Danisal had gathered everyone near an area designated for evacuation. If the station was truly in danger, the large doors beyond them would open and give them access to the escape ships beyond.

It only took one sweep of the noisy group for Hesarium to see Rain was missing.

"Danisal, where is Rain?" he shouted at the warrior.

She turned to gaze at him then surveyed the group. "She must have been left behind," Danisal called back. "She was right behind us. Check the room. I'll put a notice in with the station."

Hesarium already knew he'd find the entire suite empty but ran there anyway. The door was open and there was no sign of Rain. He stood in the doorway for a moment, thinking. This had to be a plot to steal Rain. The thieves probably hadn't targeted his human specifically but set out to grab the most convenient one, and Rain was the unlucky individual.

Moving back into the hall, he looked up and down the corridor before unclipping his Ident and pulling up a map of the station. At first, he didn't see a second way to gain access to the jadik sector until he switched to a maintenance overlay. Narrow hallways started not far from the room Mia and Iris were using.

It was then that he realized he hadn't seen either of them in the group. Had all three been taken?

Worry and anger made his back plates smack down with a combination of a war rattle and a buzzing rattle of anger. Ident still in his hand, he ran for the maintenance corridors, not at all surprised to find the door wide open despite standard procedure.

Unlike the rest of the station with numerous signs and markers to indicate location and the direction of various parts of the station, the maintenance corridors were bare. At every intersection he was forced to stop and check the cube. The place was a warren of dead ends and poorly lit areas. There were a few spots so narrow it was difficult for him to squeeze through. He had to backtrack several times, all the while listening for the distinct sound of a human voice.

The last thing he expected was to turn a corner and find Iris holding Mia. Mia's eyes were half closed, and as he watched, she drifted off then roused herself only to drift off again. It was odd to see the active little girl unsuccessfully attempt to remain awake.

Then he saw Rain and all thoughts of Mia flew out of his head. Walking next to Iris was Palathum, carrying Rain in her arms. His sweet human's jaw was badly swollen and starting to discolor. There was dried blood on her lips and chin, and her expression was tight from pain.

Letting loose with a loud challenging rattle, Hesarium rushed at Palathum and grabbed Rain away.

"Hey, Hes," she whispered, moving her mouth very little as she spoke through swollen lips. "It's good to see you."

"What have you done?" Hesarium roared at Palathum, cradling Rain gently in his arms. "I'll see you dead in a challenge for this!"

"She didn't do anything," Rain said, then winced and pressed a hand against her face.

"Palathum saved us," Iris said, moving to stand in front of Palathum, as if to shield the much larger Talin from Hesarium's anger. "There are two bodies back there because of her. Those are the guys you should be rattling at."

"You didn't do this to my Rain?" he pressed, quieting his rattle.

"No, Citizen Hesarium," Palathum said with conviction. "I'd never strike a human. The male who hurt her will never hurt another."

"May his soul forever be locked out of the Domicile of the Souls," Hesarium spat out.

"Of that, there is no question," she agreed.

It relieved Hesarium to know the kidnappers were dead, but how had Palathum ended up being a rescuer? This place was far too deep inside the bowls of Falsof Station for her to have happened upon the kidnapping. There was something suspicious going on, but now wasn't the time for him to question the wealthy Talin.

"Palathum, if you can pick up Iris and Mia, we can make better time to the medical suite," he said, nodding his head at the two humans while Rain relaxed into his grip with a sad little huffing moan.

Hesarium expected Palathum to simply scoop up Iris, but she turned to the human and asked a question instead. "Will you let me carry you and Mia?"

"Sure," Iris agreed with a small smile. Mia roused enough to giggle as she and Iris were picked up. Then the little girl mumbled something and went right back to sleep.

"Keep up with me," he ordered Palathum. Impatient to check on Rain's health, Hesarium set out at the fastest jog he could that wouldn't jostle Rain. Palathum easily kept up with him, her bloody claws cradling Iris and Mia with tender care. Both of them kept up rumbles of comfort the entire way.

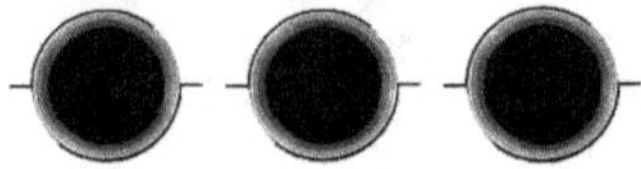

Hesarium

They'd been in the medical suite for three marks and still Hesarium couldn't bring himself to set Rain down. Mia and Iris were in the bed next to them with Palathum seated on the far side. She had a member of her staff bring items for the two and they were now fast asleep, covered in soft, fluffy nano-infused blankets and self-adjusting pillows.

Due to her injuries, Rain was required to stay awake and respond to the healer's questions. She was pleasant at first but turned irritated as the marks had gone by.

"Please tell me what the name of your owner is," the healer asked, peering at something on his Ident.

"Hessie," Rain answered.

The healer sounded a worried rumble. "That's incorrect, Rain. Do you know the name of the humans in the next bed?"

"Humans give those they are fond of nicknames," Hesarium explained to the healer. "She often calls me Hes instead of Hesarium."

"But Hessie is different," the healer protested.

"It's within the same sound category," Hesarium assured him. Then he leaned over and put his lips to her ear. "Please tell him what he wants to hear or we might have to spend more than one rotation in here."

"Fine," she grumped, then patted his arm, careful to avoid his quills. "This is Hesarium, but he's Hes to the humans, and Hessie to me now because I like how it sounds." She pointed to the next bed. "They're Iris and Mia."

The healer took notes on his Ident. "Very good. How do you feel?"

Rain sighed. "My head doesn't hurt anymore, and my tooth doesn't feel so loose. I'm really tired though. Can you let me get some sleep?"

"Soon," the healer said with a soothing rumble. "We need to make sure the serums we gave you don't have adverse effects we might not notice if you're unconscious. It'll only be another mark and then you can slumber for as long as you like."

After he finished the assessment, the healer returned to his station where he could see most of the beds in the room as he worked with his Ident. Most of the station was on their rest cycle so the lights in medical were dim, and there was almost no one walking around. The quiet allowed him to hear a whispered conversation from the hall outside medical, then the door slid open to reveal Danisal.

Good, now he might get some answers!

The warrior strode across medical to stand next to the bed. She'd glanced at Palathum, Iris, and Mia, but then focused her gaze on him. "I have information to share."

Rain remained quiet as Hesarium addressed Danisal. "How serious is the threat?"

"Moderate," Danisal answered. "We believe the two males were acting alone. One of them used to work on the station and had sufficient knowledge to both navigate the maintenance corridors and also manipulate the alarm system."

"What was their end goal?" Hesarium asked.

"They wanted to sell us." Rain answered. "They said they were going to leave the station with us and find a buyer."

"That's logical," Danisal agreed, then turned her gaze on Palathum who'd been watching them intensely. She spoke loud enough for the other Talin to hear her next statement. "What I still don't understand is why Palathum was the one who found you."

"I was passing by and heard Rain and Iris shouting," Palathum said, repeating the same thing she'd told Hesarium when he'd asked earlier.

The careful way she chose her words made it clear to Hesarium that there was something Palathum didn't want to tell them. It might not have anything to do with the abduction though. It could be as simple as Palathum having a secretive meeting with a lover or perhaps discussing a political or business deal with a rival.

"She was coming to visit me and Mia," Iris said, surprising them all. Not only was Iris awake, but she was sitting up with care so as to keep from waking Mia. Once she'd extracted herself, she moved to the edge of the bed and waved Palathum around the end of the bed to stand next to her.

"Mia and I really liked visiting with her the day we met all the lottery winners," Iris explained, taking hold of Palathum's hand in hers. "She's a really nice Talin and Mia wanted to play with her more."

"I didn't see her outside the jadik suites," Danisal said.

"You were busy," Iris said, narrowing her eyes at the warrior. "She realized we were missing. She searched for us before anyone else noticed." The condemnation in her tone was strong, making Danisal stiffen.

"I'm sorry you suffered, Iris," Danisal said, her tone formal. "I can promise steps are being taken to make sure nothing like this happens again. This incident taught us valuable lessons about how best to keep humans safe."

"Your lesson almost got Mia, Rain, and I sent off to some unknown buyer," Iris retorted. "You're lucky Palathum was there to do your job for you. She was magnificent. She fought two of them at once!"

"She did?" Danisal murmured, pinning Palathum with an intense stare. "Both men were military trained. They weren't specialists or decorated warriors, but they received good marks during their time as soldiers. I don't believe you ever served, Palathum. How is it you were able to fend off, not one, but two Talins with training?"

"I might not have been in the military, but I do train," Palathum answered with confidence. "It's every Talin's duty to be war ready should our empire face a threat greater than our military is prepared to meet."

Although there was nothing overtly wrong with her statement, it was a sentiment more commonly assigned to an era long ago, when the Talin Empire hadn't possessed the vast military they had today. There were some that still believed every citizen, no matter their profession, should be ready to go to war at a moment's notice. Most no longer thought it prudent or practical.

Danisal graced her with a traditional compliment. "Your dedication makes our ancestors proud."

"Yeah, she's dedicated," Iris commented with a half grin. "Dedicated to kicking ass!"

Rain stifled a laugh. "You're going to make me wake up Mia."

Iris shrugged. "Sorry, it had to be said." She raised her gaze to Danisal. "Are we good now? Or do you want to make some more accusations against the person who rescued us?"

"Danisal is simply doing her job," Palathum said gently.

"Well, she can do it somewhere else," Iris said. "I don't trust anyone to keep Mia safe except you."

Palathum sounded a rattle of surprise for a submark before she must have remembered Mia was asleep and silenced her backplates. "Do you mean that, Iris human? After, uh, after everything that happened?"

Iris hesitated to answer. "The *everything* is what convinced me."

It was as if they were speaking in riddles, but Rain was nodding her head in agreement. Hes was determined to find out what they weren't telling him, but not yet. He respected Rain too much to push her while Danisal and the healers were within hearing range.

Palathum started up a soothing rumble. "I could stay with you and Mia. Not only here, but later when you return to your rooms. I could sit outside your rooms and guard."

"You don't need to go that far. There's plenty of space in our suite. It's got four rooms, and we're only using one. You can have one of the other ones." Iris suddenly looked nervous and shifted her gaze to him. "If it's okay with Hes."

"I have no issue with Palathum staying in your suite if that's what you need to feel secure," he agreed. "She's already proven herself as capable."

"Yeah," Iris said with an emphatic nod of her head. "Super capable."

"Great," Rain said, stifling a yawn. "Now that that's all settled, can we get the healer over here to check me one last time so I can get some sleep?"

"Certainly," Danisal said, then looked to Hesarium. "I'll have a full report by sixth mark tomorrow." With that, she strode to the healer, said a few words, then left the medical suite.

Palathum urged Iris to lie back down, then tucked the human in, sounding a comforting rumble the entire time.

"I expect answers later," Hesarium whispered in Rain's ear as the healer made his way over.

"Later," Rain agreed. "After sleep, food, and a private conversation with Iris."

Hesarium didn't get a chance to voice a counter demand because the healer was there, asking his questions and noting Rain's response. When he gave her permission to slumber, she relaxed against him and was asleep before the healer made it back to his station.

CHAPTER 31

Rain

A day later, Rain walked into Iris and Mia's suite to an unexpected sight. The little girl was shrieking with laughter while Palathum pretended to stalk the girl. The Talin was on her hands and knees, making sounds like some kind of wild beast. She was moving slowly to give Mia plenty of time to jump from spot to spot.

"Rain!" Mia shouted as she clambered up onto a chair. "Watch out or the bog beast will get you!"

Iris was perched on a chair in the corner, laughing. "According to Mia, this bog beast can't climb. You're safe if you're on furniture."

"What happens if the bog beast captures you?" Rain asked.

"You get tossed in the air!" Mia yelled and sprinted from one spot to another. Rain watched the little girl deliberately run right next to Palathum. Grabbing Mia around the waist, Palathum picked her up and held her high in the air.

"I've got you!" Palathum declared.

Mia laughed and flailed her arms and legs. "Palathum, save me!"

The Talin lowered the girl until she was at chest height, purring loudly. "I've got you, little Mia. I won't ever let any beast eat you."

Mia wrapped her arms around Palathum's neck. "You saved me!"

"Always," Palathum promised, then set the child down so they could start playing again.

"Rain, come play with us!" Mia called out as she jumped onto one of the many pillows scattered on the floor.

"I will later," Rain promised. "I need to talk to Iris first."

"Ooooookaaaaay!" Mia said, before laughing and running to another pillow.

"If you wish to speak privately, I can remain here with Mia," Palathum offered. "The pup is safe with me."

"Thanks, Palathum," Iris said, getting off the chair she was perched on. "I'll be quick. And don't let Mia talk you into giving her any sweets. Too many will hurt her stomach."

Palathum sounded a rattle of agreement while never taking her eyes off Mia. Rain followed Iris into the room she shared with Mia.

"I want to talk about Palathum," Iris started the moment the door slid shut behind them.

"I had to tell Hes what really happened, but he agreed that Palathum wasn't really at fault," Rain assured her. "He's not going to say anything."

Iris waved her hand, dismissing the topic. "I'm not worried about that. Mia and I want to stay with Palathum."

It took a moment for Rain to process Iris's words. "Stay with Palathum? As in live with her on Talarian?"

Iris's expression turned stubborn. "No, we aren't going back to Talarian. I want to go out and see things, and Palathum travels all over the place for work. She's got an entire big ship and crew. If Auntie is going off to explore the universe with Tor and Vee, I want to go with Palathum."

Rain's first instinct was to argue with Iris. She hated the idea of losing any more people. It had been a hard enough blow when Auntie came to her and told her about Tor and

Vee, but now Iris and Mia were leaving also? Rain knew it was illogical, but she was starting to feel abandoned.

"Are you sure you want to do this?" Rain asked, fighting hard to keep her tone neutral.

"Yeah, I'm positive. I don't want to go to Talarian," Iris said with an emphatic nod of her head. "I don't trust these Talins except for Hes and Palathum. Don't you see, Rain? They'll do anything to us without listening because it's *for our own good*. Or for their advantage."

"So could Palathum," Rain argued. "She's the reason we got kidnapped in the first place."

"That's why I know I can trust her," Iris countered with confidence. "When she realized what had happened, she fought those men. She wanted Mia in her life more than anything, but she still fought them. Think about that Rain. Pretend someone offered you something you wanted as much as she wanted Mia. Then you find out that what you're being offered was stolen. How tempted would you be to abandon your principles? Palathum didn't, and then put herself in danger to defend us. She's a protector I can trust."

"Hes would've done the same thing," Rain pointed out. "He fought the Gorlags when they attacked. He put himself in danger multiple times, remember?"

"I know," Iris agreed. "But if he could only save one person and he had to pick between you or Mia, he'd pick you. I want Mia to be someone's first, not second."

Rain wanted to argue that it wasn't a choice that Hes would ever be forced to make. The recent kidnapping made it very clear that, even within the mighty Talin Empire, there was crime and a potential for danger.

Iris took hold of Rain's hands in hers, gripping her tightly. "Don't get me wrong, Hes is great. I think he's doing the best for all of us, but even in non-emergency situations he has to divide his attention between you and everyone else. I want Mia to be someone's entire world, not one human of many."

Rain felt tears gathering in her eyes. It was hard, but she put herself in Iris's place. Hes was devoted to her, first and foremost. He cared about all the other humans, but he'd always favor Rain. Iris wanted what Rain had—a Talin devoted only to her and Mia. After being the focus of Hes's care, Rain couldn't fault Iris for wanting the same.

"I don't want you to go," Rain said, letting the tears fall. She pulled her hands out of Iris's grip and pulled the other woman into a fierce hug.

"I'm going to miss you, but Palathum is giving me everything I ever wanted," Iris whispered, voice thick with unshed tears. "A devoted guardian for Mia and travel. I'm with Auntie. I want to see the universe before I die."

"I guess I'm boring," Rain said with a wet laugh, pulling away from Iris. "All I want is to see everyone settled and their families in a stable environment."

"That's not boring," Iris murmured, a wide smile spreading across her face. "That's love."

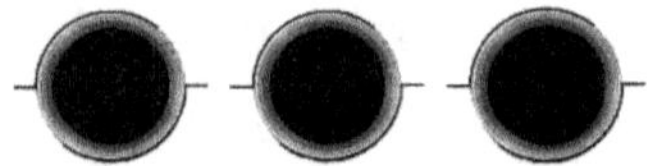

Hesarium

When Rain walked back into their room, Hesarium saw she was upset.

"Senior Specialist Dimtorum, I'm afraid I must end our meeting early," he said to the active display on the wall in front of him.

The sound of Dimtorum's rattle of agreement came through the display clearly. "I see your human has returned. You must want to check in with her. Please contact me at a later time when your human slumbers so she isn't disturbed by our conversation. Have a fruitful rotation, Hesarium."

"I wish you a fruitful rotation also, Senor Specialist Dimtorum," Hesarium responded and ended the meeting.

"Disturbed?" Rain asked as she walked up to him. "What are you guys talking about that's so disturbing?"

He opened his arms and started up a soothing rumble. Rain accepted the invitation and climbed into his lap. "We were discussing traveling from the port to our property on

Talarian. Dimtorum is in charge of traffic and logistics on Talarian. Normally he doesn't concern himself with something as small as our group, but he wants to make sure the humans aren't bombarded by Talin attention."

"I'm not disturbed, but I'm not excited about the idea of a gawking crowd either," Rain said as she snuggled up against Hesarium's chest.

"He plans to have a large industrial transport ready to collect all of you at the port so none of you need to be separated into individual vehicles. He's also working with the city's flow system to close off access to certain roads so the transport doesn't need to yield to other vehicles."

"That all sounds like too much fuss," she murmured, putting her lips to the bare patch of skin on his neck.

"He's also insisting he needs to ride with us." Hesarium started rubbing his hand up and down her back. Rain relaxed against him even more.

"So it's a ploy," Rain commented.

"Only partially," Hesarium said. "The transport will be a military one, and we'll have an armed escort. This level of security and protection isn't necessary for Talarian, but after the abduction, everyone is on edge. Something similar happened to Ari on the mining station. It seems the biggest threat to human pets are other Talins."

"Scarce commodities are always fought over," Rain murmured.

"Scarce and treasured," Hesarium corrected. "Why do you seem sad?"

Rain was silent for a moment and Hesarium worried he'd misjudged her expression. Then she let out a long sigh.

"Iris wants to take Mia and leave with Palathum."

Hesarium sounded a strong, negative rattle. "No!"

"Don't worry, I already went through all the betrayed and hurt feelings for both of us," Rain said, her warm breath wafting across his exposed skin as she spoke. The sensation was comforting even as her words filled him with displeasure.

"She and Mia can't leave," he protested. "They're like your family."

"And sometimes we have to let family go," Rain responded. "I've already given my blessing to Auntie. I couldn't refuse Iris for wanting the same thing. And honestly, Palathum will be a good protector. You didn't see her fighting, Hes. She was as skilled and fast as you. It was as impressive as it was scary."

"I've come across an interesting rumor," Hesarium said as he rubbed one of his scent glands into Rain's hair. "Palathum might be Tor Tiron."

"What, or who, is Tor Tiron?" Rain asked, making Hesarium feel foolish. Of course she didn't know what that was.

"Tor Tiron is a secret society," Hesarium explained. "No one knows very much, but it's believed that one of their purposes is to train to be Protectors of the Lineage."

"That's about as clear as the bog on a cold day," Rain teased.

"About fifteen hundred years ago, we had a sudden death of a monarch with no successor, and there was great discord. Eventually a new monarch was decided on, but only after several years of war. Legend says, to keep anything like that from happening again, the Tor Tiron were created. Their job is to ensure there is always a monarch and an heir."

"Ah, I get the Protector of the Lineage thing now," Rain said. "But what does that have to do with fighting?"

"There are supposedly different factions of the Tor Tiron, and one of them is to counter assassins. That faction is said to train as hard or harder than those in the military. They're also supposed to be experts at killing one on one as opposed to combat-scale warfare."

"That makes sense," Rain mused. "The best way to catch an assassin would be to think like an assassin. It also fits with the way she killed one of the guys. She knew exactly what she was doing and didn't hesitate."

"The healer who examined the bodies said both kills took impressive claw accuracy," Hesarium said. "Between that and the rumor I heard, I have no doubt she's Tor Tiron."

"One thing is certain, she won't let anyone hurt Iris or Mia," Rain stated with confidence. "She'll die protecting them, and I think that's what Iris needs right now."

Hesarium felt hurt. "Does she not have confidence in my skills?"

Rain made a soothing sound. "Don't take it personally. I think she's more concerned that you'll be too busy rescuing me or Royal to get to her and Mia in time."

"I suppose she's correct," Hesarium admitted reluctantly. "If you are content to let them leave with Palathum, then I'll enter into a contract with her."

"Do you really have to give her ownership?" Rain asked.

"I will make Palathum a co-owner," he explained. "Our legal and political system is still figuring out how human ownership works, especially when they aren't on Talarian. It will be safer for Iris and Mia if Palathum can legally act as their owner."

"Co-owner doesn't sound too bad," Rain agreed, her eyes drifting shut. "We leave tomorrow, and I'm going to have to say goodbye. I hate goodbyes."

"That's because you haven't had much practice," Hesarium commented.

Rain let out a sleepy chuckle. "True. How do you guys say goodbye?"

"For this type of goodbye, we would say *'Be well my friend. We will meet again, either on our feet or among the Ancestors.'*"

"I like that," Rain murmured, her voice fading as sleep pulled at her. She hadn't slept well that evening. Between the healers and nightmares, she'd woken every mark. The last rotation had taken a toll and his human needed rest.

"Sleep," Hesarium urged. "Tomorrow we leave, and soon after that, you'll be home."

CHAPTER 32

Rain didn't want to let go of Auntie. The woman had been a second mother to her, and this would be the first time in their lives they were more than a walking distance apart. Vee and Tor promised to bring her back to Talarian for visits, but the first one could be years in the future. The males had a full work schedule and Talins didn't really do vacations.

"Don't cry," Auntie ordered, but Rain could hear tears in the older woman's voice.

Rain sniffled. "Too late."

"Same," Auntie said and sniffled also.

Rain hugged Auntie tighter. "I'm going to miss you so much. I don't know how I'm going to survive without you."

"Don't be laying that kind of guilt on me," Auntie admonished, squeezing Rain just as tightly. "You're going to have Talins from all over ready to dote on you and the kids. They're even shutting down the streets so all of you can parade to your new home without the inconvenience of traffic slowing you down. I think you'll survive without me there."

"I know," Rain said, pulling away from the hug to meet Auntie's gaze. "I shouldn't be whining. It's just, everything is so perfect for all of us that I'm scared something bad is going to happen."

"No, sweetie," Auntie said with a shake of her head. "We paid for this good fortune in advance with all the people we've lost. I know they're all looking down at us and smilin'."

Rain could picture Mom and Dad holding hands, whispering to each other like they'd done when she was young. "I bet they are," Rain agreed. "And maybe everyone else too."

Auntie frowned fiercely. "Except David. He can rot in hell!"

"I'm sure he is," Rain responded with a frown. "You have to promise to visit us."

"I already have," Auntie reminded her.

"Hey, what about me?"

Rain turned to find Iris standing behind her. Next to Iris was Palathum with Mia cradled in her arms. The little girl was pointing at things as she talked excitedly. Palathum kept making rumbles of interest and asking Mia to describe what she was seeing. Rain could feel the affection for Mia pouring off the Talin. The three of them had been on Honored, saying their last goodbyes to everyone already onboard.

Rain grinned and let go of Auntie's hands so she could open up her arms to invite Iris in for a hug. "I was hoping you'd get distracted and forget to leave the ship."

Iris snorted. "Unlikely. Palathum had her Ident set to give us a bunch of reminders to leave."

"We have a ship of our own," Palathum told Rain, as if she couldn't remember that simple fact. "We don't need to travel on the royal ship back to Talarian."

Rain managed to keep a straight face, barely. "Hes told me Talarian is perfect. You should follow us in your ship."

"We have a vast distance to travel and a station to inspect," Palathum began, and Rain knew what she was going to say next from the many times Palathum had repeated it to her and all the other humans. "I know you'll miss Iris and Mia, but I'll take good care of them."

A warning sounded around them as Hesarium stepped out from the open loading doors of the monarch's personal vessel. "I'm sorry, Rain, but you must finish with your goodbyes."

Rain grabbed both Auntie and Iris by the hands. Auntie grabbed Iris's hand with her free one. With the three women linked, they let the silence hang between them for a second.

"I knew this was going to be hard," Iris said, blinking rapidly. "But I didn't think it would be this hard."

"We're family," Auntie said. "No amount of distance will change that."

"No matter how far apart," Rain whispered, "we'll be close at heart."

The warning blared out again, this time louder and more insistent. Vee stepped up behind Auntie and gently tugged her hands free, wrapped his arms around her, and folded her into a full-body hug. Palathum moved close to Iris so Mia could demand cuddles from both of them.

Rain didn't protest when Hes leaned over and lifted her into his arms, purring loudly. Everyone shouted goodbyes as he carried her onto the ship that would take them to their new home.

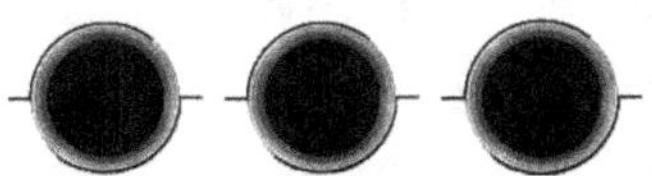

Georgia

They were all forced to move down the corridor and into the safety of the main station before The Honored could undock and start the process of leaving. As if reading her mind, Vee guided her to stand near an observation window so she could watch the ship slowly unlock and be pulled by automated tug ships away from Falsof. Iris, Palathum, and Mia followed her to get a last look at The Honored.

Iris leaned in close. "We're not being selfish, are we?"

"Sure we are," Georgia answered, smiling down at Iris. "But we're allowed to be. Our entire lives have been about taking care of the community. Now is the first time we get to think about the individual instead of the group. I promise, Rain understands."

"Georgia, our ship will be leaving soon also," Vee said with a purr. "We need to make our way to a different slip."

Georgia turned to face Iris. "Have a good trip and remember to send messages. I want to know all the best places you visit so maybe I can get Vee and Tor to take me there."

"If you do the same," Iris bargained. They hugged and then Vee and Tor were guiding her away from Iris, Mia, and Palathum.

It wasn't long until they joined a long line of passengers boarding a commercial transport. The line was moving slow but steady, and conversations were buzzing all around her.

"We aren't wealthy enough to own a ship," Tor commented as they took a measured pace forward. "Do you regret not traveling with your fellow humans on The Honored or joining Iris and Mia with Palathum? Both options are far more luxurious than what we can offer."

"Not at all," Georgia assured him. Out of the two Talins who were now her co-owners along with Hes, she'd found that Tor was the more sensitive one. He was quick to pick up on the moods of others and was already very good at judging her facial expressions.

"Are you sure?" Tor pressed.

"Absolutely," she answered, then gestured at the line of Talins in front of them. "Can we leave our room and interact with others? Or do Talins tend to stay to themselves?"

"There is a communal dining area that will be lively once a rotation," Vee explained. "And I'm sure there'll be—"

"Is this a human?" a voice behind them interrupted with an inquisitive rattle. Conversation around them stopped. Looking around, Georgia realized that about twenty nearby Talins were all staring at them.

"I apologize," the Talin who asked said to Vee and Tor with a regretful rumble. "I shouldn't have spoken with such haste. I'm Olistarium of the Klow Family within the Tolf Clan. I've seen some of the informational vids produced by the Committee of Pet Welfare and I was curious if this was a human."

"I'm a human," Georgia answered. She expected a comment from Olistarium but what she got was a barrage of questions from everyone around them.

"Can I pet her?"

"I've heard they can't rumble or rattle, is that true?"

"Does she bite?"

"Her skin and mane are darker than the humans in the vids. Does that mean she's healthier?"

"Is her mane as soft as it appears?"

"I've heard humans have trouble maintaining their temperatures. Is she wearing enough clothing for this area?"

"Is she chilled? I could ask the ship's stewards to let you pass through and get her to a cabin quickly."

Far from feeling overwhelmed or intimidated, Georgia had never felt so special or important in her life. Vee sounded a loud rattle that bounced off the walls of the corridor, making everyone quiet down.

"I'm Varlum of the Salmik Family within the Delk Clan," he announced loudly. "This is Toreum of the Orif family within Delk Clan. We own Georgia human. Humans can become distraught easily, especially in stressful situations involving crowds."

Georgia wanted to object and say everyone could ask her questions, but he continued speaking before she could voice her enjoyment of the attention.

"We are traveling to Starnum station," Vee explained to the crowd. "If Georgia feels comfortable with it, we'll eat at our assigned table in the communal galley at mealtime.

Please talk to the ship's steward about being assigned to our table so you can interact with her."

The Talins all fell back a few paces and grabbed their Idents, furiously tapping at the glowing surfaces. The poor ship's steward was about to get inundated with requests for their table.

"If we speak gently, can we talk to her here?" one of them asked.

Georgia tugged at Tor's arm. He lowered his head so she could whisper in his earhole. "We're not doing anything else in line; let me talk to them."

Tor sounded a rattle of agreement. "Georgia would like to interact but only one of you at a time."

The Talins around them were so quick to queue up behind the three of them that there was space left in front of them. There was some angry muttering from the Talins in the far back, but nothing distinct enough for her to understand. Talins were the most organized species Georgia had ever met. She couldn't imagine any other group organizing themselves so quickly, or who'd find talking to her fascinating.

"Hello, Georgia human," the first one who'd started the line greeted her. He didn't bother giving her his family or clan name. Instead he held his arms out. "Would you like to clutch or cling to me?"

Georgia shook her head at the same time Tor sounded an angry rattle. "Georgia is bonded to us and might not want anyone else to touch her. Humans are particular like that."

The Talin's purr went silent and Georgia felt bad for him. She held out her right hand between them. "Some humans hold hands briefly," she explained. "It's a form of greeting."

Eagerly, he placed his palm against hers and started purring again. "Like this?"

She wrapped her smaller hand around his and moved their joined limbs up and down once before letting go; his hand remained stiffly open the entire time. "Just like that."

"It's a hand clutch," the Talin declared. "How charming."

"I'd like to hand clutch," the next Talin in line said, nudging the other Talin out of the way and sticking his arm out.

"I will see you at the daily meal," the first Talin said as he gave way to the next one.

That's how it went for about twenty minutes as they all slowly moved up the ramp to the waiting ship. She hadn't finished meeting everyone in line by the time they reached the check in point. Vee pressed his Ident to the display at the hatch, then Tor did the same, only he tapped on the display a few times.

"We're logged in," Tor said, placing a hand on Georgia's back to guide her deeper into the ship. The Talins behind them had become silent, watching Vee and Tor check in.

Acting on impulse, Georgia faced the remaining Talins and saw that some who'd already met her had retreated to get back in line for a second interaction.

"I hope to talk to all of you on our journey," she declared and received a wave of purring from the group. She wasn't surprised when Vee picked her up while sounding a rumble of amusement.

"Troublemaker," he murmured as Tor moved to walk behind them, acting as an added barrier to the Talins who wanted to follow them.

"I've never been special before," she told him. "I'm sorry if I broke the rules."

"You didn't break any rules, sweet human," Vee assured her.

"We'll find a way for you to meet and talk with the other passengers in a manner that keeps you safe," Tor promised. "But you might want to reserve time for seeing the other interesting things on this ship. There's a historical display on the same deck as the galley."

"Every few rotations, one of the crew will give a tour and lecture on this class of transport," Vee added. "There will be many things to occupy your time when we aren't in the cabin."

"Sounds educational," Georgia said, hiding her smile against Vee's neck. "I bet I'll have as much fun in the cabin as outside it."

"We certainly hope so," Tor and Vee said at the same time.

Georgia's heart swelled. "I'm the luckiest human alive."

"And we're the most fortunate of Talins," they said with a purr.

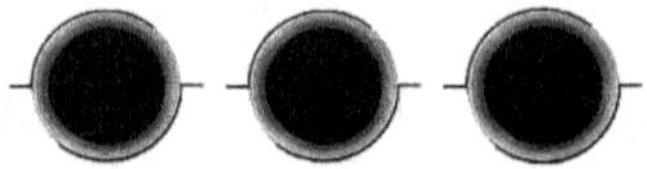

Iris

Palathum's ship was far smaller than the one Rain or Georgia left on, so they had to cover a good amount of distance to get to the docks that accommodated smaller vessels. Palathum offered to hire a specialized cart to carry her, but Iris declined. After a lifetime of hard labor, a casual stroll through the station wasn't difficult at all. She wasn't even carrying Mia. The little girl was happily clinging to Palathum as they walked.

"A few droplets of water leaked from your eyes," Palathum commented as they walked. "I read that humans do that when they're in pain. I have a healer aboard my ship; we can visit her first before I take you and Mia to your room."

Iris shook her head. "The pain can be physical or mental. It hurt a little to say goodbye to everyone. I've known those people my entire life."

"Will you become despondent without them?" Palathum asked, sounding a concerned rumble. "Could this cause you ill health?"

Iris was touched by her care. "I'll be fine. And they gave me this." She held up the information square containing vids of everyone telling stories or remembering their shared past. Rain had arranged one for her and one for Auntie, so if they ever got lonely, there would be a part of the group with them. Leave it to Rain to think of something so thoughtful.

"I have Tor and Vee's Ident codes. While they're in Talin-controlled space, I can send them messages. It can take a long time for the messages to track them down, but it will still be possible to contact them and Auntie human if necessary."

"That's good," Iris said. "Maybe we can meet up with them on some faraway station."

"I'm sure that can be arranged," Palathum promised. "After my next assignment, I don't have another one lined up. We will be free to explore and travel at will."

While Palathum worked, Iris planned to spend the time researching and making a list of places she wanted to see. "That sounds perfect."

There weren't many Talin in the area they walked through, but once they got to the hatch of Palathum's ship, there was a line of fifteen Talins waiting for them. They were all standing shoulder to shoulder, with their arms held stiffly at their sides. This had to be the crew.

"Admirus Citizen Palathum, as soon as you board, we will be ready to embark," one of them said.

"Very good, Captain Nomium," Palathum answered, then she addressed the rest of the crew. "This is Mia and Iris, my new humans. I'll be giving a longer, more formal, lecture about the proper care of humans at eighth mark. Captain Nomium has assured me everyone will be able to attend by then. Unless it's an emergency, don't interact with the humans until you've attended my lecture. Do we all understand?"

The crew sounded a rattle of agreement and didn't even look too closely at Iris or Mia.

"The crew is eager to create a safe and enriching environment for the humans," Captain Nomium said. "I can promise they will listen to your lecture and take all your instructions to heart. For now, I suggest confining the humans to their cabin."

That was fine by Iris. She was mentally exhausted and eager for some quiet time where she could read on her information square or mindlessly watch one of Mia's favorite vids.

"Excellent, Captain, I'll take them there now," Palathum said as she swept by the crew with Mia in her arms. Iris stayed at her side and soon they were walking into a suite almost as big as the one she and Mia had on the station.

"This is for you two," Palathum said as she set Mia down. The little girl immediately started exploring.

"It's so big," Iris murmured, then turned to Palathum. "Are you staying in here also?"

"No, I have the cabin across the hall," Palathum told her. "But if you become frightened or worried, you can join me in that cabin, or I can come over here. There is only a hallway between us and both of you can cross that space any time you need."

"Thanks, Palathum," Iris said, reaching out to give the Talin a quick hug around the waist. "I'm really happy to be here."

Palathum started purring. "I'm joyful also."

Suddenly Mia was there, squeezing between the two of them. "And I here!"

Palathum sounded a rumble of amusement before going back to purring. "Yes, little Mia. You're a jewel among us."

"Because I glitter?" she asked, pointing to the little collar she was wearing. At first no one planned to have the children wear collars, but Mia had gotten upset at being left out. Hes had found a necklace that looked similar to their collars, and Mia was overjoyed at her jeweled *collar*.

"Yes, exactly! You glitter, sparkle, and gleam," Iris declared with a soft laugh. "Just like our new life."

CHAPTER 33

Hesarium

Of all the things Hesarium expected to happen when they reached Talarian, having four Mavins march onto the ship and put Tolvern into restraints wasn't one of them.

"One of the humans is very attached to this young male," Hesarium protested. He pointed to where Sunny was weeping loudly and clinging to Tolvern. "She could have health issues if he's removed."

The Mavins weren't swayed.

"The Clan Authorities Council has issued a Call-For-Transit on this male," Chief Mavin explained with a regretful rumble. "We have no choice but to abide by it. Once he's returned to his colony, you can submit a request for re-assessment of his crimes. Nothing can be done until then."

Hesarium had been afraid of this. He crouched down next to Sunny and sounded a rumble of comfort. "Sunshine, you have to let go of Tolvern."

"They're going to hurt him!" Sunny argued and Hesarium could see real concern on her face.

"No, they won't," Hesarium assured her. "Mavins are held to a high standard. They are the guards of civil order and would never do anything to cause harm to someone in their custody."

"It's true," Chief Mavin said with an encouraging rattle. "The Clan Authorities Council has an unblemished record going back two thousand years."

"I don't care about two thousand years ago!" Sunny pulled one hand free of Tolvern to point to his restraints. "I care about now. You put him in chains!"

Chief Mavin was quick to defend himself. "Only because it's procedure. Once we're aboard the ship, I'll remove the restraints. He'll be as free as any other passenger."

"We're going to be on a very nice ship," another Mavin said. "There'll be many things he can do to occupy his time while we travel."

"We won't need to put restraints on him when we arrive either," a third Mavin explained. "We'll be at his home colony and rejoining his clan."

"His mother and father will be there, little human," the last Mavin assured her. "Don't you like being with your sire and dam? Think of the comfort they'll be able to provide him."

It was obvious all four Mavins wanted to release Tolvern and leave him with Sunny, but they were bound by a strict code of conduct. Mavins never went against orders.

"We could even arrange for him to message you during the trip," Chief Mavin offered. "We'll have access to a comms array while passing Stalt Station."

Sunny wouldn't be consoled by any of them until Tolvern finally spoke up. "Sunshine, please look up."

Blinking away tears, Sunny turned her gaze to him. "I won't let go of you," she promised.

"You must," he told her, his tone gentle and a comforting rumbling coming out of him. "The Mavins will stand here all day if necessary. Nothing will change if you continue to clutch and cling to me. They will simply wait until you're fatigued and take me away once you're forced to let go."

"You know how important Hesarium is to Rain?" she asked. Tolvern interrupted his comforting rumbles to sound a soft rumble of agreement. "That's how important you are to me."

"You haven't known me long," Tolvern protested.

"Sometimes we humans just know," Sunny declared, then her expression changed to one of pleading. "I don't want you to leave."

"Leaving doesn't mean we'll be separated forever," he promised her. "Think of me like Auntie, Iris, or Mia. I'll only be absent from your life for a set amount of time."

"Do you promise?"

Tolvern's tone turned formal. "I swear to you I'll return; let the Ancestors hear my vow."

It was the strongest promise a Talin could make, but it was obvious to Hesarium that Sunny didn't realize it because she tried to smile up at him. "You better come back, or I'll steal a ship, hunt you down, and put sorka gel under your backplates."

"This human makes good threats," Chief Mavin said with an amused rumble. "Young Tolvern will return to you, his ancestral pledge is proof of that. Will you release him, human? The sooner we get him back to his colony, the sooner the process of bringing him back here can begin."

Sunny focused her gaze on Chief Mavin. "You need to vow too! Vow that he'll be safe on the trip."

"Barring acts of the universe," Chief Mavin stated without hesitation, "Tolvern will arrive at his colony as you see him here, fit of body and mind. Let the Ancestors hear my vow."

Rain, Cherish, and Wind were all standing behind Hesarium. Royal was with Gris and his family, playing with their daughter on the far side of the shuttle that had brought them to the planet's port. Sensing the scene was coming to an end, the twins hurried forward to stand on either side of Sunny as she let go of Tolvern.

The Mavins didn't give her a chance to grab hold of him again. They were quick to haul Tolvern away and up the ramp to a nearby shuttle. Rain stepped up to stand next to Hesarium and tangled her fingers with his.

"You did your best," she murmured as they all watched the shuttle ramp retract and the hatch close. "We knew it was unlikely they'd let Tolvern stay."

"I'd still hoped to change the outcome," Hesarium admitted, wrapping his arms around Rain. Except for the Mavins and the guards who'd rushed up to greet them when they'd first disembarked, there was suspiciously little activity in this area of Talarian's largest and busiest port. The port officials must have cordoned off this area for their arrival.

"The transport is here!" Danisal called out. "You and Rain need to board."

Danisal had decided Rain needed to do everything first to show all the other humans it was safe. Hesarium didn't understand where Danisal got the idea, but Rain didn't mind, and the other humans found it amusing.

"Time to see our new home," Rain murmured as they all started toward Danisal.

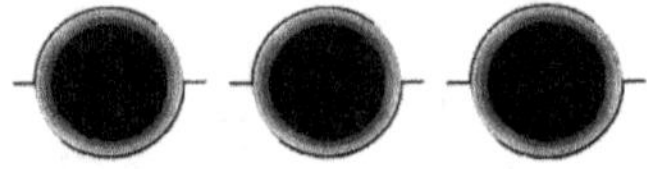

Rain

To her surprise, the inside of the large industrial-looking transport was decorated with brightly colored pillows and pads. Standing at the open door was a human woman with long black hair and dark skin and features that made Rain think of vids from Latin America she'd watched growing up.

It felt surreal to meet a human she hadn't grown up with. It took Rain a moment to pull the correct word to the front of her brain. Stranger. This woman was a stranger to her! It was such a novel concept, Rain giggled.

"What? Do I have something on my face?" the woman asked, slapping both hands over her cheeks.

"No, sorry!" Rain said quickly, rushing up the two steps of the vehicle to meet the new woman. In her haste, she caught a toe on the last stair and pitched forward. She heard

Hes sound a rattle of surprise from behind her at the same time strong hands grabbed and righted her.

"Are you well, human?" an unfamiliar Talin asked with a concerned rumble as he steadied her inside the vehicle.

"She might have twisted an ankle. You should carry her to a seat," the woman urged.

"Let me," Hes insisted, snatching her up with a warning rattle at the Talin.

"Calm down, Hes, we weren't going to steal her!" the woman teased.

"This must be Rain," the strange Talin said with an amused rumble as he backed away. "I'm happy to see you have a human of your own, Hesarium."

"Oh, you're Rain!" the human said with a large welcoming smile. "I'm Ari and this is Baz."

"Ari was very eager to meet everyone," Baz said to Hes. "I tried to talk her out of coming to the port, but she refused."

"Of course I did!" Ari exclaimed, stepping forward with her arms open. "I want to clutch the new humans!"

With a laugh, Rain wiggled in Hes's grip. "My ankle's fine; it was only a trip."

"Do not move so quickly again," he ordered as he set her down.

Stepping into the embrace of the shorter woman, Rain could smell the strong scent of Baz's bonding oil in Ari's hair. Being so close made her head start to ache so she withdrew from the hug but kept the grin.

"It's nice to meet you, fellow human," she said with the formal cadence of Talin speech.

Ari laughed. "I'm pleased with our introduction as well."

"Why is everyone not loading up?" Danisal asked loudly from outside. "It's cold. The humans shouldn't remain exposed to the elements."

The weather was far warmer than Rain or any of the others were used to on Omanal, but Hes and Baz obligingly ushered her and Ari further into the vehicle. There weren't

any windows, but soft artificial light illuminated the inside
well enough for Rain to pick her way through the mess of
pillows.

"Talins sure love pillows," she commented as the four
of them settled down at the front of the vehicle. There was a
glowing bank of displays with control options over her head,
probably a way to put the vehicle into manual operation
when necessary. Everyone else started climbing in and
finding their own spots, talking cheerfully with each other
and occasionally pointing at Ari.

"They do have a thing for pillows," Ari agreed. "But
they also think we love to make nests out of pillows, so they
tend to put pillows everywhere."

Still sniffling, Sunny settled down next to Rain.
Wrapping an arm around the girl, she held her close while
Cherish, Wind, and Royal all settled near her.

Baz let out a worried rumble. "You're leaking fluid
from your eyes, human. Do we need to take her directly to a
healer?"

"No," Rain said. "Her heart is a little bruised, that's
all."

"Her heart is bruised?" Baz shouted and reached for
his Ident, probably to interface with the controls and reroute
them to the nearest healers.

"I believe Rain is being metaphorical," Hes said with
a loud purr. He reached around Rain to give the girl a soft pat
on the head as he spoke to Sunny in a soft, kind voice.
"We're going to send a message to Tolvern's colony,
remember? I'm sure we can find an avenue by which he'll be
allowed back here."

"What happened?" Baz asked, settling back in a
relaxed, seated position.

As Hes explained the whole ordeal, Ari addressed
Rain. "It feels so weird to see another human," she said with
a chuckle.

"Same!" Rain answered with a laugh. "And then I
tripped and almost face-planted at your feet. Great first
impression."

"At least you have an INT! When my group first met the Talins, none of us had one and theirs didn't have the capacity to learn languages. There were some tense moments."

Rain's eyes went wide. "You didn't have an INT? How is that possible?"

Ari shook her head with a wry grin. "Because the mining company we worked for were cheap bastards. It's a whole thing, but at least we survived. No one else on Earth did."

"Then it really happened?" Rain asked, heart sinking. "Earth is gone?"

Ari blinked. "You didn't know?"

"My grandmother got a bunch of people to leave Earth and settle on Omanal roughly sixty years ago. Sending messages all the way back to Earth was too expensive, so we couldn't keep up with what was going on. We heard about a Final Cataclysm, but we'd all hoped it was an exaggeration."

"Your grandmother was a brilliant woman," Ari said with admiration. "I can tell you everything that happened because me and my group were some of the last to make it offplanet. But let's save that for another time and maybe some alcohol."

"There's alcohol?" Rain asked, leaning in a little closer. "I know Talins have a type of wine, but they wouldn't let us have any."

"We make our own," Ari whispered, rolling her eyes to make sure Baz and Hes were still distracted. "Don't say anything."

"You're going to want to meet Zuri," Rain said and pointed to the woman being snuggled securely on Kasium's lap. "She's an expert at moonshine."

Ari clapped with delight. "You guys are bringing in some valuable skills!"

Rain already knew she and Ari were going to be good friends. As they talked, the last of her tension vanished. Although Rain never saw herself as a leader of her group, she'd worried like a leader. Ari was quick to give her details about their life on Talarian that clearly indicated Hes had been absolutely honest about everything.

Her worrying days were over.

CHAPTER 34

Rain

The only word Rain could think of to describe their new home was paradise. The place had to be at least a few hectares. The area was a combination of open space covered in lush green ground cover, thick woods, and paths crisscrossed all over the place.

The vehicle had stopped at the end of a designated road in the center of the property. To her right was a massive domicile large enough to fit five or six of the ones she'd grown up in. Farther back was a cluster of smaller domiciles that must be dwellings for individuals.

Right in front of her were several rows of what looked like enclosures at a zoo. Each one probably had the same footprint as a large crawler. As she watched, humans streamed out from the open doors of the enclosures with smiles and words of greetings on their lips.

"These humans might be territorial. We should keep the two populations separate," Danisal said with a warning rattle and tried to grab Royal from Cherish.

The girl was quick to duck to the side with a shake of her head. "Calm down, Danisal. We're not going to get into a fight."

Royal was wiggling in her arms, frantic to be set down so he could meet all the new people. The moment he was on his feet, he ran to the nearest new person and proudly held up his multi-tech. The person laughed and crouched down to admire the tool.

"Ah, the presence of young must indicate peace," Danisal said with an inquisitive rumble.

"Yeah, sure," Cherish quipped as she stepped forward to start meeting her new community.

The two groups came together and were quick to introduce themselves. Rain held back, staying close to Hesarium. It wasn't that she was afraid of meeting new people. It was that she was feeling a little overwhelmed with happiness.

"It's not the same as your farmland, but we could perhaps set aside a section for food production," Hes offered as he wrapped his arms around her. She leaned back against him, enjoying the solid feel of his body against her back.

"A few people might like that, but I'll be happy to never grow anything ever again," Rain admitted. She studied the closest enclosure. The inside had the same lush green ground cover she was standing on, along with pots of flowering plants. There was a three-sided shelter made of stone with what looked like a section of expanding wall that would be pulled across to create a fully enclosed space. Inside the shelter was a pallet on the floor, surrounded by pillows and colorful blankets. She wasn't sure, but there looked to be some toys or trinkets laying around the space. All in all, it looked cozy and restful.

"Am I going to have to sleep in one of those?" she asked, frowning. She didn't want to be separated from Hes, but she'd known going in that they'd have to make sacrifices to keep up the illusion of her being nothing more than a pet.

"That's my home over there," Hes said, raising an arm to point to one of the small domiciles behind the main building. "You'll be staying there with me. After all, you're very sensitive and become panicked if you can't see me."

"Oh, I didn't know I was like that," Rain teased with a chuckle. "It's a good thing you're such a dedicated owner."

"Rain," Wind called out, getting her attention. When she looked up, it was to find Wind, Cherish, and Sunny standing next to a smiling woman. "Aspen is going to show us the empty spots so we can pick the ones we want."

"I get a space to myself!" Cherish crowed with a little happy dance.

"We all do," Sunny agreed and tried for a smile.

"Where's—" Rain started to ask where Royal was but then saw him holding the hand of another adult and determinedly leading them to one of the enclosures. He probably wanted to show them how the multi-tech could measure the density of the stone inside. The adult was holding a baby and looked excited to be included. When she looked up, she caught Rain's eye and smiled.

"I'm Daniella," she called back. "Royal and I are going to measure some things!"

There was nothing for Rain to do. Everyone was talking, exploring, and happy. She didn't need to find them places to sleep or procure food. She didn't need to set up any kind of systems or mediate an altercation. There was no labor to be done.

Everything was taken care of.

Turning around in Hes's embrace, she snuggled up against him. "Show me your domicile," she demanded. "I want to either sleep, eat, or fuck."

"Can I persuade you to engage in all three?" Hes asked with an amused rumble. Sweeping her up into his arms, he nuzzled her hair. "Not all at the same time, and preferably in reverse order."

"I am open to negotiation," she answered with a chuckle. The sounds of her friends and family laughing and talking in the background was the perfect accompaniment as Hes carried her off to their new home.

AUTHOR'S NOTE

Dear Readers,

Thank you for reading *Gossamer Chains*. If you want more in the Origins series, the next book, *Golden Cages*, is available for pre-order.

I hope you enjoyed *Gossamer Chains* enough to leave a review! As an indie writer without the support of a publishing company, I need all the help I can get. Your good reviews keep me writing.

If you have any questions, comments, or suggestions, feel free to contact me via email: author@rk-munin.com

Want to see artwork, chat, and have some fun? Join my Facebook group, Munin's Magpies: https://www.facebook.com/groups/2106029053097927/

I'm also on Instagram, Tiktok, and Bookbub, or check out my website: www.rk-munin.com

Signing up for my newsletters is the best way to stay up to date on new releases and free book deals. You also might receive a deleted scene not available anywhere else. Plus, you can get a free book, *Tender Captivity* https://dl.bookfunnel.com/ndn50yaxb0
(*Tender Captivity* takes place after *Fighting Captivity*, the fourth book in the Human Pets of Talin series. However you can read any of my books or novellas out of order. They are all written to be read as standalones.)

Have a fruitful rotation,
Rye

OTHER BOOKS BY RK MUNIN

-Science Fiction-

Hissa Warrior Series
Rescuing Halin (Mian and Halin)
Buying Tiran (Mara and Tiran)
Tempting Selon (Lara and Selon)
Defying Kilan (Deena and Kilan)
Healing Mavito (Raleen and Mavito)
Claiming Yopin (Mouse and Yopin)
Teasing Woken (Safena and Woken)
Defending Revin (Kamaril and Revin) – Coming soon

Human Pets of Talin Series
Loving Captivity (Sora and Searin)
Escaping Captivity (Lakin and Dalt)
Negotiating Captivity (Nalia and Derani)
Fighting Captivity (Zia and Palforma)
Tender Captivity (Jinna and Holian - This is a novella you can
get for free by signing up for my newsletter)
Craving Captivity (Lasha and Tamerin)
The Twelve Nights of Halloheen: A holiday mashup novella
(Isla and Tisuran)
Stealing Captivity – Coming soon

Origins (A Human Pets of Talin Series)
Creating Captivity (Ari and Bazium)
Gossamer Chains (Rain and Hesarium)
Golden Cages – Coming soon

-Paranormal /Urban Fantasy-

Ours Evermore Series
Two Wolves for Soren (Soren, Kalli, and Quinn)
A Hacker, Vampire, and Chimera Walk into a Bar….(Tobias, Briar, and Memphis)
When Darkness Meets Dawn (Imani, Lex, and Mac)
Tag, You're It (Short Story)
Kidnapping Their Third (Cora, Pike, and Kimble) – Coming soon
Pastries on a Plate and Blood in a Mug (Novella) – Coming soon

Alpha Series
Alpha Mage (Emma and Kade)
His Alpha Mage (Avery and Jason – Novella)
Alpha King (Cathleen and Lazlo)

New Clan Series
Stray Wolf (Steph and Eli)
Lost Lion (Maeve and Cyrus)
Reluctant Cervid (Tavi and Donovan)
Broken Thorn (Sabina and Theodosius)